HER WAYS ARE DEATH

By the same Author

RECKLESS COULSON
COULSON GOES SOUTH
DETECTIVE COULSON
COULSON ALONE
DEAD MAN'S CHEST
GEES' FIRST CASE
GREY SHAPES
NIGHTMARE FARM
THE KLEINERT CASE
MAKER OF SHADOWS
THE NINTH LIFE
THE GLASS TOO MANY

WRIGHT & BROWN, LTD.
4 Farringdon Avenue, London, E.C.4

Her Ways are Death

By

Jack Mann

Author of
" Maker of Shadows," " The Ninth Life,"
etc.

WILDSIDE PRESS

First Printed, Wright & Brown, Ltd.,
London, 1941

Printed and bound in Great Britain by
Redwood Burn Limited, Trowbridge & Esher

To

CLAIRE

Because of Peter, and . . .

G.

4. 12. 40

NOTE BY THE AUTHOR

I AM largely indebted, and also grateful, to Mr. A. C. Cox, one of the Hardy players, for the assistance he has so kindly given me over the use of Dorset dialect. I may add that I have not tried to render that dialect either in the purity of form that one finds in William Barnes' work, or to pervert it quite to the 'bus-and-cinema monstrosity that has grown out of attempts at combining gangster slang and Hollywood wisecracks with the original Dorset idiom. Rather have I tried to steer a mean course between the two, with the very kind help of Mr. Cox's monograph on the subject, and also with the realisation that it is virtually impossible to render dialect by means of attempted phonetic spelling. For instance, Barnes' "hwoam" and "sheädes" would convey entirely different sounds to two different readers of his work: bearing this in mind, I have tried to give "Dorset" as I have heard and know it.

And, Dorset readers will probably tell me, have failed. I shall not love them or their county any the less for it, but will remind any caviller that there is a vast difference between the dialect round Blandford and behind Bridport, and on the eastern and western fringes of the county. The nuances are fine, but perceptible, between village and village, even. Dorset men—and women—bear it as best you can!

J. M.

CONTENTS

CHAPTER		PAGE
I.	THE MAN WHO SAID IT . . .	9
II.	IRA—NAYLOR'S ESTIMATE . .	22
III.	PETER	47
IV.	IRA—SIDELIGHTS	63
V.	NEW MAGIC IS OLD . . .	77
VI.	EMPIRIC THEORY	92
VII.	"THERE IS NO MAGIC" . . .	106
VIII.	AN ERROR OF JUDGMENT . .	120
IX.	RETURN	134
X.	"I DIDN'T CALL"	148
XI.	ENCHANTMENT	164
XII.	ROLLO	179
XIII.	IRA, HERSELF	197
XIV.	THE MADNESS OF JEROME NAYLOR .	211
XV.	THE LAST FANTASY . . .	225
XVI.	THE HAMMER	241
XVII.	THE SHATTERED ROD . . .	255
XVIII.	"I SHALL NEVER——" . . .	273

HER WAYS ARE DEATH

I

OVER lunch at *The Three Choughs* at Yeovil, Gregory George Gordon Green read through again the letter that had started him on his journey from London. Had he been in any hurry to complete that journey, he would have taken the Dorchester road out from Salisbury, but the letter suggested an appointment that gave him plenty of time, and, on the word of his friend Tony Briggs of the Foreign Office, the cuisine and cellar of *The Three Choughs* justified one in making a point of lunching there. So, over coffee and a spot of liqueur brandy in the dining room—and a cigarette, of course—Gees took out the letter and read again—

Troyarbour Hall,
Blandford,
Dorset.

Messrs. Gees (G. Green, Esq.)
    Confidential Agents
37 Little Oakfield Street
    London, S.W.1.

DEAR SIR,

I have been recommended to you by a Mr. Hunter, of Denlandham, Shropshire, whose name and address will, I believe, be easy for you to recall to memory.

Mr. Hunter, on hearing the story I had to tell him, at once recommended me to you, as one who had carried out for him a most unusual and difficult series of investigations and brought them to a highly satisfactory end.

I should be glad if you could see your way to call on me at the above address at the earliest possible date, with a view to giving me, at the least, your advice, and if possible your aid in connection with a problem which I have no intention of putting in writing. If you can see your way to visiting me, not before mid-afternoon (which would involve putting up for the night, probably) I should be happy to pay all your expenses, and, in addition, the two guineas which I understand is your fee for an initial consultation.

Yours very truly,
J. St. Pol Naylor.

Gregory George Gordon Green, otherwise known as "Gees," refolded the letter and put it in his pocket. It was undated, he had noted on first reading it: if he had not been naturally observant—which he was— the two years he had spent in the police force would have taught him to note trifles, whether apparent or real. In actual fact, the letter was a week old: he had had what looked like another promising investigation on hand, and thus had not troubled to answer this communication until, this same autumn morning, he had found himself at a loose end owing to the fizzling out—as he would have expressed it—of that other affair, and so had wired J. St. Pol Naylor to announce that he would arrive at 3.30 to 4 p.m. Whether that were convenient or no to this possible client was not a point over which Gees troubled himself: if people wanted to consult him, they could fit it in at such time as he chose: otherwise—well, they did not want to consult him, obviously.

He spread his very large but well-shaped hands out on the table-cloth, cocked his cigarette-holder at an angle beside his long nose, and reflected. Eve Madeleine, his secretary—Miss Brandon, when he addressed her, and "Eve Madeleine" only in her absence—had looked up this Naylor person for him, and had ascertained that he was what Gees would have called a big noise in Nigerian tin. That is to say, he was not a mere landowner, like Gees' own father, finding his possessions more of liabilities than assets. It appeared that, if he wanted a thing, he could afford to pay for it, which for a man living in a country mansion designated as "hall" is a rare thing to-day. Unmarried, aged forty-five, member of Quinlon's, one of the most exclusive clubs in London, also of the Junior Counties—that caravanserai of elderly bores—and a fellow of two societies entitled to call themselves "Royal," he appeared enviably placed. All these things, and some others which for the moment Gees forgot, the highly efficient and also very attractive Eve Madeleine had dug out and placed before her employer, and then, lacking other occupation at the time, had gone back to her desk and got on reading Winston Churchill's monumental work on his ancestor Marlborough. She had read so many novels to pass the time in that Little Oakfield Street office that she was satiated with fiction, and so turned to more serious stuff.

Now, having considered the potentialities of this possible client, Gees called for and paid his bill, after which he pushed back his chair and got up, displaying a pair of feet which hinted, to say the least of it, that he ought not to have resigned from the police force. Presently, one of those noteworthily though not abnormally large feet was playing on the accelerator pedal of the grey, black-winged Rolls-Bentley which helped to prove that Gees had made a financial success of his first case, and the nose of the open car pointed south-east by south as its owner—and driver—cogitated over the man who had written that letter. That is to say, he cogitated part of the time.

For his way, after he had got well out from Yeovil, lay over the downlands that, perhaps, are richest in all that history of Britain which is so old as to be out of history, and, a sensitive, as he undoubtedly was, he felt the influences by which he was surrounded. For there on the downs sleep the very old dead, the first reasoning beings to tread and hunt and fight over the land which then was part of Europe—when Dover cliffs and Gris-Nez facing them reared high and distant over the river that flowed toward the fertile valleys now lying fathoms down under the English Channel. Sometimes they sleep uneasily, those old ones. Gees, driving past their resting places, sensed their unease, felt them as not dead at all, but sentient, watchful—of what? He put that question to himself as the letter in his pocket recurred to his mind: the letter of a pedant, almost, of a man careful of his words, of his dignity—over-careful of all that maintained him in his place. Troyarbour Hall. Troyarbour. Obviously —*trois arbres*. A corruption from the old French. And Naylor? Nailer—one who nailed things, or possibly made nails: until Doctor Johnson compiled his "dixonary," there was no standardised spelling for the

English language, and "Nailer" might spell himself anyhow—as might "Smith" spell himself "Smythe" or "Smyth" or any other variation that appealed to him. "Naylor" was in old time merely a nailer, an artisan, and so his descendant, risen to "county" rank, was mightily jealous of his dignity: if he married, his descendants also would be very jealous of their dignity: it was in the blood, that of the enriched commoner, who sought to make himself level with Howards, and Neviles, and St. Olaves, and—maybe—Voronzoff-Dashkoffs, de Polignacs, Cabots and Lapeyracs. Gees grinned as he thought of these later names: it would be all one to a Naylor, to whom a "Green" would be a mere circumstance. Strictly non-committal, that "Green". Ah, well!

Trois arbres. The three trees would have vanished, long since. They had probably rotted away ages before Naylors got hold of the hall—thanks to Eve Madeleine, Gees knew that Naylors had inhabited there since the days of the second Charles—admirable girl, Eve Madeleine: she got just the facts he wanted, the things that facilitated his quest for atmosphere. He felt that he knew what to expect in meeting this J. St. Pol Naylor before seeing the man—knew what type of being he would find. Through his secretary, and also through the writing and phrasing of that letter: not that he visioned the physical personality of the man, but that he knew the mentality, the spiritual essence, so to speak, of the one who wanted his advice. And, possibly, his aid. That remained to be seen: meanwhile, he would sting this Naylor—St. Pol Naylor—in the matter of expenses, and so make certain that he was fully two guineas to the good, even if nothing further came of the adventure. He told himself, rather jesuitically, that two guineas was his fee for an initial consultation in his own office: if he took the trouble of driving a hundred miles or so out of London, and bit pieces out of two days to visit a possible client, that two ought to be increased to ten, a sum which to such a man as this Naylor would not even amount to a fleabite.

This Naylor! Gees told himself that he was in danger of going to this interview with a prejudice against the man: something in the phrasing of that letter was ruffling, irritant: he sensed pomposity. . . .

And saw, on a signpost—"Troyarbour, 3. Blandford, 15." Indicating that the village was twelve miles distant from its post town. Well, these Dorset villages were widely spaced—it was not a populous county: the open downland stretched for miles with hardly a house in view, and such towns as existed—like Blandford—snuggled down in the valleys for the sake of water—and, secondarily, for shelter. The very old ones had lived differently: such monuments of theirs as could be traced—mere lines on the face of the downs, except for such tremendous and enduring works as Mai-Dun by Dorchester—pointed to settlements on the uplands. They had had to guard their sheep, and had made the misnamed dew-ponds to get water. For some few centuries they had had a different climate, too much rain rather than too little, and in that period many of the valleys would have been untenable.

Another signpost, marking the divergence of a mere lane from the well-tended road Gees had so far followed, bore the legend—"Troyarbour Only. No Through Road." He took to the lane, and eased his rate of travel for the sake of his springs and shock-

absorbers. Ruts had been partly filled in with granite
chips, loose and crunchy under the tyres of the car.
There was width for vehicles to pass each other only
at intervals, and, if two met between the widenings,
one or other would be compelled to back. The lane
went up and down, winding not too steeply until
shoulders of the bare downland folded it into a wind-
less stillness.

A lone farmhouse with its outbuildings appeared on
an acre or so of flat, unfenced from the lane, and
hens chirrawked away from the passing car, while an
enormous sow with her litter of piglets eyed the vehicle
momentarily, and then ignored it. Down and yet down,
with the farmstead invisible behind, and Gees reflected
that the man who had measured off that three miles
must have ignored the windings of the lane and marked
up the crow-flight distance. Well, the afternoon was
young, yet, and in the placid October sunshine this
valley was a pleasant thing, with a mildness in its
still air that was also invigorating.

At the end of the twisted descent the shouldering
heights that had enclosed the lane receded, leaving a
pocket of almost-flatness in which were set an inn,
with a signboard picturing three hawthorn trees in the
full bloom of May—it was a fairly well-executed piece
of work, with no lettering on the board: a general
store and post-office—three wires came over the downs
to descend to its roof and mark it a telegraph office,
and two wires went on, up the ascent to which Gees
faced: five cottages, and a bay-windowed, rather
modern-looking house standing by itself to face all
the rest. And this, Gees decided, was Troyarbour.

When he got out from the car to inquire the where-
abouts of the Hall, the post-office sign confirmed his

belief, and also informed him that Martha Kilmain was the presiding genius there. Since the inn was closed at this hour he entered the store, and found that the goods for sale ranged from drapery and even shamelessly-displayed lingerie, by way of bread and cakes to cheese, bacon, and hob-nailed boots. It was quite impossible that a place of such meagre dimensions could hold and exhibit such a variety of wares, yet there they were, on show. And, emerging from a bacon-festooned doorway, a mighty female of middle age, a very Amazon of a woman with bare, muscular arms, an utterly expressionless face, and—almost an absurdity on such a one—a wealth of rippling, corn-coloured hair. Martha herself, Gees concluded.

"Could you be so good as to direct me to Troyarbour Hall?" he asked, and made the question as ingratiating as possible. Tobacco and cigarettes were among the articles purveyed here, and he might want to overhaul the stock, later—if a case resulted from his interview.

She pointed through the wall of the shop, in the direction which the Rolls-Bentley faced. She said—"Foller the road, you can't go wrong." Whereon he thanked her and went out again, for the manner of her reply had indicated that she did not want to be troubled any more.

He drove on. Beyond the valley bottom the lane, ascending again, was a mere cleft between two massy slopes, with abrupt windings that hid what lay ahead, and the pair of wires from the post-office carried on poles beside it. Here, though, it had been cut to two-vehicle width at some time. A half-mile or more of fairly steep ascent, and then the car bonnet faced a pair of iron gates swung on stone pillars, and beyond the gates was a short drive, gravelled and well-kept, rising gently to the Hall frontage, that too of grey stone. Two-storied, with ground-floor windows a good ten feet in height, the structure nested into the hills at the far side of a little plateau, on which were clumps of rhododendrons, yellow-leaved laurels, and single-standing monkey-puzzlers and other trees exotic to Dorset. Hawthorns, easily recognisable by their berries, flanked the drive and made it an avenue, and the place as a whole gave evidence of scrupulous tendance: here, it said in effect, is wealth, and one who does not fear to use it.

Gees said to himself as he got out to open the gates —there was no lodge at the entrance—"Yes, ten guineas, for a certainty—*and* expenses at top level!" and knew, as after driving through he got out again and closed the gates, that he had a distinct prejudice against the owner of this place—without having seen the man.

For a minute or less the scrollwork of the gates themselves held him: sixteenth or seventeenth-century Italian work, he felt sure: there was a delicate artistry, a strengthening balance in the work from top to bottom, such as English iron-fashioners seldom compass without a certain clumsiness, which betrays the intent to combine strength with decorative effect. Here, he knew as he gazed, was the work of an artist in iron, one sensitive enough to be content with nothing less than perfect work.

He got back into the car, and swung it to a stand-still opposite the pillared portico, over which was a shield in low relief on the stone, bearing the initials— "I. R. N." and the date "1701." The panelled, black-green, massive door was in keeping with the date, and

Gees, pulling a bell-handle beside it, noted that the
door swung back as silently as easily, to reveal a
parlourmaid, young and pretty, and rather over-
daintily attired for her part—it was a stage costume,
rather than a working dress.

He asked—"Mr. Naylor?" and with no inquiry of
any kind she asked in turn—"Will you come this
way, sir?" took and deposited his shabby old felt hat
and shabbier overcoat, and conducted him through the
high-ceiled hall, decorated with stags' heads and rams'
heads, moose heads and tiger heads—and even an
elephant's head—to another door in a corridor at the
back of the hall, where she halted to ask—"Mr. Green,
isn't it?"

He said—"Yes," and on that she opened the door
and announced him. Entering, he saw the reverse of
his expectation: he had looked for a beefy, Squire
Westernish sort of man, and found himself facing one
thin and small and delicate, with finely-shaped hands
and feet, soft, appealing brown eyes, and very pale
lips. A shy, anaemic sort of man, at first sight, who
greeted his caller with a charming smile, and, offering
his hand, said—"Mr. Green? I'm so glad you were
able to get here. It's rather early for tea, but—shall
I ring?"

"Thank you, no," Gees answered. "I've lunched
not long since, and don't feel like tea yet. If you
don't mind."

"Why, certainly not. A business man, evidently,
in spite of the nature of your business—I speak of that
from hearsay, and you must forgive me if I trespass
too far."

Again Naylor smiled, that very charming expression
of friendliness which Gees found a little disturbing. He

had an instant's memory of those entrance gates, all artistry, and yet concealed in it was tremendous strength. So here—perhaps! He was far from sure as to whether his first impressions of this man were to be trusted. *Amba gachle,* as the Zulus say—tread softly!

He said—"I don't see where the trespass comes in. Do you mind my asking where you got those marvellous gates at your boundary?"

"Picked them up in Milan, for not merely a song, but one line of the first verse," Naylor answered readily, and laughed a little. "I'm glad you noticed them. Not many people have the seeing eye."

"Very few could miss such a pair," Gees assured him. "But—you wanted—what?" He put it as bluntly as he could, being determined not to yield to any spell this strange man could weave. For the man *was* strange: he was as exotic, here, as the monkey-puzzlers in front of his Hall: he was small and frail, yet he had power: Gees felt it.

He said—"Ah, yes! You have not much time, perhaps. And that fee of yours for initial consultation—two guineas. All very well if one comes to you in London, but your coming here—taking the trouble, I mean. Shall we make that two into a ten?"

"My own idea," Gees assured him promptly, and saw the thin, delicate features harden slightly at his apparent rapacity. "And expenses, of course. Eight, say—eighteen guineas for the total."

He put it as brutally as he could, determined as he was to give this man not one inch of advantage—the prejudice against, with which he had driven here, was growing stronger and yet stronger. Naylor nodded a rather frigid assent to his estimate.

"Eighteen—yes. I will write you the cheque before you leave."

"Very good of you," Gees told him. "And now—what is it you want of me? Something you wouldn't put in writing, I understood from your letter." He saw the thin, delicate hands of the man facing him quiver as he put the blunt question, and divined that Naylor was afraid—of something. Though why one in his position should fear—

"I am going on what Hunter—Hunter of Denlandham—told me about you," Naylor said slowly, as if he chose his words very carefully. "You—you can, it appears, lay ghosts. So I gathered, from what he told me. But—I am not afflicted by ghosts, but by something worse."

"There are many worse things than ghosts," Gees said soberly.

"Yes. Yes. Mr. Green, do you believe in witchcraft?"

"Believe in it—no," Gees said promptly. "In the possibility that there is such a thing—yes. Obeah, Voodoo, the evidence is——"

"No!" Naylor interrupted rather peremptorily. "Not African magic—or hoodoo, if it is that. Witchcraft, for which women used to be drowned, and burned, and all the rest. That sort, I mean."

"I believe it did exist," Gees answered cautiously.

"Supposing I tell you it still exists?" Naylor said. "Here, in Troyarbour—and directed against me?"

"Then," Gees answered steadily, "I'd advise you to consult a mental specialist, not a confidential agent like myself."

"Will you let me try to convince you?" Naylor asked earnestly.

Gees nodded assent. "But I'm tough," he pointed out. "I take an awful lot of convincing. Who and what is your witch—or wizard?"

"Witch!" Naylor made an exclamation of the word. "Witch, if ever there was one! Here, in Troyarbour, and—and—her ways are death!"

II

IRA—NAYLOR'S ESTIMATE

"YOU seem to have a certain respect for the potentialities of this lady, whoever she may be," Gees said
calmly. "In fact—well!" He left it at that, except
for an inquiring glance at Naylor.

"Her ways are death!" Naylor repeated emphatically.

"That's two deaths, and how many ways?" Gees
queried, in matter-of-fact fashion. "Who is the lady
with the deadly ways, anyhow?"

He wanted to keep this interview on a light note,
if possible. Naylor's fingers were clasping and unclasp-
ing, and altogether the man looked as if he believed
what he said—as if he were in fear. Yet, Gees felt
sure, he was a strong character, and not altogether a
likable one at that. If he maintained this intensity,
things looked like being difficult: he might, too, be
attaching far too much weight to nothing at all. Ever
has an accusation of witchcraft been hard to prove:
nineteen out of twenty times it has had no foundation
in fact, but has been dictated by envy, covetousness,
or mere spite.

Naylor said, doubtfully—"It is a long story, I'm
afraid."

"The night is young," Gees rejoined cheerfully. "In
fact, it isn't tea time, yet, and I'm going to hunt
quarters in this locality when it threatens to get dark
—not go back to London."

"I believe you could get a room at the Three Thorns," Naylor informed him. "They take in tourists, sometimes—hikers, I believe the people call themselves. Men and girls with knapsacks——" he broke off, obviously embarrassed. Gees reflected that, by the look of this place, there must be dozens of empty bedrooms, and made no comment.

He said—"This long story, now? Or have you changed your mind?"

"No—Oh, no!" It was a hasty, almost frantic denial—the man was far too intense, Gees knew. "It goes back—well, a long way. I said it was a long story. Are you in any way conversant with mythology? With ancient beliefs, and all that sort of thing, you know?"

"The *Golden Bough*," Gees told him solemnly, "is one of the fondest things I'm of. I sometimes make it a bedside book."

"Then"—Naylor frowned at the levity of the reply, but made no comment—"you will know the Norse legends, I expect?"

"Witchcraft enough there," Gees observed, more gravely.

"And—and other things," Naylor amended. "Such as—both the Valkyrs and the Volsungs owned Odin as their father. I am more particularly concerned with the Volsung race—Wagner used that legend in his Germanised version of a Norse myth—as it is considered."

"And as, of course, it is," Gees added.

Naylor shook his head. "Oh, no!" he dissented, and again there was evident in him an intensity which, on the face of it, the subject did not warrant. "The gods of Norse legend actually existed—not as immortals, but as heroes of the race, originally. They were deified and given attributes of godhead by later generations, but Odin and Thor, and Baldur—existed. And Loki—he too was real."

"A prehistoric confidence trickster," Gee suggested.

Naylor not only frowned, this time, but voiced his objection to such flippancy with regard to a subject on which, evidently, he was far from flippant. He said—"I don't like your tone, Mr. Green. Loki was real evil, personified. A power, in his time."

"And there you have it—in his time," Gees retorted calmly. "A swindler of any sort—a person who thrives on deceit—is a real evil in any time, and you yourself own that the gods of Norse mythology were not immortals at all, but heroes subsequently deified. And I'm not going to use a kow-towing tone over any one of them, especially Loki, to please you or anybody."

"You will please yourself, of course." To Gees' surprise, the rejoinder was almost meek. "I am going into this matter of the Norse gods, and especially of the Volsung half-gods, children of Odin by a mortal woman, as, say a foundation for what I wish to tell you—over which I felt you might possibly advise me, at the least."

Gees felt all his prejudice against J. St. Pol Naylor returning. That speech was like the man's letter—far too much like it. Didactic, each word chosen carefully —he was on his dignity again.

"The Volsungs—yes. Well? Not a very creditable crowd, were they? That is, by modern standards," Gees said reflectively.

"I am a Volsung," Naylor replied coldly.

"Is that so?" Gees did not sound impressed. "Well, if I were you, I should keep it dark. Difficult to prove, too——"

"Mr. Green!" The interruption was angrily harsh. "I am sorry I ever asked you to call on me here. I will write your cheque for eighteen guineas as arranged, and bid you good-day." And he got on his feet in pursuance of the intent.

Gees said—"Pity you haven't got a fire here."

Pausing, turning about in curiosity over the remark, Naylor asked—"Why?" A sharply frosty monosyllable, he made it.

"To save me the trouble of striking a match to burn said cheque," Gees answered coolly. "I don't take money I haven't earned."

"You—you——" Naylor sat down again. "I *am* a Volsung, I tell you!" he reiterated, and now there was fierce intensity in the claim.

"And I tell you it would be difficult to prove it," Gees retorted. "In any case, what does it matter? I don't see——"

"I'll tell you." Naylor appeared to have forgotten his outburst of anger. "Volsung Sigurd took and carried off Wulfruna, wife to Oger the Nailer, so called because, when he killed an enemy, he cut off the right hand of the dead man and nailed it over the doorway of his great hall. This Wulfruna was still a very lovely woman when Sigurd stole her, for which Oger—to-day, that name would be Hugo, of course— for which Oger eventually killed him. Wulfruna was left with child by Sigurd, and she hid away and eventually bore the child, a daughter. Except for the sex of the child, this is the story of Siegmund and Sieglinde as Wagner tells it in the *Valkyrie*."

"Obviously," Gees observed, "except also that those two were brother and sister. This Sigurd and Wulfruna were not, I take it."

"They were that, or very nearly that," Naylor answered slowly—reluctantly, it seemed. "They were both Volsungs. All this is out of history, of course, purely legendary. Yet—believe me—true."

"Most legends have a foundation in fact," Gees remarked primly.

"This *is* fact," Naylor insisted earnestly. "To finish that story, though. Wulfruna, before Sigurd came and tempted her away, had borne a male child to Oger, one who was named Oger Ogersson, as was the fashion of naming in those times. Which is evidence, though not proof, that the elder Oger was founder of the family through Wulfruna his wife, because he does not appear to have been called anyone's son, but only Oger the Nailer. And my name, you note, is Naylor."

"There will be missing shoots on that family tree," Gees commented.

"Believe it or not, as you like," Naylor said sourly. "Oger Ogersson dropped the 'Nailer' from his titles, but it was resumed by his grandson, who went viking, and nailed the hands of his dead enemies round the prow of his long ship. And from then on, in various forms according to the time, the name—or nickname, if you like—stuck to the family, so that when surnames became common, after the Norman Conquest, we became Nailers with all the variants of spelling, till with the building of this hall my forebears finally adopted the spelling that I retain. And that is half the story I have to tell."

"You said it was a long one," Gees observed rather caustically.

"I am descended from Oger Ogersson," Naylor claimed yet again. "Now, to complete that first half of the story, Oger Ogersson was a Baresark—and I think I need not tell you what that means."

"It was a useful quality, in his time," Gees commented.

"But"—Naylor made a long pause—"it would be far from useful to-day. Which"—another long pause—"is part of my reason for asking your advice, at the least. Your help, if—if you are the man Hunter of Denlandham said you were. If, that is, you have the qualities with which he credited you in speaking of you to me."

Again Gees heard the didactic precision of phrase that roused in him prejudice against this man. He said —"I claim to be a specialist in certain directions. We keep wandering from this story of yours, though. What have Oger's baresark habits to do with it?"

"The—the attribute, call it—is transmissible," Naylor said.

"Runs in the family, you'd say," Gees suggested.

"Intermittently. Has persisted down to this present day, in our case, but will miss out two or three—or more—generations, and then recur. Not—not mere anger or unreasonableness, but a blind fury of which one is totally unconscious after the fit has passed. One becomes a different being altogether, and wakens at the end to know nothing of it—nothing of what one has done or said while it lasted."

"I believe that was the case," Gees conceded thoughtfully. "By your way of putting it, it seems as if you——" He did not end it.

"Yes," Naylor said quietly, "and that brings me to the second part of the story, which begins with

Wulfruna's daughter by Sigurd—and both that child's parents were of the Volsung breed, remember."

"You claim that you are, too," Gees reminded him.

"That is so—but Sigurd was not my ancestor," Naylor rejoined. "He was that daughter's father, and through him—though he was dead before Wulfruna bore the child—through him she inherited and developed the qualities that make the witch. There was pre-natal influence, and I believe there was, too, the unholy communion that goes with possession of the powers that girl had—you get an outline of it in the tale of the witch of En-Dor. Power to commune with the dead."

For a moment Gees' thoughts went back to his drive to this place, and how, as he went over the downlands, he had sensed unease among the very old dead, as if they stirred in their barrows. He asked— "What is the legend of her—what was she called?"

"Lagny. Dark Lagny, because of her hair," Naylor answered slowly. "Because Oger had killed her father, she devoted her life to vengeance on his son—part of her life, that is. Because she had many lovers, and brought harm to them all—ruin to some and death to some. That is a long story in itself, but it is not part of mine that I am telling you now. She was evil and beautiful—the two often go together—and in the end she contrived a spell that drew Oger Ogersson's long viking ship to wreckage on the Northumbrian coast, not far south from Iona. I have seen the place where the ship broke up on the rocks——"

"Where legend says it broke up," Gees interpolated, for again, in telling this story, Naylor was verging on unnatural intensity.

"All that was written down," Naylor insisted. "I have a verbatim copy—it is bad Latin of the second century. The general impression is that the vikings did not come to ravage this country till after the Roman occupation ended, but that is wrong. Oger came, and was drawn toward the rocks by Lagny's witch spells. It was in a night of storm, and only three of Oger's men came out alive—half-alive, say, to recover enough to tell their tale. I want you to believe, Mr. Green, that I have devoted enough time to search and research to unearth all the facts of this story I am telling you —all the facts, that is, still ascertainable. Palimpsests, fragments of old chronicles, bits of monkish gossip in bad Latin, written in black letter to make it worse— everything I could find, to piece it together and—as far as possible—get this story in full, because of—but I am coming to that."

"You'd got to the wreck of Oger's long ship," Gees reminded him.

"Yes, and the three live men washed ashore. They said—and each of them confirmed the other two—that as the ship was driving on they saw Dark Lagny riding a Valkyr horse in the storm—choosing the dead, that is. Saw her beckoning Oger on, riding high over him as he steered his long ship—whether he too saw her is past telling. They said, too, that at the time she was in reality asleep in the arms of her last lover, a Roman officer of the garrison at Eboracum—York—many miles away from the point where the long ship was wrecked. Yet they said it was Dark Lagny they saw, past question, but younger and more alive and lovely than she was then—because by that time she had borne children who had nearly grown up, and was past her best. But all three say they saw her, and that it was her spells which caused the wreck."

"Men were credulous, in those days," Gees observed reflectively.

"Ye-es," Naylor half drawled. "So much so that, less than a year after Oger's death—and with no reference whatever to that incident—Dark Lagny was crucified by order of the Roman commander at Eboracum, being found guilty of unholy spells and practices by which men had been compelled to kill each other, or themselves."

"A *lamia*, apparently," Gees commented. "Yet the Romans were a practical people. Materialists to the *n*th, as a rule."

"*Lamia* perhaps," Naylor half-conceded, "but certainly Volsung—and, if you accept that story told by the three men who escaped from the wreck, Valkyr too. Beloved of Odin, admitted to all the mysteries of that old faith, and so given powers—these things are, Mr. Green." He broke off from his tale to make an earnest insistence of the statement. "You can see stark evil walking the earth to-day, if you look."

"And so they crucified Dark Lagny," Gees mused.

"They should have put an end to her before she bore children," Naylor said sombrely. "Because—her death was not the end."

"Else, you would not be telling this tale," Gees surmised, seeing in part the point to which the story was driving.

"Else I should not be telling it," Naylor admitted. "You know, in spite of—of—well, a certain irritating way you have—you are an understanding soul. I feel I *can* tell this to you."

Not merely prejudice, but distrust of the man wakened as Gees heard the rather fulsome comment on himself. He said—"That may be. This is, as you said, a long story, and I haven't heard it all, yet."

"Dark Lagny left children," Naylor went on. "There were two sons in this country—she spent a good part of her life in Britain—and there were others, sons or daughters, who grew up and settled—and married—in or near where Trondjhem stands to-day. On that fiord. That branch of her family is all that counts in this tale of mine. You know Norse is Norman, of course—the Norsemen came to Normandy, and in due time Harold of England fell into Duke William's hands —this part of it is child's history—and swore away his kingdom. Senlac, and the Conquest—and among Duke William's followers was a descendant of Sigurd and Dark Lagny, Hugo Main de Fer—because at some time after Senlac he lost his left hand, and had it replaced by an iron hook. He was a mere man-at-arms, but he got a knighthood or some patent of nobility from the Conqueror over the devastation of the north—when William laid all Yorkshire waste in revenge for the attempted rising. Also, this Hugo found and subsequently married one of the descendants of Dark Lagny's British-born sons. Now I expect you have heard of William de Warenne, the Conqueror's favourite who got so much out of his master?"

Gees nodded assent. "He had manors all over England," he said.

"Yes," Naylor assented, "and this of Troyarbour—trois arbres—was one of them. To carry on the story —Hugo Main de Fer died, and his wife became mistress of William de Warenne, for a little while. Through that—they were lax over such things in those days—her son became known as a de Warenne—not as a surname, because there were no surnames at that time, but as belonging to William de Warenne. And William so much favoured him as to give him this manor of Troyarbour—to call it by its present name, and get a barony for him from the Conqueror—am I making this clear to you?"

"Quite clear," Gees told him. "Carry on with the tale."

"My forebears—later to be called Naylors—had won pardon of a sort from the Norman authorities, and settled somewhere near here before Hugo's son was granted this manor," Naylor went on. "That Hugo, remember, was descended from Wulfruna and Sigurd. My forebears were descended from Oger Ogersson and Wulfruna—you see?"

"There was—well, a sort of removed cousinship," Gees commented.

"There was the deadliest of enmities," Naylor said emphatically. "Also, on their side, the tendency to—possibility of, rather—the use of witchcraft against us Naylors, as I will call us from this point onward, and on our side the intermittent curse of running baresark. As instance. In the time of the first Henry a witch developed among the de Warennes of Troyarbour, and set her wits to ruining the family of Naylors of that day—Saxons, by Norman reckoning, and freemen holding a stead in tenure under a neighbouring manor—between here and where Blandford now is. The cattle and sheep died and the crops failed—it was all in pursuance of the old feud beween the two families that began when Oger killed Sigurd—and then the eldest son of that Naylor wasted away through her spells——"

"Got tuberculosis, most likely," Gees interposed.

"As may be," Naylor said, making the remark utterly sceptical. "Whether that were so or no, one night the boy's father went baresark, and instead of going out as a freeman of those days should, took an axe and flint and steel and tinder, and went off alone. He fired the gatehouse of these de Warennes—it was a wooden structure, apparently—and killed three men before his fit wore off. A naked man with an axe against three or more armed men, remember. Now— and here comes the part of the story that counts— the king's justiciar of those days judged the case— Henry Beauclerc was strong on forms of law. This was a case of Saxon rebellion against Norman authority, on the face of it, and the Norman in question a sort of connection of the great William de Warenne. Yet— yet!—the baresark Naylor was not hanged, or sub- jected to torture as one might expect, such as being broken on the wheel or pressed to death. He was let off with the loss of his right eye and right hand, and lived to be a very old man. Meanwhile Ira de Warenne —the first woman of the family to be given that name—was burned at the stake as a witch, although she was allegedly of noble birth. Condemned, not by the justiciar, but by ecclesiastical jurisdiction, and, as I say, burned at the stake. Unique, I believe."

"Possibly." Gees made it a non-committal comment. "Is any part of this—this family history, call it— documented?"

"In other words, you think I am telling fairy tales," Naylor accused with acrid coldness. "It was all docu-

mented, up to the time of the Civil War—about the
time of the siege of Corfe, it would be. The Naylor
of that day was a Parliament man—he served with
some distinction under Ireton—and the Warenns—as
they had then become, having lost their title during
the wars of the Roses—were Royalists. Naylor got
here with a troop, and managed to sack and burn the
castle that stood where this house stands now, and most
of the old records went up in smoke—the Parliament
men were all iconoclasts, as you know. But that Naylor
left children who knew the tale, and most of it is
available to me in old letters and diaries. One has to
read between the lines to a certain extent, but to us—
to me, since I am the only one surviving, now—it is
all clear."

"I see." There may have been a tinge of scepticism
in the rejoinder. "And still, all this is story. I don't
see the point, yet."

"I am coming now to the point," Naylor said. "It
is that once in so many generations—once in a century, perhaps, or it may be once in two centuries—a
Warenn, father or mother or both, names a daughter
Ira, as if they had prescience, foreknowledge, of what
was to come in the lifetime of that daughter. Simul-
taneously—within a few years either way, that is—a
son is born to a Naylor, and on him is the Baresark
curse. It is no less than a curse, believe me. And the
old feud is renewed. The Ira Warenn, descended from
Sigurd and Wulfruna, sets herself to destroy the descendant of Oger and Wulfruna, to rob him of all he
values and in the end drive him baresark, so that he
may suffer the penalty for wanton killing, as men
kill when they are in that state. As surely as a daughter
of that family is named Ira——"

He broke off, and sat silent, evidently trying to read what impression his story had made on his auditor. But Gees, keeping a poker face, quoted softly—

" 'Dies irae, dies illa,
    Solvet sœclum in favilla——' "

"So!" Naylor said, as if satisfied. " 'Ira.' That is, wrath. And she is, whenever she recurs. I see it as a reincarnation—of hate. Time after time has an 'Ira' been named, and each time a Naylor has been cursed with the baresark fits, developing when the Ira Warenn of that time has come to womanhood and full powers. Whether she induces the fits—I don't know. None of us has known."

"You mean—through contact with you?" Gees asked. He was growing interested in this fantastic story. The man who was telling it evidently believed it all, and was influenced by it.

"Not necessarily," Naylor answered. "As instance —all my contact with this Ira Warenn has consisted of quarrels, threats on her side and utterly useless attempts to placate her on mine. It was my fault in the first place, of course——" He broke off, rather nervously.

"I'd better have the whole story," Gees encouraged him.

"Yes. Yes!" He wakened from a moment's reverie—not a pleasant one, by his expression. "The whole story. There have been—this is the thirteenth 'Ira,' since that first one who was burned as a witch. And I am the thirteenth—let that wait, though. My own part in this comes last. I told you they lost their barony during the Wars of the Roses—they were

Lancastrians, because always the de Warennes, and Warenns as they call themselves now, have held to the old order, no matter what that order may be. So they held to Lancaster, and lost all but Troyarbour when Earl Warwick lost Barnet Field. They kept Troyarbour till a Warenn followed the man Charles Stuart, and went down with Charles Stuart. That is—he was not beheaded, but escaped to France, to come back at the Restoration and try to remind the second Charles Stuart that his father had sacrificed everything to the Royalist cause. And that second Charles was—well, a Stuart. Warenn begged in vain —he was a very old man, then—and a son of his came here. The homing instinct, I suppose you'd call it. He brought enough worldly goods with him to become tenant to us Naylors—I haven't told you, but out of revenge against the Warenns, I take it, the Naylor of Cromwell's time somehow got possession of this manor, and we have held it ever since. Naylors ousting those Warenns, and then their coming back as tenants of the manor they had owned. It must have been bitter for them, proud beggars that they are."

That last sentence defined for Gees his own dislike of the man. There was a smug satisfaction in it, revenge accomplished, no matter what its victims might do. Past question, J. St. Pol Naylor kept and nourished a hate, whatever might be the feeling of these Warenns.

"That was—in the time of the second Charles," Gees said.

"And to this day," Naylor added, almost gloatingly. "But——" his tone changed—"now I come to why I asked for an interview with you—my own part in this story. They—that is, the far greater number of

villagers who lived in Troyarbour in those days—flung
an Ira Warenn into a running stream to sink or swim
—for witchcraft, of course—when the foundations of
this Hall were being dug. She sank, and drowned—
that test is as futile as it is foolish. Because she *was*
a witch. She was drowned after the Mrs. Naylor of
that time had given birth to a dead infant, and half
the cattle belonging to us had died of some disease
not diagnosed, and—and that Naylor went baresark
and set fire to the barn at the farm, which in turn
fired two ricks of corn, and the story goes that it took
six men to get him under control and prevent him
from killing the witch before the fit passed, and pretty
much all the justices of the peace in the county to
hush up the scandal—though drowning Ira Warenn—
you note the accent is on the 'enn,' always—put an
end to his troubles, in every way. He was quite a
normal man, after that."

Spoken with placid satisfaction, that last sentence.
Gees felt his prejudice growing again. Was this man
quite sane?

"Then they named another 'Ira' about the end of
the eighteenth century," Naylor went on. "She was
found drowned—that was a coroner's inquest verdict
—with nothing to show how she came by her death.
Whether my great-great-grandfather were baresark or
no I do not know. He left no records, and died of
apoplexy. The normal, hard-drinking country squire
—not in the least a Volsung."

"That is, as far as you know," Gees observed.

"I *know!*" Again he evinced intensity. "Such of
us as hark back to that beginning—such of us as know
the story of Oger and Sigurd is real—we are—but I'm
wandering from the point again. My own part in it.

I was eight years old when the Warenns at the farm
—you must have passed that farm before coming to
the village—when they named a daughter Ira—the
thirteenth Ira. As long as my father lived all went
well. I was here very little—I went shooting in the
African game preserves after I came down from Cambridge, and did the modern grand tour. And then—
there was a woman."

On that he broke off, and Gees saw his mobile face
harden, grow almost ugly. Then he smiled, and again
was a very attractive man—superficially. He said—
"I suppose that is true of every man, sooner or later.
She was married, and she came to me. We went away
together—it was the year my father died. My mother
had been dead a long time. Her—the woman's hus-
band was vindictive. He refused to divorce her. We
had a child—a girl child——"

He broke off, there, and now Gees did not dislike,
but pitied him. After a while he roused from his
memories, and spoke again—

"We came back here—I had to come back, to take
over all my father had left. He had not been a good
business man, and there was much for me—that is
not part of the story, though. What is part of it is
that for the last four years before his death Warenn,
this Ira's father, had paid no rent. It is not that I
need the money, but—well, you can't let one tenant
off and compel the others to pay. I went to see him—
and did not. He was then dying, and I saw . . .
Ira."

"Well?" Gees asked it after a long silence.

"I—I almost forgot you were here," Naylor confessed. "Yes, Ira Warenn. Dark Lagny—unutterable
allure—I knew all the legends were true, when I saw

her that day. Yet, to me, hateful—I was near on
baresark then. You see, that curse has come down to
me. Which is why I called on you, to see if there is
any way——"

"You should see a mental specialist, not me," Gees
said gravely.

"Damn all mental specialists!" Naylor broke out
with sudden, bitter passion. "Wait, though! I told
that girl I could not make an exception of her father,
because of others—I could not run this estate as a
charitable institution. I remember I used just those
words. It was reasonable, but—her father was dying
even then. She knew it—I did not. She told me the
manor of Troyarbour was his and hers, by right, not
mine at all. She told me she was Wulfruna's daughter
—daughter, mind you!—and she would leave me with
nothing I valued, and when she had taken all would
destroy me, myself. She would leave me not even the
dog I had with me that day—it was a red setter I
loved more than any other dog I ever knew. She called
the curse of Odin on me, and told me she would take
from me all that I loved. And all the time I saw her
as Dark Lagny, allure unutterable—I could have lost
all reason in her arms, and yet hated her the while.
Perhaps you cannot understand that—because it is
beyond my own understanding. Dark Lagny, daughter
of Wulfruna who was mother of my race as of hers.
This is a thing of the Volsung breed, where brother
and sister mate as the Incas and Pharaohs mated. You
will not understand it—I cannot explain it."

"Perhaps I understand more than you think," Gees
said dissentingly.

"As may be," Naylor retorted, half-angrily. "Listen,
man! In a week the red setter was dead, and I mourned

over it as over the loss of a friend. The vet who post-
mortemed it said its heart had failed, and he could not
tell why. *I* could tell! Within six months, the only
woman who ever meant anything to me died—double
pneumonia, in high summer! In high summer, I tell
you! Within a month of her death, our little daughter
was taken away—scarlet fever and diphtheria—and
never another case of it that summer within thirty
miles of this village! She came back in her coffin,
and lies beside her mother—I think my heart lies
there too. And I was then—wait, and let me show
you. Not as you see me now."

He went to a desk under the high window, opened
a drawer, and took out what Gees recognised as a
snapshot album. Returning, he handed it over.
"Look at them," he said, "and see if you recognise
me."

Beginning with the first page, Gees saw photographs
of a massively-built, middle-aged man, and in one of
them his arm was laid over the shoulders of a slight,
small, grey-haired woman. Naylor said—"My father
and mother—and now you come to me," and
Gees turned over and asked—"You were an only
child?"

"No, the second of three. The other two died in
infancy."

Looking out from the page to which Gees had turned
was a broad-shouldered, hefty-looking boy of about
sixteen, who, although the photograph was an amateur
snapshot, apparently, had posed for his picture and
smirked self-consciously—and self-approvingly. Naylor said—"That was nearly two years before I went up
to Cambridge," and Gees turned over to see the same
boy, older now and developing to vigorous, athletic

adolescence, in rowing kit, football shorts, tennis flannels, and corduroys with a gun in the crook of his arm.

"You all the time?" Gees asked.

"All the time," Naylor answered. "You will see why, later—or I can tell you now. *She* wished it. She mounted all those photographs."

In silence Gees went on turning the pages. They formed a picture chronicle of growth to manhood, and the "she" of whom Naylor had spoken in a tone verging on reverence came in as a woman who stood beside him, tall as himself and, as nearly as the monotone of a photograph told, fair-haired and more than normally attractive. And Naylor himself showed as far different from the man Gees saw now, though he was recognisable as the same man. He was more virile, physically robust and a bigger, stronger man than this. So he remained through the rest of the series, which included views evidently taken abroad—probably in Riviera resorts, though two or three appeared north African, by the clarity of the light and sharp-edged shadows. The last picture of all showed him bending over a cot in which an infant lay, and he took the album out from Gees' hands and closed it abruptly, almost rudely.

"Not that one," he said. "I wanted you to see—all this has changed me. Do you realise it—that I am changed?"

"You're more—ascetic, say," Gees answered.

"A polite way of saying I'm half the man I was then. Which is quite true. And—let me tell you this too—I'm pariah, you'll find. Because of—of her and the child. Content to be so—she was all to me, and since I was all to her we were happy until—until Ira

Warenn took her away from me. Only the people who would know me for my possessions would come here to see me now—and if they come they' get turned away. The social life my father and mother knew— the people who make up that life will never know me, because of—because to their thinking she and I lived in sin. Though we did not. But—I am quite alone. I'm still a member of Quinlon's, but I've not been in the club since—since she came to me."

"And that is all the story?" Gees asked.

"All the story—yes," Naylor answered. "Except —say it is the outline of the story. I have yet to tell you why I want your advice."

"Perhaps I can guess, but won't," Gees told him. "Do you mind if I summarise what you have told me, from a practical viewpoint?"

"Do so, by all means. I should like to know your view."•

"You wouldn't—won't," Gees said rather grimly, "but I'll give it you. For a beginning, I will discount all this legend of Dark Lagny, and her mother Wulfruna, who you claim is ancestress both to you and these Warenns. I will rule all that out, and to a certain extent will ignore your allegation that withchcraft has run in the Warenn family all the way up to Cromwell's time. Because wherever a feud persisted between two families, accusations of that sort were likely to be made, and superstition was strong enough to establish them on very slight evidence—without actual proof. Many an innocent man and woman has suffered death on that charge, as probably you know."

"I do know it," Naylor agreed. "But——"

"Wait!" Gees interrupted. "I am giving you my view. When your Naylor of the Cromwell period

seized on this manor of Troyarbour, the Warenns of
that day obviously had a grudge against him—there
was already the feud between the two families. The
Warenns had a way of perpetuating a rather uncommon
name for a girl—but it is no more uncommon than
your own 'St. Pol.' They very foolishly—I should
call it that—came back here as tenants of the family
they had cause to hate, since they regarded that family
as dispossessing them. On your side, you Naylors
were only too ready to attribute any trouble that came
your way to some sinister influence exerted by a
Warenn——"

"Always by an Ira Warenn," Naylor interposed.

"Or by no Warenn at all," Gees insisted. "I tell
you, you have no proof. In all you have told me I
can find no proof. If I take your own story—and
forgive me if I put it rather brutally—there were in
succession a dog, a woman, and a child, all three
dying after a probably neurotic woman—or girl
—who has some knowledge of the old legend that
oppresses you, had made a vague threat against you.
Can you trace any actual contact between that Ira
Warenn and any one of those three?   Any contact
whatever?"

"No-o." Naylor owned it reluctantly, dubiously.
"But——"

"No," Gees went on, "you can't. You have as
little proof against her, over these three deaths which
can be attributed to purely natural causes, as your
ancestors had against the other Warenn women whom
they accused of witchcraft, or—I'm anticipating what
you would say—got up enough prejudice to cause the
accusation to come from independent sources. And
now you've lived here alone and brooded till that old

legend and the feud between you Naylors and those Warenns have become the principal interests of your life. You want my advice—I'll give it you now. Shut up this place for, say a year. Go abroad again, do anything rather than stay brooding here alone. Get among normal people and revive normal interests— be a normal man among others, as you were meant to be. And come back to laugh at this Ira Warenn and regard her as merely foolish, not a witch or potent."

Naylor shook his head. "I—I cannot do that," he said.

"You mean you think you can't do it," Gees amended for him.

"No—it is not thinking. Because—as is always the case when a girl of that family is named Ira—I—I am a Baresark."

For a brief interval Gees wanted to shout laughter. If a rabbit had proclaimed its power to roar like a lion, the assertion would not have seemed more absurd. This smallish, delicate, even anaemic-looking being, going ravening with axe or club, was not merely an incredibility, but a preposterous impossibility! The man was mad.

"And what advice did you intend asking?" Gees inquired after a long,long pause, in which he could hear Naylor's uneven breathing.

"How to—how to neutralise her powers—Ira Warenn's powers," Naylor answered, dubiously and nervously.

"That's easy—just don't believe in 'em," Gees said bluntly. "As I see it, you're a case of self-hypnosis. You dislike the woman and know she dislikes you— you own that you gave her cause——"

"I have seen her since," Naylor interrupted, "and done my best to remove the cause. Offered to do all I could for her as my tenant——" He broke off, rather than ended the sentence, and though Gees waited he did not end it.

"How did she take the offers?" Gees asked at last.

"Laughed at them—and at me. Renewed her threats."

"Why not turn the woman out—get rid of her?"

"I can't. They hold on lease—over eight years of it to run."

"Then, as I said before, go yourself, and come back cured of these fears—these utterly groundless fears—of yours."

"I can't do that either, and they are not groundless."

Gees stood up. "You merely emphasise the truth of an old saying, that the only advice people will take is that which coincides with their own inclinations," he said. "I can offer you no other than what I have already given—and if I get to the main road before dark I can be back in London to-night."

"I see-e." Naylor, also on his feet, spoke very coldly. "Just one minute while I write you your cheque. Eighteen guineas, I think."

"Thank you, that is the amount." Gees spoke equally coldly.

Naylor took up the album, which he had put down on the floor, and with it went to the desk from which he had taken it. He put it away again and, taking out a cheque-book, wrote the cheque and handed it to Gees, who glanced at it and crumpled it into his pocket.

"Thank you very much, Mr. Naylor—and good-bye."

"I—I can't offer you any refreshment, I suppose?"
With the offer, Naylor unbent, evinced some slight
cordiality. Gees shook his head.

"No, thank you. It must be within an hour of
sunset, and—well, that lane! A merciful man is merciful to his car. No, don't trouble to ring—I know my
way out. Good-bye."

III

ABOUT to open the driving side door of his car and seat himself at the wheel, Gees paused, holding the door handle, and staring at the seat. He drew a long breath and murmured—"Holy mackerel!"

For, curled in somnolent comfort on his seat, lay a black cat. A sleek, healthy-looking cat, with his lengthy tail so adjusted that the tip was just under his nose. Reaching in and leaning over, Gees tickled the animal behind its ear, and it wakened to look up at him—gratefully, he thought. He said—"If you could drive, feller, it'd be a different thing. But I guess I'd better plant you where you belong."

He reached farther in and got a hand under the cat, which, unfolding itself, disclosed a small white shirt-front on the blackness of its chest. When he lifted it to hold it against his own chest, it got a paw up on his shoulder and climbed round to the back of his neck, knocking his hat off as it rubbed against his head, purring the while. He stooped to pick up the hat, and the cat retained its place, as it did when he went up to the front door of the Hall and rang the bell.

The same attractive-looking parlourmaid opened the door, and, as Gees reached up to lift the cat down, ejaculated—"Goodness!"

"He was in my car," Gees explained. "I thought I'd better hand him back so you'd know he's safe, before driving off——"

47

"Oh, no, sir!" She backed away as with difficulty he pulled the cat from its perch to hold it out to her. "Mr. Naylor'd go mad if that cat came in here—he would, really! It's Peter!"

"And what's wrong with Peter?" Gees asked curiously.

"He—he belongs to Miss Warenn, sir."

"But—but that's the other side of the village," Gees objected.

"Yes, I know, sir, but Peter goes everywhere."

"Oh, he does, does he?" Gees lifted a paw of which the claws were going through his coat to stick in his shoulder, and held it. "Does he often come here to call?"

"He's only been once before, sir, as far as I know, and then I got the gardener's boy to stone him away. Because Mr. Naylor would recognise the cat if he saw it, and we'd all get in trouble."

"I see. That's all, thank you."

He turned his back on her and, taking Peter to the side of the car, dropped him in and got in himself. The buzz of the starter appeared to worry Peter slightly, but Gees reached down and stroked him as he sat facing the pedals, and then engaged gear and moved off. As he neared the gates, Peter jumped up on the seat beside him and put a paw on his arm as if to claim some attention, and he spared a hand to respond, noting a lad—possibly that same gardener's boy, opening the gates for him. He thanked the boy as he passed, but, keeping a hand and an eye on Peter, had no chance to get out a tip. It was all one, he thought: there was no need for him to lay up treasure at Troyarbour Hall, for he had no intention of returning there. He disliked Naylor too much: the man believed the

story he had told, but, in Gees' opinion, he had gone
cracked on it, let it become an obsession.

And now Peter, friendly Peter, provided an oppor-
tunity of seeing this Ira Warenn: he could pull in at
the farm and deliver the cat—even ask to see her, if
she did not appear herself in reply to his knock at
the farmhouse door. Since this was her cat, Gees told
himself, she was not a witch: Peter was no witch's
cat: he was too sociable, too likeable. That paw of his,
soft and with retracted claws, came out to pat Gees
on the arm if he neglected too long to stroke his
passenger: Peter had adopted him, meant to own him
—and yet, Gees felt, all this was especial favour.
Peter would not own everybody he met, but was
making an exception: perhaps he remembered that
on his previous visit to the Hall he had been stoned
away, and appreciated the different reception this
human had given him.

So thinking, Gees drove through the village, and
in a fold of the heights, back from the inn, sighted
a squat little church and the chimneys and roofs of
more cottages. He said—"Y'know, Peter feller, if
they had a jail and a pawnshop, this place'd be very
nearly civilised." To which Peter responded with a
tremendous yawn: unlike nearly all cats, apparently,
he did not object to riding in a car, but was quite
happy over it. Gees tickled him behind his ear, and
he leaned hard on to the tickle to turn it into a scratch:
he liked it.

So, climbing out slowly from the village—slowly,
because of the bad surface of the lane, they came to
sight of the lone farmhouse, and Gees turned aside
to halt on the level before the shabby, discoloured
frontage. The two ground-floor windows were veiled

by casement cloth curtains, but the three above them
were bare and stark-looking. The door, as Gees
approached it, declared its need of paint, as did the
window frames. Peter lay quiescent in this new
friend's hold, and Gees was about to stretch out to
knock on the door with his knuckles, but a click of
the latch and the door's opening forestalled him. He
knew, as he gazed, that he was facing Ira Warenn.
Or Dark Lagny?

There are moments in life that stretch out to prove
the swiftness of thought: this, for him, was such a
moment. He saw a slip of a girl with coiled hair of
a bluish blackness, the night-black hair that is hardly
ever seen on the women of Caucasian stock. There
were little curls of it about her ears, and it was loose
and wavy over her forehead—over her eyes that were
like still sea-pools under the light of the moon. So
he would have defined the eyes, but neither then nor
at any time could he have told what was their colour:
they were dark, so dark that pupil and iris were only
just distinguishable. She used lipstick, he could see,
but what other make-up she had used he, being only
a man, could not tell. A plain black dress, dark
silk stockings and sandals, and round her neck a thin
gold chain from which was suspended a tiny pendant,
in which a circular, turquoise-blue stone was set in
white metal—not a thing of value, but quaint and
attractive. He even noted faint intaglio lines, defined
in gold, on the stone.

Thus, if he had been asked for a description, he
would have catalogued this girl—or woman—and
what she wore, and would have known the while
that he was not describing her. "Allure unutterable,"
Naylor had said, and in this first sight of her Gees

knew the man had given her no more than her due.
Naylor, thus defining her, must have seen her inimical,
hating him: Gees saw her slightly amused, quite self-
possessed, and coolly assessing him as her wonderful
eyes directed the allure that was hers at him, with
such a challenge as Lilith must have flung at Adam
in the very dawn of woman's conquest of man.

She said—"O, Peter!" and her voice was soft and
deep as were her eyes. The cat struggled, fell from
Gees' hold and, going to her, lifted himself in one
bound to her shoulder, to curve himself round the
back of her slender, finely-modelled neck and look
coldly at Gees.

"He did that to me," Gees said, "when I found
him in the car."

She said—"It was very good of you to bring him
back—but quite unnecessary. He goes for long expedi-
tions, and always comes back."

"If I hadn't fetched him, he might have been
stoned," he told her.

The sow, with her litter of piglets, came grunting
and snorting toward the doorway. The girl said—"No,
Irene—go away!" and the ungainly beast, with a
deep grunt that sounded very much like disgust,
turned about and lumbered jerkily away, her brood
following.

Gees said—"You might have named her Violet, or
Lily."

"Then you haven't read W. H. Hudson," she
suggested.

"Oh, yes!" He made it a triumphant assertion. "I
know—if man had taken and trained the pig as he
has the dog, for the last two hundred years, he would
now have a friend just as brave and loyal, and far

more intelligent. That was the sense of what he said
—I don't remember the exact words. But—Irene!
Well, it's not my sow."

"You saw how she did as she was told. She's
highly intelligent—all her kind are. They're debased
and uglified to make them fat, and the courage they
have in a wild state is almost atrophied, now, but
still they have the next largest brain to that of man,
relatively to their size and that of other animals."

He said—"I don't know if I'm talking to Miss
Warenn, but I believe I am. I stopped to bring
Peter home, but never expected to get as far as Hud-
son and the brain content of the genus *sus*. Or may
I say I never hoped to get as far? This is an un-
expected pleasure."

"Talking about the genus *sus?*" she asked, with
innocent gravity.

"No—meeting you," he answered.

"Is it?" The dark, wonderful eyes mocked him,
then. "When you found out where Peter belonged—
keep your claws in, Peter!—when you found that
out, you brought him here with the express—but not
expressed—intention of finding out what Ira Warenn is
like. So you did expect to meet me, if not to talk
about Hudson and the genus *sus*."

"That doesn't lessen the unexpectedness of the
pleasure," he said.

"Will it if I—if I tell you I sent Peter there, intending that you should find him and bring him back?"

"No-o." He half-breathed the reply. "But—you
can't send a cat. You can't own a cat. The cat
owns you, every time."

"And yet, Mr. Green, I sent Peter—and you are
here!"

Allure unutterable—it was in her night-dark eyes, in the tempting music of her voice. Gees replied with—"Why, and how did you know my name?" and made the questions harsh, because he was afraid of her.

"Why?" she echoed the question with a note of amusement. "Because I wanted to know what sort of man Jerome Naylor asked to drive me out. And your name—and address—were lying on the post-office counter for anyone to see when I went in for——"

"For what?" he asked, as she hesitated.

"If you must know—cigarettes," she answered.

He produced his case with the suddenness of a conjuring trick, and held it opened before her. "Do have one," he offered.

She shook her head as a grizzled, elderly man came round the corner of the house and advanced toward them.

"Have you fed Adolphus, Ephraim?" she asked.

He said—"Yes'm," and pulled at his scanty forelock in a way reminiscent of half a century or more ago.

"Thank you. I'll attend to Irene, later—you may go. Good-night."

"Good arternoon, 'm," he corrected severely, and turned to tramp off toward the village, with just a glance at Gees as he went.

"Adolphus being——? or am I not supposed to question?" Gees asked.

"Being an illustration of the truth of Hudson's theory—a boar," she answered. "But don't you think we have talked long enough on my doorstep? Jerome Naylor would—if he knew, he'd go baresark."

Gees managed to take the revelation of that final sentence with a poker face, though inwardly he questioned whether she had used the last word with no special meaning, or had intended to tell him that she knew all about Naylor's obsession. He glanced at his wrist watch and, turning his head momentarily, saw how shadows were deepening in the folds of the hills. If he made the main road before dark, he would be more than lucky—or might break a spring and be unlucky.

"Quite right," he said. "I've detained you quite long enough, and won't trespass any more. So—goodnight, Miss Warenn."

"I didn't mean that!" She spoke with the first note of emphasis of any kind that he had heard in her voice. "I was going to suggest that you come in and try my cowslip wine before going on. As a— as a sort of expression of gratitude for bringing Peter back. I know he's grateful too—tell him so, Peter!"

Slowly, lazily, Peter uncurled himself from about her neck, where he had lain all the while, and dropped to the ground to yawn and stretch himself, and then pad in leisurely fashion until he was directly in front of Gees. There he sat up, and looked up, almost as if asking a question. Gees, looking down at him, nodded the answer.

He said—"All right, Peter—you win. And if I go back to the village, Miss Warenn——" he looked up at her again—"I suppose the pub could put me up, or shake me down for the night?"

"Harry Todd will be glad of you," she assured him. "So——" A gesture, inviting him to enter, finished the sentence.

He had to stoop to cross the threshold. When she

had closed the door, Peter having made up his mind
to enter too, the low-ceiled, narrow hallway of the
house was almost in darkness, for there was no tran-
som, and only the faint light from a doorway on the
right relieved the gloom. Through that doorway he
followed the girl, to a room of which he could have
touched the ceiling without raising his arm to its full
stretch, and, since she said—"Just one minute, please,"
and left him alone there, he had time to take in the
quality of the room.

With the exception of one piece, the furniture was
mid-Victorian, shabby and valueless. There was a
claw-legged, circular table in the middle of the room,
its bare surface scratched and dingy: the four dining
chairs and one carving chair, mahogany-framed, were
horsehair seated. The black marble clock on the
mantel, and its flanking ornaments, were late nine-
teenth-century abominations—and the clock had
stopped. A four-tiered bookcase along the wall facing
the window was evidently of deal, painted and grained
to a bad imitation of oak: it was not merely filled,
but crowded with books—Gees recognised the volumes
of *The Golden Bough,* and Eliphaz Levi's treatises,
without making any close inspection of the shelves.
The one piece of furniture that contrasted with the
rest attracted him more than the bookcase, and he went
to stand before it. A black chest—at first he thought
it was ebony—with three-panelled front, a keyhole
which suggested an enormous lock, and a lid on which
were carved, in low relief, three trees. Bending over
to look closely at them, Gees saw that they were
thorn trees, with bunches of berries on their branches,
and, in spite of the lack of colour—for the carving
was black as the rest of the chest's surface—the work

was so finely done that the trees seemed alive. And now, with his eyes close to the wood, Gees saw that it was oak, age-darkened to blackness and its graining smoothed to a silken gloss. Here was a surface that no polish nor artificial staining could have produced: centuries had gone by since the artist—for artist in truth he must have been—had looked on his work and seen that it was good. For only by age and human touch may oak be brought to such perfection of surface as Gees saw here: other woods may be surfaced by tools and artificial means, but oak retains the indentations of its grain under such treatment, and darkens and takes on a glacial evenness only in the course of ages.

He stood erect and turned, conscious that he was no longer alone, though he had not heard the girl enter the room. She put down on the centre table an ugly, squat black bottle, and two stemmed wine-glasses, of which the stems were mere threads, and the bowls of paper thinness.

She said—"I made the wine. Taste it."

He watched her fill the glasses: the fluid was ruby-dark, and, as he saw it rise oilily in one glass and then the other, he remembered MacMorn, maker of shadows, and the reason-destroying drink that had made an hour of Elysian illusion[1] for him and one other.

He said—"I have been admiring that chest of yours."

"Yes?" There was a reflective note in the half-question, and as she spoke she held out one of the filled glasses to him. "All we have left to us, the chest and what is in it."

[1] *See Maker of Shadows*, by the same author. Wright & Brown, Ltd., Publishers.

"All you have left?" he asked. "I don't see——"

"Try my wine," she suggested, and held up her own glass to the light. "They say Dark Lagny made wine like this. Try it."

He held up his glass as she was holding hers, and saw that the deep-red, translucent fluid was not still in it, but a moving current circled from top to bottom and from bottom to top of the glass. He said—"It looks perilously alive, to me."

"Pure imagination on your part. Still!" She waved her free hand toward his glass, and the movement within it ceased.

"I shall soon begin to believe——" he breathed rather than spoke, and did not end it, but stared at her. The dark eyes laughed at him, though her lips did not curve. There was mockery in the laugh.

"Jerome Naylor?" she asked. "Believe, then. I drink! To all who believe beyond the sight of the eyes, know more than they are taught—whose lives of yesterday give them guidance for to-day."

"That is, to yourself," he said, and laughed. "Yes, then—to you. And perhaps, in some small measure, to me."

He drank with her, emptied the glass and put it down. The wine was a soft fire, a tingling sweetness that effervesced on his tongue—or so it seemed—and, momentarily, gave him an illusion that the girl who faced him was clothed, not in a black dress of to-day, but in some garment that was made of tiny, overlapping plates of gold or polished brass. Only for a moment did the illusion hold, and then he saw her as before, but slightly smiling with her lips, now, while the dark eyes were unlighted, sombre—and surely the room had darkened! He must go back to the inn: in mercy to the car, he must not attempt the deeply shadowed lane, even with headlights on.

"I think—yes, to you too," she said. "I thought it when I saw you looking at the chest there."

"Old, that," he said. "As old as—as what?"

She shook her head. "I know only that it is very old," she answered. "When Jerome Hold-the-Faith Naylor brought his troop to destroy our castle of Troy-arbour—the Naylors built their Hall with the stones of the castle—when he completed our ruin, the Warenn of that day saved only the chest and what it holds. Nothing else—we lost all but that—and the last Naylor lives there to-day."

"The chest and what it holds," Gees mused aloud.

"This Naylor would give half his possessions for what it holds," she told him. "When my father was dying, he came here to get what is in the chest. Threatened to turn me out if I would not give it up. I did *not* give it up, and Jerome Naylor went away afraid. He is still afraid. That is why he sent for you. I know."

He wanted to ask how she knew. Instead, he asked —"What is in the chest, then—what is it he wants so much?"

Passing him, she went to the chest and lifted its lid. He turned and looked inside, saw the massive, antique lock, and down within the chest rolls of parchment, tape-tied—ten or more of them—together with a white-handled axe, of which the head had rusted to a brownish black, and a long, heavy sword, cross-hilted and unscabbarded, of which the blade was shining, bluish-tempered steel, apparently.

"Can you read runes?" the girl asked abruptly.

"With difficulty," he answered. "It depends on the script, too."

"Yes. The handle of that axe—it is narwhal horn, I understand—is covered with them. Twice covered. Dark Lagny began the record, inscribing round and round the haft, and then it was carried on and on, till the last of it is scribed lengthways of the shaft, crossing the first characters as people used to cross the writing in their letters. You may take it out, if you like."

He lifted the axe and poised it to test its balance. The head, he saw, was deeply eaten with rust, which had been oiled over at some time. The haft was of shining bone, yellowed with age, but still having its tensile strength: its end widened to a knob to give good grip, and was pierced for a wrist-thong. And from end to end the haft was covered with incised characters that Gees knew as runes, lengthways and crossways of the shaft, and so small and intersecting that he could make nothing of them—except for one word that he translated as "Gunnar," near where the haft was set in the head.

"Who was Gunnar—do you know?" he asked.

She took the weapon from him and put it back in the chest. "Since you could read that, you might read more—more than I wish," she said. "And that— the axe—is what Jerome Naylor wants but cannot have. All the knowledge Dark Lagny had, knowledge that goes far beyond the sight of the eyes—my father taught me to read the runes when I was only a small child. There are Latin translations of some of them on the parchments, but I keep them only because they are old things—things of value, now. Not—not as I keep the axe and sword."

"Runes on the sword, too?" he asked.

"No—it was forged long later. When the first crusade

was being preached, I think. But it is a singing sword
—one of Thor's own descendants forged it. Not pure
steel, but an alloy—I have seen my father take the
point round to touch the hilt, and it springs back, so
fine is the tempering. He said—my father said—the
smith who forged it alloyed the steel with glass, but
that may not be true."

"And may be," Gees said. "Glass is the most elastic
substance known, though how it could be alloyed with
steel——"

"Many arts are lost," she reflected. "How were
the monoliths balanced to stand century after century?
And how were tree trunks interwoven to make them
unite as they grew, joined into wanted shapes more
surely than tools or human hands could join them?"

"And that," he said, "is a new one on me. Welding
living trees, apparently. But you said—Thor's own
descendant."

"A mighty smith was Thor—no wonder they made
him a god." Her soft, deep voice took on a dreamy
note. "A mighty lover, too. Wulfruna was of his
breeding—we go far back—O, very far back! Volsungs and children of the Hammer——" She checked
herself and, looking at him, laughed—at herself, he
knew. The laugh was music. She said—"The night
is darkening on us. How long have we talked?"

"A few seconds," he answered. "Have we really
begun to talk?"

"Or is all said?" Her lovely voice was sombre,
now. "You know so much, too much, I think."
Abruptly she pointed at the squat bottle on the table,
a dim thing, now, in the gloom that gathered with
night's approach. "More?" she asked, and moved
a step toward the table.

"No," he answered resolutely. "That stuff—cowslip wine, you called it. Who ever saw dark red cowslips? Are you a witch, Miss Warenn?"

"I am Dark Lagny's child," she answered. "Why do you call my wine 'that stuff'? Was it so unpleasant to your taste?"

"It was so pleasant that I'm afraid of it, and half afraid of you," he said. "When I took that axe in my hand I felt the hands of others who had held it—killed with it. Did you mean me to feel them?"

She shook her head. "No. It is—you know too much. See beyond the sight of the eyes. I would not have had you feel those hands. I would have Jerome Naylor feel them, but not on the axe handle. Grasping his hand, leading him out, making him mad——" The last words were whispered, yet they seemed to poise echoing in the gloom.

"Then you are a witch," Gees said harshly.

She faced him, her eyes not far from his own—dark pools of the sea under the light of the full moon, nearly luminous and quite distinctly seen, though the light in the room had almost gone. "Is not every woman a witch?" she asked. "If all of us knew our power! *I* know, therefore I am a witch. What of it?"

"So much do you hate Jerome St. Pol Naylor?" he asked.

"That?" The syllable was a mere note of mocking laughter. "Why, it has been in the blood of my people since Dark Lagny hung on a cross outside the wall of Eboracum—since Wulfruna took Sigurd's head on her knees before she bound the hell-shoes on his feet —and kissed the blood from his dead lips! Hate? It is more than hate!"

He said—"I'm going, Miss Warenn. I've stayed too long, talked too much—where did you get those marvellous glasses, though?"

She laughed. "Must you know everything? A Varangian brought them from Byzantium. All that I have is old—I too am very old——"

"Harry Todd—wasn't that the innkeeper's name as you said it?" he interrupted. For now the gloom had so far deepened that he saw her face only as a framing for the eyes that retained their distinctness, and her night-black hair blended into the shadows behind her.

"That is his name," she answered. "I shall see you again, then?"

"I don't know. To tell you the truth, I hope not."

"Afraid of me?" She laughed, softly and amusedly.

"Good night, Miss Warenn."

He got out to his car, somehow, and turned to drive back to the village of Troyarbour and the *Three Thorns*. As he drove, it seemed that the soft music of her laughter pursued him, and on the gloom of approaching night he saw twin pools of deeper darkness—the luminous mystery of her eyes.

She was a witch. Yes, she *was* a witch!

IV

THE light had just begun to fail when Ephraim Knapper entered the bar-room of the *Three Thorns* and clacked across the red-brick floor in his heavy, hob-nailed boots to face Harry Todd, the proprietor, with whom business was not brisk enough to justify his keeping a barman. There was only this one bar, a fairly large room with the old-style conventional sand on the floor, and earthenware spittoons available for such as felt inclined to use them. But, following on the campaign against tuberculosis, nobody spat, in these days: the earthen vessels were mere ornaments, the sand a superfluity.

Four worthies, who made the pub a club, as did Ephraim Knapper, occupied a bench on the right—that is, in relation to the door—as he entered. They gave him grave greeting: Sam Thatcher, immediately facing the door, nodded and grunted—he was simon-pure Dorset. Phil Hodden grunted without nodding. Jacob Cowder, third along the bench, said, " 'Do, Ephraim," and Fred Carphin, nearest the bar, merely grinned and pointed at his glass, of which not more than a fifth of the contents remained unsunk. As a scrounger, Fred had a reputation, and Ephraim knew it—had had years in which to learn it. He shook his head mutely, and spoke to Harry Todd:

"One ha'f pint, Mr. Todd. Look like a fisher throwed a line, but I ain't rizin'. *One* ha'f pint, I do tell 'ee."

Todd drew the half-pint from the barrel back of the bar, and had to loosen the spile-pin to fill the glass. Ephraim put down his pennies, took up the glass, and meandered slowly to the table at which the four sat. He seated himself on the bench facing them all.

"Heer's to I," he said, and drank.

"Theer were a furriner tu the Hall," Sam Thatcher observed with the gravity of one imparting weighty news. "In a moty-car. Yu zeed 'un?"

"Aye," said Ephraim, with equal solemnity.

"He went back, happen it were a hour zince," Sam pursued.

"Happen he coom from Dorchester," Jacob Cowder chimed in.

"Or from Lunnon," Fred Carphin suggested. "T'were a valiant car, sure-ly."

" 'Valiant?' Sure-*ly?*" Sam Thatcher snickered a little. "Zuzzex born, yu du zhow yurzelf, Fred Carphin."

"Happen I du." Fred sounded a trifle defiant over it. "My Nettie coom hoam a hour back for a crack wi' the missis, an' she towd us the furriner found Peter when he coom out arter seein' Squire Naylor."

"I rackon Squire'd zhoot Peter, zo be he dast," Sam surmised.

"Niver know wheer that cat'll goo next," Phil Hodden broke silence to remark, and took a sip from his glass.

"Yure Nettie zay what the furriner wanted 'ith Squire?" Sam inquired.

"My Nettie got a good job theer wi' Squire," Fred told him severely. "She keep her mouth shet over what goo on."

Into the following silence Ephraim Knapper launched

his bombshell. "The furriner took Peter hoam," he said. "He were standin' talkin' wi' Miss Warenn, a front o' the house, an' I left 'em talkin' arter she towd me I might goo an' said good-night tu me."

"Goddlemighty!" Sam Thatcher made the comment after a lengthy silence. "If Zquire heerd that, now!"

"Happen the furriner coom to make it oop atween 'em," Jacob suggested. "Squire can't git her outer the farm, zo——" He left it incomplete.

"Happen pigs might fly," Sam remarked caustically.

"Peegs—aye," Jacob said, to cover a certain discomfiture. "That theer owd bore at the farm started talkin' yit, Ephraim?"

"Next tu it," Ephraim admitted. "She'll let it out an' goo round the farm, an' it'll foller her jest like a sheep-collie. Du anything she tell it. 'Dolphus! An' the sow's nearly as bad."

"What she can't du wi' animals beeant noobery's business," Fred Carphin stated. "When I were theer at the farm afore yu, Ephraim, that theer Peter were a little kitten, an' near as sune as it'd lap milk she'd make 'en set up like sayin' prayers. I rackon if she kep' a lion, she'd make it meek an' foller her around."

"We don't want no lions heer," Sam Thatcher reproved him. "If so be she was to heear yu say that, happen she'd git one."

"I ain't sayin' it so it'd git to her ears," Fred protested.

"Yu gotter be ceareful," Sam said warningly. "She got long ears."

"Rackon the farm don't pay enough f'r her to keep lions," Fred pointed out. "She got a dunnamany beasts now."

" 'Dunnamany!' " Sam gibed, and snickered again. "Zuzzex, yu du be."

"An' ain't I niver to heear the last on it?" Fred demanded angrily.

Sam's mouth had opened for the retort discourteous when the opening of the bar door reduced them all to silence, for a stranger—*the* stranger, evidently— entered and, closing the door again, advanced to the bar, where Harry Todd had been leaning to enjoy the conversation of his regular customers. Discussion of local affairs among them in the hearing of a furriner was utterly taboo: they sat mute, and waited to learn what had brought him to the inn.

He faced Todd, who gave him a courteous "Good-evenin', sir," and straightened from his leaning posture in anticipation of an order.

"Good evening," Gees responded cheerfully. "I was recommended to you by a resident here. Mr. Todd, isn't it?"

"I'm him," Harry admitted—rather cautiously, since he was not quite easy in his mind over the observance of closing hours and a surreptitious dilution of spirits sold over the bar.

"Ah!" Gees smiled at him. "Do you think you could stable my car for me and give me a bed for the night, Mr. Todd?"

"Why, cert'ny, sir," he answered with far more cordiality. "That is, if ye don't mind runnin' the car inter my open shed at the back—stand it next the wagon. An' I got a room all ready."

"Splendid! I'll go and run the car into the shed, and then come back here. You might have a pint of bitter waiting for me."

He went out. The five habitués looked at each

other, and Sam Thatcher nodded with a world of meaning in the gesture. Ephraim said—"It wur a hour agoo I zeed 'un talkin' to her."

"Zquire zent un, to maake it oop," Jacob Cowder insisted.

Sam shook his head. That possibility had already been denied, and he was not going to waste words repeating the denial. Besides, the furriner had only gone to put his car away, and might be back at any moment. Harry Todd drew a pint of bitter, and placed it on the bar.

Then Gees came back. He put down a shilling with "Thank you, Mr. Todd," and placed on the brick floor beside him the small suitcase he had taken from the car. Then he took up the glass tankard and drank, and drank, to put it down again empty, while the eyes of the worthies widened as they stared in silent wonderment.

"Very good bitter," Gees observed. "I'll have another like that, now it's washed the dust away. Yes, excellent bitter. A free house?"

"'Tis that, sir," Todd assented, busy at the barrel.

"Makes all the difference," Gees remarked, and, noting the change from his shilling, put down enough coppers to complete payment for the second pint. "And you're not a native to these parts, eh?"

"Been here twenty year, sir. I was born an' bred Winchester way. But how d'you reckon to know I don't belong round here?"

"By your accent—that's easy," Gees told him. "I'll bet you're still what they call a furriner—and always will be." He turned to look at the five figures, still and silent as dummies, at the table beside the wall. Being interested in what he had already seen of Troy-

arbour, he wanted to know more, and here, if anywhere, he could learn it, if he could get those five
talking.

He said, ingratiatingly—"Our friends here all seem
to be near the end of what they've got." And waited
till, as he had expected, five pairs of eyes questioned
what he might mean. Then—"Can I ask you all to
have drinks with me—anything you like to call?"

Dead silence, while four pairs of eyes turned to
those of Sam Thatcher, as *doyen* of their society, and
therefore the one by whose decision they would abide.
Sam thought for a few seconds longer, and then replied
—"Yazzur, I reckon it be very kind o' yu."

"Take their orders, Mr. Todd, and don't fail to
have one yourself at the same time." He put down a
ten-shilling note and, taking up his tankard, turned
to look round the bar-room. Sam, leader of the five,
decided on another ha'f pint, and in turn each of the
others followed suit until Fred Carphin, last to call,
said—"A pint, Mus' Todd," quite boldly, whereat
the others almost groaned aloud. The scrounger had
got away with it: they also might have had pints, had
they had the courage to call for them—but it was
too late, now.

Taking no notice while the drinks were being
served, Gees went across the room, glass in hand, to
a notice board on which was pinned a sheet of paper.
He read the particulars of a darts competition, and
noted the first five names on the list. Ephraim Knapper
he knew would be the one to whom Ira Warenn had
spoken at the farm: of the other four he knew nothing,
but, as in Ephraim's case, their surnames indicated
the callings their ancestors had followed, and declared
three of them of the soil and one of artisan descent.

For Hodden was corrupted from "hodman," almost certainly, and denoted a brick-carrier. Cowder, with equal almost-certainty, derived from "cowherder," and Thatcher declared himself with no alteration. Carphin was puzzling: probably it went back to the middle ages when carp was a fish of commerce and repute, and this man's forefather of that day had been "carp hind" on the establishment of some monastery or manor—one who had to see that the stock of fish was maintained for his masters and not poached by others or destroyed by otters and like enemies.

Two Smiths and a Butcher completed the list, and they needed no study nor thought. Gees turned back in time to hear Sam Thatcher's—"Yure very good heealth, zur," and the murmur of "Aye!" from the others. He said—"Good health to you all," and returned to stand beside Ephraim, who looked up in a scared way, as if remembering his sins.

"Any flint pits round these parts, do you know?" Gees asked.

Ephraim frowned over the unexpected question, taking it in gradually.

"Flint pits, zur," he echoed eventually. "Aye. Thur be one oop back o' Wren's. 'Tis all blackb'ries, now."

"Dewberries, Ephraim," Sam Thatcher corrected severely.

"Brumbles, anyway," Ephraim said. "How be yu wanter know, zur?"

"Your name," Gees told him. "You're native to these parts, eh?"

"Bred an' born heer," Ephraim conceded. "Yazzur."

"I went by your name," Gees explained. "Knapper—flint knapper in the old days, of course. In that very pit, most likely."

"I 'member my owd gran'fer tellin ov me," Sam Thatcher contributed, "how his gran'fer towd him how it wur afore Boney's time theer wur a rare lot o' flint pits along these heer downs. Mostly filled in, they wur, arter the trade died out. Along o' caps f'r the sogers' guns, an' they stopped usin' the flint-locks. An' f'r tinder-boxes."

"I allus carr' a tinder box," Ephraim boasted. "Cheaper'n these heer matches, I finds en. Gimme tinder, says I."

Proof, Gees felt, that the man was descended from a family of flint knappers. But he went off on a more promising tack.

"Wren's, you said," he observed. "Where is that?"

"Why, wheer Miss Wren du live now," Ephraim answered. "Yu seen her, I know. Yu an' she was talkin' when I left to-night. Arternoon, it wur then. Her people had that farm f'r everlastin'."

"Not all that, Ephraim," Sam corrected him. "The Hall, it wur the Wrens', afore Zquire Naylor—zome owd Zquire Naylor long back—avore Naylors come theer. All o' Troyarbour, them Wrens had."

"Yes, I did see Miss Warenn," Gees admitted with a thoughtful intonation. "I took her cat back from the Hall—a cherry-coloured cat with a rose-coloured weskit. Friendly sort of cat, too."

Four mouths gaped wide over the obvious lie, for all knew that he had taken Peter back, and no other cat. The fifth, Fred Carphin, said—"Well, if that beeant a master one, sure-*ly!* Cherry-coloured— Mister, theer ain't no sech cat as that in Dorset, let alone heer."

"Ever hear of black cherries and white roses?" Gees inquired.

The old schoolboy jape was new to them, and as one they snickered and chuckled over it—no one of them so far forgot himself as to laugh outright. Then Ephraim said—"Aye, it wur Peter, zurely."

"Peter's moz'ly wanderin'," Sam Thatcher observed rather sadly—and Gees knew, by the free comment, that he was admitted, strictly on furriner status, to their fraternity. He said, sagely—"Cats mostly do. They're never really tame."

"'Less Miss Wren gits howd on 'em," Fred Carphin amended. "She'd taame the davvle hisself, I rackon. She got a owd bore up theer, an' yu'd rackon it wur a dawg, way it foller her around."

"A boar pig?" Gees made it an incredulous query.

"Aye, a bore peeg," Fred confirmed him enthusiastically, and the other four frowned heavily at this betrayal of local secrets to a furriner. But then, Fred himself, hailing from Zuzzex, was a furriner too, and thus capable of all indecencies: no Dorset man would be guilty of such revealments. "An' a owd sow," Fred went on, "as'll du all 'tis towd—by her, mind, not by noobery else. Peegs, mindin' what they're towd! An' 't'ain't only that. I've *heerd her laugh!*"

He made of the last sentence no more than a fearful undertone, and looked to right and left as if he feared he might be overheard. Sam Thatcher said—"It don't du f'r a maan tu hev tu many pints," and Phil and Jacob chuckled at the hit. But Fred spoke mulishly—"I tell 'ee, I've heerd her laugh, when she'm been miles away. Like—like a ghoast. Lordy, don't I know? I worked theer f'r her father yeers enough, an' f'r her tu, afore Ephraim took my plaace. I've heerd it."

"An' what du yu think made her laugh?" Sam inquired caustically.

"Us wur talkin' about her," Fred explained sulkily, and went silent.

Sam shook his head. "Tu many pints," he said again.

In the utter silence that followed Gees noted the disapproval on the faces of the other four. Fred had outraged all manners and rules of good society: he had talked about his late employer before a stranger: he had talked of local things before that stranger, which was never done in Dorset: and, in attempting to create a sensation, he had obviously lied. Condemnation of such a one was unanimous and bitter.

Then, into the silence, came a sound that Gees recognised with a little, fearful thrill, a sense of the uncanny. From somewhere near the door it came, deep-toned and musical, the sound of Ira Warenn's laughter. There are voices that are unmistakeable, even in laughter, and he knew this as her laugh, though he had only seen and talked with her for an hour or less. Almost involuntarily he turned his head to see no more than had been there since he entered for the second time. And then he noted that all other eyes had turned toward the laugh—he had heard, not imagined that he heard it.

"Theer!" Fred Carphin ejaculated, and pointed. "'Tis—theer!"

"A boord craaked," Sam Thatcher said—but there was no conviction in the statement. "I heerd en. It wur a boord."

"Wheer?" Fred demanded, with angry defiance. "Theer's bricks underfoot in heer, an' the walls— they'm brick, else lath an' plaster. That theer door ain't moved, I'll taake my oath. She laughed!"

"Sign the pledge," Sam advised drily. The Zuzzex furriner was letting them all down, he felt, and had to be put in his place.

But Fred stood up, knocking over more than half of his free pint, and taking no heed of the overturned glass tankard. "Mus' Todd?" he demanded loudly and harshly. "Yu heerd that laugh?"

"I heard somethin'," Todd responded uneasily, and after a pause for thought. "But when there's nobody to laugh, there can't be no laughin'. Can there, now? A mouse behind the plaster, mayhap."

"Du mice laugh, then?" Fred asked bitterly. "Yu, sir!" He turned on Gees. "Yu heerd it, sure-ly! A laugh, it wur, wurn't it?"

"Maybe one of you is a ventriloquist," Gees suggested, trying to evade direct reply. "You know—one of those chaps who chucks his voice into the hayloft and a pitchfork screams back at him."

"Beggin' yure pardon, sir, that ain't no moor'n fulish, that ain't," Fred said, with deep injury in his tone. "I rackon yu dedn't goo to see Squire an' her i' the one day f'r nothin'——"

"Fred Carphin!" Sam Thatcher's voice had in it angry authority. "Yu'm zaid enough—*an'* moor. Mister —whatever yu're name may be—we beg yure pardon f'r this *furriner*——" he put stinging, bitter emphasis on the word,—"an' hoap yu unnerstand we niver heerd the like i' Troyarbour afoore. Talkin' o' a laady ahind hur back—they du zay yu got tu know a man yeers, an' then yu don't rightly know him—an' 'tis true. Niver till this night ded I know Fred Carphin, an' now I don't wanter know him no moor. Zuzzex boorn!"

The contempt of the last two words was well-nigh

intolerable. Fred picked up his empty tankard, and looked as if about to hurl it.

"Aye, t'row it," Sam urged coldly. "I'm twenty year older'n yu, Fred Carphin, an' ha'f crippled along o' rheumatics. Yu'm safe to t'row it." He stood up to present a better mark. "Goo on!"

Fred put the tankard down on the table, edged out from behind it, and went to the door. Opening it, he stood holding the handle.

"She *did* laugh!" he said, and went out.

Again a dead silence, and, again, into it, came the deep, musical sound of laughter—and Gees saw Sam Thatcher's jaw drop as he stared in fear, and Todd craned over his bar, and Jacob Cowder stood up to stare fearfully at the door. The silence held for a full minute after the weird laughter had ceased, and then Gees moved toward the bar.

"One more pint, I think, Todd," he said easily, "and if any of these chaps would like another, or a stiff whisky to steady him and stop him from hearing things, you can put it on me."

"But she did laugh, sir," Todd said, in an awed way.

"Aye." From behind Gees, Sam Thatcher echoed it. "She ded laugh."

"Is—that—so?" Gees put all the mockery he could into the question. "Then, whoever she is, ask the lady to step forward, and I'll buy *her* a drink. Anything she likes to name, except cowslip wine. I bar cowslip wine—do you keep it?"

"Nun-no, sir." Todd backed from the bar, for there was vicious savagery in the query. Though he did not know it, Gees' anger was not against him, but against the woman who was fooling these rustics.

"I'm sorry. Drinks all round again, on me. Ah! That's my change there, of course. Well, weigh out the drinks, not forgetting yourself, and let me know if that's enough. And then, what have you got to eat?"

"Well, sir——" Todd came out from his hallowed area to collect empty glasses and take orders—"there's some cheese."

"Pickled onions?" Gees asked. "Dorset butter?"

"I've just remembered, sir—there's ham."

"And eggs—or did nobody massage the hens today?" Gees asked.

"I dunno about massage, sir—there is some eggs."

"Are some eggs, you mean—never mind. I'm a purist—don't ask me what that is—it doesn't mean religion. Now let's see. Cheese, pickled onions, ham, eggs, Dorset butter, beer, and sundry other fluids. To be served with a laugh—listen!"

He stood quite still and cocked his ear, so to speak. Todd, with the empty glasses from the table in his hand and the orders registered in his mind—easily, for they had all called for pints—also stood still, and gazed unhappily toward the door. The best part of a minute went by, and then Gees put his tankard on the bar.

"The lady will not oblige," he said. "In fact, we're all hearing what didn't happen, and waiting for it to happen again. Death and the income tax are the only real things in life, and nobody likes realities. Which may be over all your heads, but I'm a very angry man, so I won't have another pint, but a double whisky and only a spoonful of water—unless you have some soda. Have you any soda?"

"Aye," said Todd, and gaped over the exordium, which, as Gees had said, was over his head—far over it!

"Then a splash in the whisky—a very small splash. Then cook the cheese—no, the ham—and I like the onions lightly fried—the eggs, I mean, and tell whoever does the cooking not to laugh. It's not safe."

He said no more. The four worthies puzzled over what he had said, and made nothing of it. Todd served the drinks, drew one for himself, and then went out to order the cooking, and, until he returned, not a word was spoken in the bar room. Then Sam Thatcher lifted his pint.

"I dunno when I drunk zo much f'r nawthen," he said, "an' fr'm a furriner, tu. But a right good furriner yu be, mister, though us doan't unnerstan' ha'f what yu been talkin'. Heer's tu yu."

"Good health," Gees responded, rather absently. He was thinking, then, of Ira Warenn and the two laughs. He would not leave Troyarbour yet: it promised to be interesting.

"She *ded* laugh," Sam said, with solemn conviction.

V

NEW MAGIC IS OLD

TODD himself conducted Gees to a bedroom which, though small, looked comfortable and adequately furnished—surprisingly so, for such an out-of-the-world hamlet as this—and observed that the door on the right at the foot of the stairs led to the coffee room, where the ham and eggs would be ready by the time Gees got there. Also pickled onions, Dorset butter, and cheese—the best he could do.

Quite good enough, Gees told him, and with that he went out. Later, following him down the stairs, Gees opened the indicated door to face an attractive-looking girl in her twenties, who, evidently, had been just about to emerge. As he stood back to make way for her, she too stood back in a sort of confused hesitancy, as if she had been caught where she ought not to be, and he had time to take in her *ensemble,* as he would have put it. The green *rayon* blouse clashed with the beige skirt: the skirt was none too long, and revealed shapely legs in silk stockings—silk, here in Troyarbour!—and her shoes were dainty and high-heeled. She was blonde, but needed another visit to her hair-dresser, for the roots of her hair were obviously darkening: her eyes were palish blue, and too closely set, while she had slightly overdone her make-up. Yet there was a certain attractiveness about her, especially in her nervous embarrassment. She had tried to make the best of herself, and had failed through lack of taste and colour sense: had she tried less, she would not have failed so badly.

Gees said—"Sorry," and held the door for her. She passed him with—"I've put your supper on the table, sir," and in the one sentence betrayed Cockney origin. Then she escaped, her heels clicking on the oilcloth, and Gees went to the table and uncovered his meal. The ham had been generously cut, and there were four eggs.

Seating himself, Gees began business, reflecting the while over the girl, over the laugh in the bar, his determination to see Naylor again before leaving this place, and equally strong determination *not* to see any more of Ira Warenn. She might be interesting—was interesting, in fact—but he felt sure she would prove dangerous, and so resolved to avoid her. He was a little afraid of her, in fact.

Taking the second pair of eggs on to his plate after disposing of the first two, he realised that something was missing, and, espying a hand-bell on the table, took it up and rang it vigorously. Almost as if he had been waiting for the summons, Todd appeared.

"I hope everything is all right, sir," he asked, before Gees could speak—and he looked at the empty dish and refilled plate.

"Nearly too good to be true," Gees told him, "but the odd spot of fluid would come in handy. From the barrel. A pint, I think."

"Right away, sir. I can get tea, if you'd like it."

"From the barrel, Todd," Gees repeated gently, and Todd went out.

To return with one of the glass tankards, and a napkin over his arm with which he wiped the base of the vessel before setting it down. By that time,

Gees had pushed his plate aside and reached for the cheese—and Todd moved the jar of pickled onions to handiness for him.

"After which," he observed, "I shall be in a fit state to breathe on my friends. You've been here quite a while, Todd."

"And still they reckon me a furriner, sir. Always will."

"How on earth did you find the place?"

"'Twas the missus's doin', sir. She was a down-land girl when I married her, an' allus hankered for the downs. Didn't bother about the loneliness—it is lonely when winter sets in, too—so I took this when I heard it was goin'. I useter hanker for the towns an' lights at first, but by-an'-bye I got used to it—there's a sort of drawin' power about the downs. They —they *get* you."

"I understand," Gees said. "And a free house, too."

"That is so. Not much of a trade, but I was in a tied house before, an' there's something about a free house—so when the missus died—five year an' more ago, it was—I felt I didn't wanter go. An' here I am—here I'll most likely finish, too."

"A lone widower." Gees remembered the girl with silk stockings. "Any children—if I'm not asking too much?"

"No, sir, you ain't. An' we had only a baby that died before it was a month old. No, a lone widower, as you say."

"Umm'!" Gees commented reflectively, while he thought, but did not say—"Not so very lone," as he remembered the silk stockings and all the rest of that would-be entrancing vision—which ought to have been out of the room, he knew, before he entered it. Abruptly he said—"What about the bar—who's looking after it?"

"Closed, sir," Todd answered—rather uncomfortably. "It's late."

It was—past ten, Gees noted, glancing at his wrist watch, and divining that the girl did not serve in the bar. Her type would not go down with Sam Thatcher and his cronies. Again he spoke—"That was rather an unpleasant little dust-up. The man—Carphin, wasn't it?"

"That's the name, sir." Glad to be off thin ice—as he knew it had been—Todd answered more easily. "But Fred'd had too much—it didn't show in his speech, I know, but what he said—if he'd been sober he'd had more sense'n to talk like that. Them others was quite right to down him the way they did. They'll get over it—he's the best hand at darts among 'em, an'—between ourselves, sir—more'n one man i' the place owe him money. A smart chap, is Master Fred Carphin."

"Used to work where Ephraim Knapper works now, I understand?" Gees suggested, and made a half-question of it.

"That's so, sir. He was theer i' the owd man's time, Mister Wren that had the farm till he died. It was Miss Wren got rid o' Fred i' the finish. He was—well, it ain't for me to say, but she turned en out sharp one day, an' the hens seemed to lay better ever since."

"Maybe he wasn't sympathetic enough—to the hens," Gees observed. "Anyhow, it's your confidence, Todd, and it stays in this room. And—you heard that laugh, I noticed. Both times, eh?"

Todd nodded. "If it was," he said. "I dunno. Queer, it was."

"The first time it happened?" Gees asked. "Or have you——?"

"No, sir—never before. Look like Fred'd heard it, by what he said. Maybe it was—her—up to tricks. Though why—it beats me."

"She gets up to tricks, then?" Gees inquired, leading the man on.

"I wouldn't say that, sir," Todd answered—honestly enough, as Gees could see. "Folk hereabout say since her father died she's got inter queer ways, but it don't take much to make Sam Thatcher's sort say all sortser things about anyone. All I know is Squire Naylor'd about give his ears to get her outer the farm, an' can't. Things get about, y'know, sir. Fred's daughter Nettie—she's parlourmaid up at the Hall, an' a right smart bit o' goods, too—she'll tell her mother things, the mother'll tell Fred, Fred'll get a drop too much, like to-night, an' then—well, things get about. So I ain't lettin' out no secrets. Squire Naylor's scared of her, an' that's a fact."

"Why?" Gees asked, reflecting the while that Fred Carphin's tongue was not more loosely swivelled—if as much so—than that of the man before him. "What is there to be scared about?"

Todd shook his head doubtfully. "She—she ain't ordinary," he said. "The way she'll handle animals —there was never anything like it, as I know. Why —four year ago, it'd be—Abram Timms had a bull. Timms' farm jines on to Wren's, you must know, sir. That bull was a killer, if ever there was one—they shot it at the finish, an' nobody in all Troyarbour dast go in the medder where it was, long afore it was shot.

But *she* went! Wanted to cross that medder one day to go to Timms', an' the bull come at her, tail up an' head down. Timms seen it, an' knew she hadn't a hope on earth—she was as good as dead. An' she stopped an' faced the bull, an' it pulled up a score yards away from her, lookin' all dazy, sorter— Timms'll tell you the tale any day. She went up to the bull—maybe she spoke to it—nobody don't know what she did. But the finish was she laid her hand on the bull's neck, an' it walked alongside her till they got to the gate, an' then she come out as cool an' cheerful as if she'd been pettin' a turtle dove. That for one thing, an' it ain't natural. She got a big owd sow an' a little owd boar, an' they're as tame an' biddable an' clever as the winnin' dog in sheep trials —they do say the boar is cleverer'n any dog. An' that cat Peter—Peter'll be heer this minute an' gone the next, an' they say she talks to him, like he was human."

"That power over animals is rare, but it exists in some people," Gees remarked. "I see nothing in it to scare a man."

"It ain't only that, wi' Squire Naylor, sir," Todd said. "He went to the farm the day her father died, an' they say he tried to make her give up somethin' —I dunno what it was. That was the beginnin' o' the trouble betwixt him an' her—I'm sayin' no more'n what folk hereabout all know. Not only she wouldn't give up whatever 'twas, but she threw back at him that by rights the Hall belonged to her people, not his, an' she cursed him an' all his. You may say there was nothin' in that, but it warn't long arter that the lady—his kep' lady—died, an' then their child died, an' he—he sorter dwindled, somehow. He'd been a upstandin' man up to then, but now he's gone all dwainy—puny, if you know what I mean, sir. He was a man to make a woman look twice, before that, but now he'd please no woman's eye if she was worth callin' one. They do say Nettie—but I allus stand up for the gal, an' all that is lies outer spite. I don't believe—well, there!"

"And why," Gees inquired blandly, "are you telling me all this?"

"Well, sir——" Todd hesitated a moment—"you got talked well over i' the bar to-night afore you come in, an' I know you seen both Squire Naylor an' Miss Wren. I reckon you as sharp as most, an' there's a sorter opinion you're out to learn all there is to learn about them two—lordamighty know why, an' I don't ast. But you might as well know the straight truth from me, rather'n a pack o' lies which is all you'll get outer people which belongs round here. I'm a furriner like yourself, sir—people native to the place'll never tell you ought but what they think they can make you swaller. Likewise, you seem to be a pleasant gentleman, an' a straight one, an' if I make money outer such a one I like to give good value. That's about why."

"And how much do you reckon on making out of me?" Gees inquired.

Todd reflected over it. He said—"Well, sir, there's supper to-night, an' the room, an' there'll be breakfast. We'll say nought about the car, because it ain't usin' up room I want for anything else. An' I ain't got no bath-room i' the place. So—would seven shillin' be too outrageous much, do you think, sir?"

Gees smiled. "Make it out at that," he concurred. "But I suggest that you add in the cost of a pair of really good silk stockings, and don't say they were on my bill when you hand them over."

Staring while comprehension grew, Todd went brick-red. At last he questioned—"Dud-do you mum-mean that, sir?"

"My middle name is sincerity, and there are two each side of it—Lord help me!" Gees answered solemnly. "That is to say, if you don't put those stockings on the bill, and get 'em, I'll crab your inn whenever anybody mentions Troyarbour. Is it a whiz?"

"I dunno what that is, sir," Todd answered puzzledly. "If you really mean me to get 'em—she told me you'd seen her which I'd told her you was not to. Because I reckoned you'd be down on me for——" He broke off, evidently unable to complete the explanation.

Gees said, softly—"*De gustibus non est disput-andum.*"

"French, sir?" Todd inquired timidly.

"French, or as good as," Gees told him. "It means —you mustn't argue with the wind. When I get go-ing, I'm a cyclone with tail up and head down, like Timms' bull when there's no Miss Wren about. And you could put all my morals on a threepenny bit and have room enough left for a fried egg. So what have you? The stockings—can do?"

"It's very good indeed of you, sir——"

"Can it, Todd," Gees interrupted. "In other words, cork it up and wire it down. If—I don't say it's likely, but if I should want to stay another night, produce me the hen that laid those eggs, or some equivalent other than more eggs. You get me, I trust?"

"I'm sorry, sir. I didn't know you don't like eggs."

"On the other hand, I've just proved I do, on four of 'em. But variety is the motive power by which the rotation of this terrestrial oblate spheroid is maintained—never mind! I'm merely saying that the vitamin content of other forms of nutriment is fully equivalent to that of the egg. Which means I like a change occasionally."

"Leave it to me, sir. I'll see you get it."

When, after a sponge-down as apology for a bath, Gees came down in the morning, he found his breakfast already on the table, and on removing the cover found two kippers, either of which might have made Gargantua himself cheerful. Beside the plate was a sealed envelope, and, opening it, Gees extracted and read his bill.

— Smith, Esq.
Dr. to H. Todd, The Three Thorns, Troyarbour.

Supper, bed, breakfast . .	£0	9 11
One pint beer		8
	£0	10 7

With compliments.

"Tactful," Gees said to himself, "but he might have made me a Montmorenci, or at least spelt it Smythe. And—two-and-eleven stockings! Not what you'd call ribaldly extortionate, huh?"

.   .   .   .   .

Again, in mid-morning, the Rolls-Bentley stood before the main entrance of Troyarbour Hall. Again

trim, attractive, and rather pert Nettie Carphin—
Todd's defence of her seemed rather ineffective, since
her whole attitude contradicted it—ushered Gees into
the lofty-ceiled library—a truly magnificent specimen
of the architecture of its period, Gees realised—where
Jerome St. Pol Naylor rose to his feet from the armchair beside the fireplace as his visitor entered. The
room was not merely warm, but hot: the fire, of
dimensions which would have neutralised arctic conditions, was an oppression on the mild October day.
Naylor looked even frailer than when Gees had seen
him the day before, and seemed, salamander-wise, to
bask in the stuffy, unnatural heat.

"How-de-do, Mr. Green?" he said, with a satiric
note in the greeting. "Am I to conclude from this
second call that you have changed your mind?
That I can count on your help, as well as your
advice?"

"I have most decidedly changed my mind," Gees
answered coolly. "That is why I am here, a second
time."

"I am very glad to hear it," Naylor said, with no
satire at all.

"Uh-huh?" Gees made the exclamation not merely
satiric, but derisive. "You've never, of course, been
in the position of a defendant consulting his defending
counsel, Mr. Naylor?"

"I should hope not!" Naylor exclaimed hastily.
"Why, though?"

"Because—I spent two years in the police force, and
learned a lot—because the defendant, if he's got any
sense at all, generally realises that it's best to tell his
counsel the truth, the whole truth, and nothing but
the truth. It always pays."

"Are you insinuating——?" Naylor asked very coldly indeed, and left the query incomplete.

"Nothing," Gees answered calmly, "knowing as I do that a truthful man has nothing to fear from insinuations, and a liar gets round 'em somehow. If I put you in the second class, it's your own fault."

"Will you please leave this room at once, Mr. Green?" Naylor asked.

"No. And I haven't seen anyone here capable of throwing me out, yet. I can be an exceedingly blunt devil, and also a disagreeable one, if I'm led up the garden, Mr. Naylor. I have seen Miss Warenn since I saw you, and have also heard what she told me confirmed by independent evidence. Why didn't you tell me you threatened her?"

"Will you please leave this room at once?" Naylor repeated.

"No, I tell you! Come off that high horse and be honest. This case interests me, and I want the truth of it. Mean to get it, either for you or against you—and I don't care which. But heaven help you if I'm against you! Why did you threaten the girl?"

"I didn't," Naylor retorted sullenly. "At least——" he broke off.

"In other words, you did," Gees said with stinging incisiveness. ' "Why? What was it you wanted of her—asked of her?"

"I didn't threaten her half as much as she threatened me," Naylor protested, and so betrayed the justice of Gees' accusation.

"That may be," Gees said, "but in admitting that you threatened her at all, you prove that you misrepresented your case to me yesterday afternoon. I don't like that sort of thing, so I'm here again."

"To—to help, did you say?" Naylor asked apprehensively.

"I have not said so. I want the truth, first. Why did you threaten the girl—what did you want of her?"

"I wanted—the rod of An," Naylor answered, half reluctantly.

"The rodofan?" Gees repeated, puzzledly. "You can search me. What is it—a patent medicine formula? It's a new one on me."

"The—rod—of—An," Naylor repeated, with evident irritation.

"Ah, now I get you!" Gees said. "An—yes. Capital of Atlantis. The mother of hewn cities, they called it —all hewn from the solid rock, not built above it like cities of to-day——"

"You know?" The interruption had in it all of Naylor's intermittent intensity. "How much do you know? How much can you tell me?"

Gees shook his head. "What is this rod?" he asked in reply.

"The rod? She has it fitted as the shaft of a viking battle-axe, and doesn't know what she has—doesn't know what is inscribed on it," Naylor answered. "She may have deciphered some of it, but not all, or else——" He broke off, oddly. "I wanted it," he ended, half-apologetically. "I'm sorry I omitted to tell you—you'll help, you say."

"I do *not* say—anything of the sort," Gees told him forcibly. "I want the truth out of you before I decide on anything. What is there inscribed on this rod, or connected with this rod, that Miss Warenn does not know? If you want my help, you've got to confess everything."

Naylor thought it over, and evidently fought down

a rising anger at the dictatorial statement. He said—
"The science of Atlantis was far in advance of that of
to-day, as perhaps you know."

"So far," Gees concurred, "that the powers who
rule the world decided that the whole continent must
be destroyed—drowned—because its rulers discovered
the secret of creation and gained power over death—
and would have misused both discoveries. I know."

"Yes, you know," Naylor admitted. "That is obvious. Whether either of those secrets was inscribed
on the rod is more than I can tell, but I do know, what
she does not, that there is on it enough to give not
merely knowledge, but control of what is generally
called the fourth dimension. The fifth, really. Time is
the fourth."

"That is to say," Gees said slowly, "for human
comprehension any object must possess four dimensions: length, breadth, thickness, and duration. Yes,
all that is alphabetical, if you get me. The fifth?"

"For that——" Naylor forgot his anger, and Gees'
judgment on him, in his interest in the subject, "it
would be better to take an analogy, since neither you
nor I can visualise this fifth dimension, living as we
do in a four-dimensional state—counting in time or
duration as one of the four, I mean. That is generally
conceded, now."

Gees took out his cigarette case and offered it, and
Naylor took one, as if from his oldest friend rather
than from a man who had only recently insulted him.
Gees said—"This promises to be very interesting indeed, but I think you've made one mistake in it."

"Do sit down!" Naylor accepted a light, and pointed
to a chair. "Hunter—Hunter of Denlandham—told
me I might depend on you, and though—if you'll for-

give my saying it—you have damned irritating ways, I believe he was right. This—this analogy—I always resort to it for comprehension of the fifth dimension. Picturing, which is fairly easy, a two-dimensional state, considering the two dimensions of length and breadth, and presupposing the possibility of consciousness in such a state. Since we live in more than two dimensions, we can comprehend living in those two, by an effort of imagination. But why—in what do you say I am wrong."

"Let's leave that alone, for the present," Gees said in answer. "Give me your theory—I think I know it, but you state it, all the same. I'm interested—this looks like being a case, to me."

But whether he would take up that case for or against Jerome St. Pol Naylor, he did not say. He had in mind the fact that the man had lied to him at the outset, and also had in mind the laughs he and others had heard in the bar-room of The Three Thorns. That laugh, though there was in it no proof, was evidence that Ira Warenn had mastered the secrets inscribed on this "rod of An," and had got control of what Naylor chose to term a fifth dimension.

"I will certainly state my theory," Naylor said, with, for him, marked cordiality. "It is—what shall I call it—an exposition of the new magic, which derides and nullifies the old."

"Is—that—so?" Gees mocked the statement, deliberately. "If our newest scientists were aware of all that the very old ones called magic, the world would be one hell of a way farther advanced than it is to-day. The very newest magic is old—etheric vibrations were used for transmitting messages when mankind was in its infancy—and we brag about the discovery of wireless transmission! How old is the telescope or explosive propellant? How old is the steam engine? No man to-day knows what electricity actually is, but the sages of Atlantis could give you the formula—and even the later Lemurians knew how a cat purrs, a thing no scientist can tell you to-day. Now go ahead—I want your two-dimensional exposition. To get your idea of it all."

He settled himself in the chair Naylor had indicated, and drew a long breath, expressive of enjoyment. He had practically insulted the man, and then had gained his point.

Naylor said, deliberately—"I don't think I could tell you anything you don't know."

"Try," said Gees.

VI

EMPIRIC THEORY

NAYLOR sat hesitant. Was this cool, masterful devil inwardly laughing at him? There was nothing new about his theory, but it had been enunciated years ago, formed the mere A B C of the subject, and Gees' reference to Lemuria and knowledge of the Atlantis legend showed that he was conversant with, if not well-up in, matters which the average man either dismisses as fantasies or regards with amused scepticism. Still, having begun, Naylor felt that he had to take up the challenge.

"The two-dimensional analogy, then," he said slowly, "considering length and breadth as the two dimensions. You get a plane surface, with its boundaries at right angles to each other—perpendicular to each other. And a surface has no thickness —in that two-dimensional state there is no such thing as height or depth—thickness. It is inconceivable, on a two-dimensional plane."

"You may say," Gees put in for him, "that the surface of which you speak has no more thickness than has a shadow cast by the sun."

"An admirable way of putting it," he conceded, and felt, more than ever, that he was talking to this man before him as if he himself were an infant—that Gees knew more than he did. Still, he went on. "We now imagine a two dimensional life—intelligent life—on that plane surface. Being two-dimensional, it has no consciousness of a third dimension, does not know there is such a thing as height above the surface, or depth beneath it. It can travel in the two directions of length and breadth, but cannot lift itself the minutest fraction of an inch above the surface on which it lives. It simply does not know there is an 'up' or a 'down' beyond its two-dimensional world."

"Quite lucid, so far," Gees commented again, and Naylor flushed slightly at the implication of the remark: it put him more in the position of a schoolboy reciting a lesson to a master than that of one who imparted information. Still, he forced himself to go on.

"We will now suppose," he said, "that a three-dimensional being comes along, looks down on the plane surface, and is enough interested in that two-dimensional being to lift it, even the smallest fraction of an inch, away from the surface on which it lives. No matter how small the lift, the two-dimensional being is instantly and completely out of its world. Since it knows nothing of up or down, it cannot look down and see that world still near: it is lost as completely as you or I would be if we were hurled off the earth's surface into space, altogether out of sight of the earth. Further to that, since neither this being nor the plane on which it has been living has thickness, it may find an entirely different world, only a thousandth part of an inch removed from its own, but still quite distinct from that first plane surface world, and out of sight of it—since the sight of the being does not extend up or down."

"Carry on," Gees urged. "It's all clear."

"Now let's come to the three-dimensional world—ignoring time as the fourth for this illustration. Our three dimensions in space are all perpendicular to each other—length, and breadth, and thickness. They are all the human mind can comprehend and visualise. In three-dimensional geometry, it is impossible to construct a figure with more than three dimensions all perpendicular to each other, and if such a figure could be constructed, the human eye would be incapable of taking it in, since the human eye is three-dimensional, just as the eye of the two-dimensional being I have been talking about would be incapable of realising the third perpendicular, height. But, though three-dimensional geometry will permit of constructing figures with only three perpendiculars—length, breadth, and height—mathematics show that there *is* a fourth perpendicular, a dimension at right angles to the three we know. We cannot see it or comprehend it, but it is *there.*"

"And if it were possible to move along that fourth perpendicular, to move in the fourth dimension," Gees amplified the statement, "we could get quite away from any point in the three we know, and—given control of ourselves and our movements in that fourth dimension, re-enter the other three at any point we liked. Which is to say that I could just enter the fourth dimension in this room, vanish from the room, and reappear in London—or New York, or the moon, for that matter. Anywhere within the confines of the earth and its satellite."

"Ah!" Naylor sighed, rather wearily. "You know as much as I do, I see, if not more. But why only the earth and the moon—why not anywhere in the whole universe, that re-entry?"

"Because," Gees told him, "there are dimensions without number, as your mathematics tell you. You can raise two to any power—the cube of it is eight, which is as far as three dimensions will take you, but mathematically you can go to the fourth, fifth, sixth power of two—to as high a power as you like. Now the Adepts of An knew what you do not appear to know, that control of the fourth dimension gives power to move, without using any of the first three dimensions, within the limits of the earth's influence—that is, say, as far as the moon, but no farther. If any one of those Adepts could have raised himself to control of the next, fifth dimension of space, he would have had power to move anywhere in the planetary system of our sun—but no one of them ever got that far, and so all their knowledge of that fifth spatial dimension remained empiric. And what control of the sixth would give no man ever knew or will know, because the human brain is capable of understanding just so much and no more. It is incapable of taking in the potentialities of six dimensions of space—comprehension of them belongs to gods, not to men."

"You, with your knowledge, let me expound the elementary beginnings of the subject to you!" Naylor said, with angry disgust.

"I wanted to know how much *you* know," Gees told him calmly.

"Where did you learn this about the Atlantean Adepts?"

Gees shook his head. "Maybe I listened to the wind on the downs, or heard a silence talking. Perhaps I dreamed it all."

"Why gibe at me?" Naylor demanded heatedly.

"Did I? I was not aware of it. I thought we were merely discussing a purely empiric theory, a possibility that man may turn to solid reality—more than solid, since it includes a perpendicular beyond the solid—

some day when he is far enough advanced. As far, say, as the Adepts of An, who for all their knowledge could not save their continent when the sixth-dimensional gods decided to drown it."

"Are *you* an Adept?" Naylor asked uneasily.

Again Gees shook his head. "I am a student," he answered. "There have been very few Adepts since —since the first pyramid was built. Very few. Solomon, who let his desires blind him and so lost his powers and ruined his kingdom in the end. Kong-fu-tze—Confucius, as he is better known. King Alfred of England, just and only just an Adept in the year of his death. A few others—very few."

"The Christ?" Naylor asked.

"Higher than them all—controller of not less than six dimensions, and probably more. Laid aside His powers for humanity's sake—and humanity has rewarded Him ever since as it does all those it cannot comprehend, denied and crucified Him over and over again from age to age." He got on his feet in a restless way as he ceased speaking: that statement of a faith—it was no less—was unfitting here, he knew. Naylor looked uneasy over it—resented it, perhaps.

"Well, perhaps," he said, with a sort of judicial coldness.

"No perhaps about it," Gees retorted brusquely. "Obvious truth."

"And now—can I count on your help?" Naylor looked up as he asked the question—he had not risen when Gees did, and his anxiety showed in his gaze as it did in his tone.

"In what way do you think I could help?" Gees parried.

"Get—recover for me—the rod of An, before that woman learns the use of it," Naylor said very slowly. "I will pay——"

"Recover, you said," Gees interrupted. "Was it once yours, then?"

Naylor dropped his gaze—there was that in Gees' eyes which he did not like to see. Gees waited, and by mere will power compelled the man to look up at him again, after a long interval.

"No," Naylor said, and the word was patently dragged from him.

"I see." Under the irony of the comment Naylor literally writhed. "You know perfectly well that Miss Warenn would never give up that rod of her own free will. You ask me to become a common thief, and offer to pay me for it. I'd sooner turn——"

"No!" Naylor started to his feet with the shrill exclamation. "Bribe her, anything—help me! I'm afraid, man—she's taken all but my reason, and she's making spells to take that too! Help me!"

Gees said—"No," and made the one syllable definite and final.

"You—you saw her yesterday," Naylor almost whispered. "Will you—do you mean you will help her?"

"No," Gees said again. "Neither of you. The feud began with Wulfruna, it seems, ancestress of you both —Dark Lagny intensified it. Now you two are left— you two only. Fight it out between you—I'm going back from here to London and everyday sanity. Now!"

With no further word at parting he turned and went to the door. There, though, he turned, and fired out— "How did you know I saw Miss Warenn yesterday? Do you keep spies here in Troyarbour."

"Nettie——" Naylor blurted out the one word, as
if he would deny the accusation of spying, and then
stopped, knowing what he had revealed.

Gees said—"Get Nettie to help you—she seems to
fulfil more than her obvious purpose here." And went
out, furious.

When he seated himself at the wheel of the car, he
cooled a little. On such a day as this the drive to
London would be a pleasure, and probably Miss
Brandon would have some other, saner case waiting
for him to take up—something to sharpen his wits and
make him forget this tiny hamlet tucked away in the
folds of the downs, where laughs came out from
nothingness and an otherwise sane man feared spells
such as went out of fashion centuries ago. He let the
car gently down to sight of the inn and village: he
had no use for Naylor, on the one hand: Ira Warenn
had no need of him, on the other. Straight through,
out to the main road, and away. He had finished with
Troyarbour.

A face looked out from the window of the room in
which he had last slept, as he passed—looked out
momentarily, and as he turned his head, vanished. A
pity the girl blonded her hair like that: by the look
of the root ends, there would be red shades in it if she
left it alone—let her keep at it: hair with red shades
was for girls like Eve Madeleine, girls of innate fineness and real worth, not for common little things like
this innkeeper's toy. Yes, let her go on blonding!

He let his mind dwell on Eve Madeleine—the perfect
secretary. No, though—Eve Madeleine the woman.
She did not care one hoot about him as man, he felt
certain: she had known of various adventures in
emotion through which he had lived in consequence

of these cases of his, when girls had fallen for him, and it had made no difference to her cool acceptance of all that he asked of her, no difference to the manner in which she met him day by day. She was quietly friendly, never resenting his moods or eccentricities, but suiting herself to them all the time. Chestnut hair with red shades in it, like sunlight on foliage in autumn: long-lashed, lovely eyes, and a restful, deep-cadenced voice—a voice to remember. Supposing Eve Madeleine—

"Oh, hell! She's Miss Brandon to me. Always must be."

He came out from his reverie, and wrenched at the steering wheel. He was almost abreast the lone farmhouse, from which emanated no sign of life. But, in the middle of the way he wanted to go, lay Irene the sow, contentedly asleep, and round her the litter of piglets rooted at the grass, grunted, chased each other, and utterly ignored the juggernaut advancing toward them—at a crawl, for Gees wished to kill none of them. He blared a warning at them, and they wouffed and, one and all, faced the source of the sound in curiosity rather than fear. Then Gees saw that, if he swung off the laneway on to the grass in front of the house, he could pass them and their somnolent mother.

The radiator lifted, swung toward the house. Round from the back came a smallish, sturdy, bristly-backed animal with a fearsome tusk protruding on each side of its jaw. It snuffed the wind—saw it, perhaps, as in some parts is said to be possible for swine—and then, advancing, planted itself squarely in front of the slowly advancing car, and said—"Urr-wouff!" In human language—"No, you don't!" or so it sounded to Gees. He stopped, puzzled, and a streak of black lightning came from nowhere, and with one mighty leap landed on his back and clung, claws deeply sunken through fabric to skin, to hold him there.

"Blast you, Peter!" Gees exclaimed, and lifted his hand to remove the cat. But Peter chewed at the lifted fingers, very gently, and began to purr. He rubbed, and Gees' hat fell over his eyes.

When he had got it off, he saw Ira Warenn standing in the farmhouse doorway. Not so much standing as leaning against the doorpost, weak with much laughter. But he felt like anything but laughter.

"What is this—a circus?" he snapped out angrily.

She stood erect. The only way to stop you," she answered. "You meant to go, and not come back, I know."

"And still mean it," he retorted, trying to lift Peter down. But the cat sat claw-tight, and Gees desisted. It was too painful.

She came out from the doorway and stood beside the car. "Please, no," she said. "A little while—an hour? Won't you?"

Some wistful note in the request changed his mind for him. It was weak, he knew: he had not meant to see her again, but there stood the boar in front of the radiator, gazing steadily at it as if he would let it run him down rather than budge: there on Gees' shoulders sat Peter, and Sindbad's old man never clung more tightly than the cat. And there stood Ira Warenn, pleading—the witch pleading!

Slowly Gees got out and faced her, and Peter, moving round from his back, leaped to her shoulder to sit on it, waving his tail like a black pennon of triumph. If he stuck his claws in to balance himself on alighting, she did not flinch: perhaps he landed clawlessly.

Gees asked—"Why?" and did not amplify it.

She said simply—"To save me the trouble of coming to you."

"Why should you? What have I to do with you, or you with me?"

"To find that out, I stopped your car," she replied.

"Planted this menagerie in my way, you mean?" Anger sounded in the half-assertion, half-question, and his gaze emphasised it.

She raised her voice slightly to say, in an authoritative, almost peremptory fashion—"Irene—go away! Adolphus, to heel!"

The sow got up and ambled off round to the back of the house, her family following and disappearing with her. The boar advanced, took a distant sniff at Gees which betokened curiosity, and then went behind his mistress and sat on his hunkers like a well-trained dog. Gees noted that, unlike the average hog, the beast was scrupulously clean: he was smallish and lean, with a hint of reversion to wild type about him, and his flanks and quarters betokened more power of muscle than likelihood of fattening. Hudson's dictum recurred to Gees' mind: let that boar beget a family, then breed from the best and most intelligent, and the third generation would develop points which would prove the pig's equality with the dog, if not superiority over it.

"Does he light the kitchen fire in the mornings?"

"Invariably." Her deep, dark eyes held mocking lights. "That is, after he has chopped the firewood and blackleaded the grate."

"And now you've made me stop, again I want to know why?"

"Because, after seeing Jerome Naylor for the second time, you would not be satisfied if you went away now," she answered, with no mockery at all. "At present, perhaps, you think you would, but your curiosity would grow and grow, and in the end you would come back to see what is happening between Dark Lagny's daughter and Oger's son. And I—I do not wish you to come back. I wish to feel that when you go from here, I shall be left in peace to do—as I will."

"With Naylor—do as you will with him," Gees completed for her. "Don't you think 'peace' a rather inappropriate word. You mean war."

"Left in peace to finish my war, then," she amended calmly.

"I see." The comment was acridly satiric. "Do we conduct the interview here, with that bristly gentleman squatting on guard behind you? If so, let's sit on my running board. It's quite clean."

"Will you come in with me, Mr. Green?" she asked coldly.

"Thank you, I will—but it's too early in the day for cowslip wine." He placed himself beside her as, turning toward the house, she left Adolphus to his own devices. When they reached the open doorway, Peter took another leap from her shoulder, landing inside the passage, and streaked up the stairs at the back. Gees heard him padding along oilcloth in some corridor above, and then entered the room he had seen the preceding evening. In full daylight it appeared dingier and less attractive than then, and the oaken chest shone out in greater contrast as its surface reflected the light from the window.

A persistent, singing note sounded and grew in

volume as the two entered. The girl turned to Gees, and he saw her lovely eyes wide with fear. The sound grew to a musical, martial clanging, and gradually died away. She went to the chest, lifted the lid, and after looking inside closed it down again. "The sword!" she said, fearfully.

"Any meaning in that solo, then?" Gees asked casually.

"It is the second singing in my lifetime," she answered. "The first was on the day my father died —the day Jerome Naylor came here."

"And you cursed him, I understand," he remarked, still keeping his voice down to casual interest. "M'yes. Who's it singing for, now?"

She shook her head. "No," she said, "I do not know. But it is a dread thing, that singing. For all of Dark Lagny's breed."

She alone was left of Dark Lagny's breed, he reflected but did not say. Instead, he said—"I think I don't like this metropolis. A sword that sings, and a bodiless voice that laughs. Was it bodiless, though?"

She gazed at him steadily, making no reply. The fear had died out from her eyes, now: a tinge of colour changed her paleness.

"You were interested, it appears," he said, "in my going to see Naylor a second time. It was rather an interesting interview. He wants your axe handle— the Rod of An, he calls it—because of a recipe or formula on it, one you have not yet discovered and he doesn't want you to discover. I am quoting him in saying that."

"He will never have the axe handle," she said inexorably.

"I told him I thought you felt like that about it, and knew as he talked—it was rather a long talk on his side—that he had made one mistake about you. I knew he had—knew it since last night."

"Yes?" The query betokened only slight interest in his words.

"Yes. In the bar parlour—tap room, or whatever you like to call it—of Todd's inn. If you hadn't discovered that formula, you could never have laughed for all of us in there to hear."

"Isn't that rather an absurd statement?" she asked.

"I think I'll get on my way," he retorted abruptly.

"No—what is it you want me to say?" She was instantly eager, persuasive, even leaning toward him as she stood before the chest. "You believe—what, of me? That I know——"

"I'd say," he answered deliberately, "that if you know all your family tree, you can go back as far behind Wulfruna as she is from you. Back, generation piled on generation, to some family of An in which were Adepts—or was an Adept—of the old cult. From whom the formula on the axe-handle originated, to be handed down and handed down till Dark Lagny scribed it on the handle—for you to decipher. I'd say you have deciphered it, too, having inherited knowledge enough."

"And why the inheritance?" she persisted.

"Well, take your ancestress' description, for one thing. Dark Lagny. So outstandingly dark as to be distinguished by that title among the fair-haired race that bred vikings. Then you, with that dead-black hair and such eyes as I have never seen—Dark Lagny's darkness persists and is reproduced in you. One conclusion only—you are of Azilian descent, and that means Atlantean. Some colony or settlement that escaped when the great inundation happened."

"To what is all this leading?" she asked.

"You have somehow got control or partial control of the fourth dimension in space," he said slowly. "Naylor knows that the secret of it is on the axe-handle —what else is on that bone, heaven and you only know, apparently. Naylor talked of it empirically— theorised. You, I believe, can state it practically— perhaps demonstrate it. I tell you, I've as great a thirst for knowledge as any man living, and I want your practical statement of this—this three-dimensional impossibility that you know as real."

She shook her head. "No," she said. And again— "No."

"Then I'll say good morning, and if those pigs of yours get in my way again, I'll drive over them. Good morning, Miss Warenn."

"Wait," she said. "I will tell you."

VII

"THERE IS NO MAGIC"

IRA WARENN pointed at the horsehair-seated carving chair, set back from the table toward the window. She asked—"Will you sit there?"

Gees took out his cigarette case and offered it. She took one, and he lighted for her and himself and then took the indicated seat. She perched herself on the edge of the circular, claw-legged table, facing him, and inhaled and exhaled—a practised smoker, he saw.

"You want—me," she said reflectively. "All of me—all I know and have done and will do. You want to add that to all you already know—to pin me in your specimen case and know yourself so much greater through adding my knowledge to yours. That is so?"

"If you hadn't spread those impediments in front of the car and stopped me, I'd have foregone the knowledge," he answered. "I was going away from here, not to come back."

She shook her head. "You would have come back," she demurred. "I know. I *know!* Yester evening, when I talked to you, I realised you as of those who know, and for all of you the increase of knowing is—you are always questing, all of you, for more. Knowing that you know so little. And you were afraid of me."

She spoke reflectively, slowly, gazing into space. Gees took a long inhalation from his cigarette, and answered—

"Of your magic—if that is the right word."

"It is not. There is no magic—and you know it!"

"That is true," he admitted. "Also it is true what you say—I wanted you—the essential you that can do—what you do. What Naylor told me you have done. I wanted—and wouldn't let myself want—to dissect you, to get at reasons. Why you, being what you are, should waste time and life on such an aim as that old feud. Near Adeptship, obviously, and yet you—I want to know why. I confess it."

"I am not—I shall never be Adept," she said. "That is reached by—prayer and fasting, as the phrase goes. One goes up stage by stage—*they* went up, painfully and slowly, knowing the final stage would compensate for all they denied themselves. As Adepts they knew *all*, through patient years of ascent along the path. I come in to the path like a blind child—I know my limitations. I have not paid the price *they* paid, and so I shall never see, but grope. Nor, I think, reap any profit. You see, I am a woman. You, I think, will yet be Adept. Ten—twenty years hence, perhaps. Thirty years hence—what are years, or what is one life? I am a woman."

"Obviously." He put a tinge of satire into the comment. "And wasting what is, equally obviously, a mentality and breadth of vision given to few women on an old hate. It *is* waste!"

He put strong emphasis on the last sentence, realising as he did that she was incredibly beyond and above her setting. Here in this lone hamlet she had the poise and knowledge of a woman of the world twice her age. In the sense in which she had used the words, he wanted her—wanted to know how such a one knew all she knew, and how she knew it. A mere farmer's

daughter, on the face of it, yet a seeress, or very near
it.   Here was a puzzle worth the solving.

"You think it waste," she said, and flicked ash
from her cigarette. "You are outside, looking in from
the outside on what Jerome Naylor has told you. I—
I am Dark Lagny's child—I am Dark Lagny herself,
for all I know. You are not yet Adept—how can you
judge the power that drives? You want me—to know
me and my motive and driving force. You cannot
know it, cannot comprehend it. An urge in the blood,
driving me—centuries of hate compressed in me. So
I tell you. You wanted me, and in so telling you I
reveal myself—you have me."

He shook his head, threw away his cigarette end,
and took out another. She too threw her stub into the
unlighted fireplace, and as he reached out the case
took one and a light after it.

He said—"Not all of you. This is a mere statement.
It needs amplifying, before I have all of you. So far,
I get your coming in to the Path by a back door,
say, stealing what Adepts earn—and for that, of course,
you will have to pay, in due course. But how you
steal in I can only guess, so far. I want to know,
not guess."

"You know, as I know, that there is no magic," she
half-questioned.

He nodded. "In the sense that the ignorant of all
the ages have seen magic in natural sequences, there
is no magic," he agreed. "Do you know, you are a
very wonderful woman?"

"I suppose I am." She regarded her cigarette end,
and smiled. "Yet I am only a small child, half-blind
and groping. On the edge of seeing, yet not seeing
fully. It is true—there is no magic. We learn the

use of a rule—of a law—and those who do not know the law say that we work magic. Is that not so?"

Again he nodded assent. "Which is why they burnt wise men at the stake, in old days," he said. "They could not comprehend. What I cannot comprehend is that you, being of the wise, pursue this feud against Naylor. You might make so much better use of your life."

"I tell you, that is beyond my control. It is my task, say. I shall destroy him in the end, as I have already destroyed all he valued. When I know a little more, have advanced a little more."

"Which means——?" A tinge of impatience sounded in the question.

"You know—you accused—there was a laugh," she said very slowly. "It is quite true. I laughed. They were so funny. I had to laugh."

"In other words, you have got control of the fourth dimension in space," he said. "That is what I want of you—we come down to practical fact, now. The first human being, I think, since——"

"Since An became a submarine height," she completed. "Perhaps. The later Adepts did not follow that path—I think, being a woman, that they might have gained more if—but I am a woman, and outside. I cannot *see* the Path, but grope, having entered it without sight."

"Through what is scribed on the axe-handle—the rod of An," he suggested. "You have got your knowledge at second-hand."

"You are a very wise man," she told him, and smiled.

"Oh, very!" He smiled too. "You were virtually admitting that you have got control of the fourth dimension. I'd have left you to it, but you stopped me. Now, Miss Warenn, for everything you get out of life there is a price to pay, and my price for your stopping me is a share in this knowledge of yours— of a fourth dimension in space."

"You must risk much," she warned him.

"I think it would be worth it," he answered.

She laughed outright. "You want magic?" she asked. "Have you four years to waste on it? On that one bit of magic?"

"Is it that?" he queried.

"Yes? Magic!" There was derision in the word. "An old woman finds out, or inherits the knowledge, that a certain herb will inspire desire in a man. A girl comes to her and asks for a potion that will give her the love of that man. The old woman makes a decoction, the girl induces the man to drink it at an opportune moment, and—magic! There is no magic. It is applied knowledge of cause and effect, whatever the case may be. Jerome Naylor fears my magic, I know, and the fear is a mere proof of his ignorance. I have given five years to this last bit of knowledge, and still I am uncertain, not fully able to use it."

"You suggested four years, I think," he remarked practically. "Now you say it took five. I'm merely asking—before going off to London."

"Five years——" she took no notice of the gibe— "since I read Dark Lagny's runes on the rod. And thought myself mistress of the world, when I had fully understood them. Let me take a parallel. Say that you want to learn to skate, and you learn from a book all the rules of skating. You put on skates, and—can you skate?"

"Personally, yes. On your parallel—no."

"So with what I learned. It gave me comprehension of what one must do—you own you want me, and I am giving you myself, in this. I learned, in theory, how to enter the fourth dimension of space, but my three-dimensional mind could make no use of the knowledge. The fourth line on which one must travel—I could not *see* it."

"I know," he said. "I've spent some hours thinking this over."

"Hours? Five years! My father spent his life, and still dared not experiment. He read the runes, and I had his knowledge to add to mine. Still it was not enough. Else, there had been no Naylor living to-day. Because that is our aim, to end them."

"You bloodthirsty crowd!" Gees ejaculated, half-involuntarily.

The door, just ajar, was pushed open then, and Peter entered and came to sit looking up at his mistress. She said—"Go to that man, Peter," and pointed at Gees as he sat in the armchair.

But Peter sat, looking up at her, disregarding the command. Then he leaped on the table and seated himself beside her, purring.

"I thought you could control animals," Gees observed caustically.

"To a point," she answered, with no discomfiture at all, and stroked the cat's ears. "Do you know you must never thwart a cat? If you do, you lose all power over it. You must never strike it."

"One thrashes dogs," he observed, "and they're better for it."

"But a cat, never. Peter settled himself in your car——" She broke off, as if she had said too much, and tickled Peter's ears.

"We're getting near it," Gees observed. "Do have another cigarette." The inevitable case opened itself under her eyes.

She shook her head. "Two is enough. Can I offer you—anything?"

"Yes. The conclusion of what you were saying when Peter interrupted us. About those five years, and what you learned."

"And what I learned." She spoke musingly, as if recalling it all. "You must understand—you do understand, I know—the Adept travels along a path that carries him through many more years than I have taken to reach—what? I myself do not yet know."

"The beginnings," Gees suggested, after waiting for the end of it.

She said—"Picture yourself a baby, groping your way into this world—this three-dimensional world—into which you must fit. At first your consciousness of material things is very vague—perhaps because you are so busy forgetting the immaterial things you have left to come to this state. For two—three—four years you are incapable of understanding what people say, what will hurt you, what is good for you—you are learning, very slowly, and in the learning you may hurt yourself. That is of three dimensions. The fourth is more difficult."

"Takes longer," he said—to induce her to go on.

"Takes longer," she echoed. She made an odd movement of her head, and for an instant he saw the sun-glint in her eyes, whose colour he was never able to determine. Then she was not there: apart from the turn of her head, he saw no movement, but knew himself alone in the room. Then she was there again, perched on the edge of the table as if she had not moved. "You see?" she went on, as if there had been no intermission. "There is no magic—there is only cause and effect."

He got his breath back with an effort. Sitting there, she looked utterly attractive, all woman—it was difficult to see her as witch, mistress of the old magic that is not magic, but a far greater thing. Yet—was she mistress of it, or subservient to it?

"Don't do that again," he said, trying to retain normality.

"It was the first thing I did—like the baby trying to walk," she told him. "I took one step, and came back. One step, in that fourth direction that you know but cannot realise, and then I came back. Quickly, gladly. I have never been so much afraid as when I saw what that one step revealed. There are presences—intelligences far beyond ours, there. And I was like the baby taking its first step in this world we know. It was a year and more before I took that one step again—I was afraid. I had my three-dimensional understanding, there in a four-dimensional world. I could not see, could not venture farther. I—tottered, and came back. Dared only to come back."

"I understand," he encouraged her. "And then?"

"If you were a child of five, you would be in this world what I am in that," she told him. "I have to learn. I think the Adepts had to learn, but they had put many years of study into a knowledge I have stolen from the axe-handle—they were prepared, able to see, perhaps, when they entered on that state. As if for years you trained a man to work a machine, taught him by pictures and drawings and lessons, and then took him to the machine. With my stolen know-

ledge, with no preparation, I face the machine, and
have to learn how to use it."

"In other words, consciousness of the fourth dimension in space does not mean control of that dimension,"
he commented thoughtfully.

"You said you wanted me—I am giving you all of
me," she said, and smiled. "Giving myself away—
isn't that the phrase? I tried the one step, and found
myself blind and helpless—that was the beginning.
As I say, I took that one step, and it was a year and
more before I had courage enough to take it again."

"And then?" he asked, watching the play of her
expressions. She was forcing herself to a confession:
why, he could not yet determine.

"I took—the step you have just seen me take. One
movement into that other world, which cuts across
this. I know, now—it cuts across this world in which
we live, and one may move into it, move in it, and
return. Not so much a fourth dimension, as I see
it now, as a fourth direction. I move in it, and as
far as you are concerned I am not——"

Her voice ceased, and again she was not there.
Gees realised a little flurry of air, as if her effacement
of herself had caused a vacuum that had to be filled,
and as he realised it she was sitting again on the table
edge, as if nothing had happened.

He said—"Don't *do* that!" with angry emphasis.

She laughed. "One step," she said. "Not a three-
dimensional step—you see, I don't move a foot or
a hand. I move along another line, one that has
no relation to the lines you know. Out of your sight
and consciousness, to return into it as I went."

Trying to retain sanity, he said—"You are a very
dangerous person. You have got not only knowledge,

but control of this other state of being. Which, as I see it, is not permitted to humanity—we have to live in the world we know. You will be destroyed, I think, as An and its Adepts were destroyed. You know too much."

"I will risk it," she retorted defiantly. "If I can first destroy Jerome Naylor, I will risk all that my knowledge brings on me. I live to that end—am devoted to that end."

"A petty, human perversion of a knowledge that might be of service to all mankind!" He contemned her with the pronouncement. "Knowing as you know, you ought to be bigger, saner. Not like this."

"I am what I am—Dark Lagny's child," she said incisively. "Set here, no matter what I might be elsewhere, to fulfil a purpose. After—I do not know, but the purpose must be fulfilled. I know! To you it is a futility, a very small and mean use of life, but who are you to say what is use and what is futility? You challenged me from the moment I first spoke with you. You towered over me, told me in effect that I faced one who knows from the beginning, while I steal in at a point far along the path, and try to steal knowledge for which I should have paid by years of patience. It is true—but I have the knowledge. I can move as you cannot—you have seen."

"Child, you are playing with a thunderbolt of the gods as if it were a toy!" he told her angrily. "You don't know what you do."

"Who are you to judge me?" she demanded with equal anger. "Give me another cigarette, and don't presume beyond your knowledge!"

The utter, practical anti-climax of the request—or command—brought a smile to his face. He proffered his case, and the lighter followed it. She leaned toward him to get a light, and again poised herself on the table edge, smiling a little. Dark Lagny's child—or Dark Lagny herself, reborn. So Gees thought, then.

"We are sane again," she remarked, with the cigarette alight.

"And that laugh, last night?" he asked after a pause.

"I laughed twice," she said frankly, and he nodded assent, but did not interrupt. "They were—you were there, you know. I stood on the edge—it is more than ever I have attempted before in darkness, though in daylight I put Peter in your car, and heard you talk to Nettie."

"I don't like this," he said, frowning. "Are you intending to haunt me? What happens when I undress? Will you be there?"

In turn she drew her brows together. "I had right," she said, and half the music went out of her voice for the claim. "Jerome Naylor had called on you, so I took Peter in my arms, and stepped out—so——" Gees gasped, for she was no longer there, but the air appeared to swirl about the table edge. Her voice came to him as if from a great distance, not raised, but a stilly ghost of a voice. "I put him in the car and soothed him to quiet—he lay quiet where you would sit, I knew. And that was all. I stepped back, here."

"How?" he asked, after a pause for thought over the incredibility.

"Just . . . so." Again she sat there, real, as if she had not moved. "You see, once you know how to move along that line—the line that is so hard to see—you can regard the three dimensions we all know as a sheet of paper—it is a poor simile—but you can go under and above and round the dimensions we all know as if they did not exist. Or rather, as if they existed as an adjunct to the line on which I am learning to travel. When I know more, am more used to it, I shall be able to control my movements along it and go where I choose. Now, I step out, and am afraid. So I step back."

"Like a child learning to walk," he said thoughtfully.

"Just like that," she assented, with obvious pleasure in his comprehension of her state. "I know it all—it is on the rod—but I have to practise the use of it. And then——"

"For the love of Mike," he said in the pause, "don't get acquainted with any burglars! If you did, it would be just too bad."

"You're laughing at me!" she accused indignantly.

"I am not," he answered, with sober gravity. "I am thinking of what you may control—when you have learned to control it fully. As I see it, you are on the way to full knowledge of one of the primal forces of the universe, and mankind is not yet sufficiently advanced to use such a knowledge as that. You have no right to it."

"I have!" she contradicted, incisively. "It was there for me to read—left to me by Dark Lagny on the bone shaft."

"You have no right to it," he repeated. "You are not Adept, even. If you persist in using this power, you will be destroyed."

"By whom?" she challenged the statement, defiantly.

"Not by any human agency." He spoke slowly, and as if thinking to make sure that every word was fitting. "It may seem to be by human denial of your right to use the power, but in reality it will not be so. There are powers beyond this fourth dimension of space, powers that watch humanity and say—'Thus far, and no farther.' Which is why spiritualists often become obsessed and silly—they have no right to go beyond human limits. Lodge and Doyle are cases in point, great intellects that became moronic, condemned by the powers beyond this fourth dimension. So you too will be condemned if you persist. I warn you— stop tampering with this thing, for the human race is not far enough advanced to use it to wise ends. It is not so far advanced as in the days of Atlantis, and the whole continent was destroyed to prevent the survival of the knowledge you have."

She shook her head. "No," she said, "but because of other knowledge that I have from the axe-handle, and dare not use—dare not even define to you, near Adept as you are. This, I think, is given me to use— I shall use it, and with it destroy my enemy."

"Perverting a mighty force to petty ends," he said. "I tell you, if you do that, you will be destroyed. It is—well, sacrilege."

"I will take the risk," she told him angrily.

He stood up. "It's up to you—I've warned you," he said. "One other word, Miss Warenn. You're asking something for nothing, in this. I tell you— that can't be done. You've got to give to get, whether you seek vengeance, or profit, or love—whatever you seek, you've got to give to get. You're trying to get without giving—to develop something that has come to you with no giving at all, and gain from it. That cannot be done—you've *got* to give to get!"

"Say it again!" she mocked him, and laughed.

He went to the door—his hat was in the car, he knew, where Peter had knocked it by rubbing against him. Now, Peter moved from his stance and sat in the doorway, looking up, as if praying this stranger to stay. Gees bent to tickle the cat's ears.

"No use, old chap," he said. "She's far too set on her course. Good-bye, Miss Warenn."

"But I wanted to tell you—ask you——" she began, and broke off.

"I said—good-bye, Miss Warenn," he repeated coldly, and went out to the car.

Since neither Irene nor Adolphus was in evidence, he drove away, along the tortuous lane, shadowed by the downs, that took him to the main road and Londonward.

VIII

AN ERROR OF JUDGMENT

THE flat, on the third floor of No. 37, Little Oakfield Street, which is an exceedingly decorous and respectable street not far from the Haymarket, consisted of four rooms—and usual domestic offices, of course. Gees reserved two rooms as his residence, maintained one as his own very comfortably-furnished office, and the fourth, on the right of the short corridor as one entered the flat, was devoted to Miss Brandon's use. She had been his secretary since, to his father's wrath, he had announced in the personal columns of otherwise unblemished newspapers that he was prepared to tackle anything from mumps to murder, and, the day after his return from Troyarbour, she sat behind the typewriter on her desk, smoking one of Gees' cigarettes, while he sat on the corner of the desk. He had dictated all he could tell her about his visits to Naylor and interviews with Ira Warenn, and now her shorthand notebook lay closed beside her, until he should see fit to go to his own room and leave her to get on with the transcription.

He appeared in no hurry, but, for him, unusually and gravely thoughtful. Miss Brandon sat silent, waiting. She was, as he had realised long since, an exceedingly attractive girl, and a clever one as well. Clever enough to hide from him the fact that he had so far grown into her life, become such a part of her thought and feeling, as to form her chief interest.

Clever enough to retain a cool, rather satiric attitude, knowing full well that any change in their relationship would end her tenancy of this room: she wanted to keep near him: some day, perhaps, he might realise that he had only to ask . .

To-day, she waited, and in the end stubbed out the cigarette in the ash-tray she had so placed that he could use it too. Instantly his case flew into his hand, and opened itself under her eyes.

She said—"No, thank you, Mr. Green. Not just now."

"Oomph! Did you get all I've been telling you?"

"I can promise you an accurate transcription," she answered coolly.

"And what have you!" he put acrid emphasis into the comment. "I meant—did you take it all in enough to discuss it?"

"I—yes, I think so, if you wish to discuss it with me. That fourth dimension part of it is rather over my head, I'm afraid. I know very little about the subject—except I know that if we could find a fourth perpendicular to the three we already comprehend, we should open up a new world, and have full control of this we know."

"That's all anyone knows," he said. "Except, perhaps, this Ira Warenn. She's found it, past doubt, but there's a vast difference between—I might find a herd of elephants, but that's not to say I could make money out of giving tuppenny rides on 'em. You get that."

She nodded, thoughtfully. "One has to learn, just as one learned to walk and talk. Yes. In a different world. New conditions—yes."

"New—presences," he added. "You've got it down —what was it she told me? Yes—intelligences far beyond ours. In the world that interpenetrates ours, the fourth perpendicular cutting across all three that we know. Obviously those intelligences must be far beyond ours, since they have full comprehension of this fourth direction—line of movement, or what you like to call it. Consider that at this moment you and I are being watched and studied, perhaps, by those far vaster intellects—and moving as they can they are able to see into our minds and spread out our very thoughts while we are restricted to speech for interpretation of what we want to express——"

"I'd rather not consider it," she interrupted.

"You prefer normality, eh? Well, I don't. I want to explore that fourth direction, learn to step out from solidity into that unknown region as she stepped out. Out and back, at will."

"Which means, you will go back to Troyarbour," she asserted.

"I shall not!" He put vigour into the denial. "A, I've paid in Naylor's cheque for eighteen guineas, told him I'll have nothing more to do with him, and so finished the case. B, I am definitely afraid of that woman—girl, for she's little more. I don't know what her age actually is, except that she's so strong an example of heredity that in development she's centuries old. I mean she has a vast inherited knowledge, a store that she hadn't to learn again at the beginning of this present life. As if Dark Lagny had come back to earth."

"I know," she said. "We all have—flashes, call them—of pre-natal memory, at times. Some of us more than others."

"You?" he asked interestedly.

"Sometimes. I may feel that I know a place, or a person, on seeing or meeting for the first time. Prenatal memory, I think."

"Probably. Almost certainly. Y'know, Miss Brandon, you make a most excellent wall for me to bounce my thoughts against. They come back all flattened out and expanded, so I can see 'em much better."

"You told me that some while ago," she observed. "My ulterior use to you, in addition to the mere secretaryship."

"Now you're getting uppish, and we're wandering clean away from all I want to discuss with you," he reproved her. "This—never mind St. Pol Naylor— I wonder why St. Pol, but it doesn't matter. He knows no more than I do about this fourth-dimensional discovery——"

"Fifth dimensional, surely," she interrupted.

"Fourth in space—I'm leaving time out of it, for simplification of my own thought. Browning had a glimpse of it—he was a seer, of course. Do you remember Abt Vogler?"

She shook her head. "Some of it. Not enough to quote."

He quoted—

"Nay, more: for there wanted not who walked in
    the glare and glow,
Presences plain in the place; or, fresh from the
    Protoplast,
Furnished for ages to come, when a kindlier wind
    should blow,
Lured now to begin and live, in a house to their
    liking at last;

Or else the wonderful Dead who have passed
   through the body and gone,
But. were back once more to breathe in an old
   world worth their new:
What never had been, was now; what was, as it
   shall be anon;
And what is—shall I say, matched both?——"

She ended the verse, very softly—" 'For I was made
perfect too.'"

"You do know it, I see," he said. "To have
written that, he must have seen, no matter how
dimly. Along that fourth direction, into the world
of those greater presences. And she's found the
way in!"

"And you——" she sounded slightly ironic—"are
not going back."

"I am not going back." He repeated it with sober
gravity. "Something else will turn up and take my
mind off this, if we wait a day or two. Meanwhile,
I've nothing else to think about, and you must admit
it's a fascinating subject. A new world all round us,
invisible, but *there*. If one could only take the step
in that fourth direction!"

"One can't," she said practically. "I wouldn't, if
I could."

"No?" The query invited her to explain.

"You said—you say you told her she would have
to pay, not being Adept. I've got it down for
transcription. I wouldn't give the years of with-
drawal from human interests that would make me
Adept, if I were a man and had the means to do
it. And her way is wrong, as you told her. She's
breaking in, burglariously, not entering by the
door."

"Other things, too," he reflected. "That axe-handle must be terrific. Not as an axe-handle, but as what I think it was originally."

"And that?" she asked, as he did not explain.

"She said it was narwhal horn. In other words, it would last not merely years, but centuries, unless it were laid out to rot through weather conditions—heat and frost. Tens of centuries—it may date back to the days when An was still above the waters, may be some symbol carried when the processions went through the mother of hewn cities. Priestly or royal—more likely belonging to some Adept."

"Mother of hewn cities?" she repeated. "Why hewn?"

"Because that city was not built as we build," he told her. "It was quarried out—you couldn't call the places and houses in it structures, because they were not constructed. They were dug in an area of solid rock—hewn, and the rock quarried and carried away to leave what was wanted. Palaces and mansions and temples—all hewn out and hollowed out, and the stone that was taken away made the triple wall—three mighty quadrangles. Gates at the corners of the outer wall, midway between the corners of the second, and two gates to each angle, halfway between the corners and the middle, in the inner one."

"But—but look at the time it would take to get inside!" she protested. "And to carve a whole city out of solid rock—Oh, no!"

"Oh, yes!" he dissented. "It was so, I assure you—An was the mother of hewn cities, so-called and so in reality. As for the carving—slaves by the ten thousand, remember, and lashes to drive them. Probably they died by the ten thousand before it was all done, but—why worry? Plenty more to replace the dead."

"How utterly inhuman!" she protested. "I thought, by what you said about them, that the Atlanteans were a civilised race."

"They were," he said rather grimly. "So civilised, so far in advance of where we stand to-day, that the whole continent had to be destroyed to prevent the use of knowledge man is not yet fit to hold. We have to grow up, yet—you'll find individuals capable of using what they know in the way it was meant to be used, but the vast majority—occasionally individuals grow up, but nations are still children. As for inhumanity, if the slaves who hewed An out of the solid died at their work, at least they served some use in dying. We of to-day—what use was it that the world of to-day killed off four or five millions of its young men between 1914 and 1918? We have no room to talk of inhumanity—nations of to-day are far behind the reasoning use of slave labour that produced the wonders of Atlantis."

"I suppose—yes, I suppose that is so," she reflected. "But one does not like to think it, naturally. That we misuse knowledge."

"As a wise old man once said to me—if the cost of two battleships were devoted to research, mankind might now have the use of this fourth dimension—lift itself that much nearer the gods. But from the renaissance period to now, far more has been devoted to means of destruction than to advancement. Have you any idea how many thousands of millions the world of to-day is spending each year on preparations for war—materials for destroying life, instead of fostering it?"

She shook her head. "That is a terrible thought," she said.

"So much so, that I'm going to have another cigarette—more destruction," he announced. "You have one too—just for fun."

He lighted for them both, and smoked in silence for a minute or more. She saw his brows drawn down in thought. Then—

"'Pears to me I've been wandering. What I meant to discuss with you, for the sake of clarifying my own ideas, was this Ira Warenn and what she's got on that ancient bone. All in runic characters, I made it to be, and mighty hard to decipher because the later inscription is crossed over the first lot, which is scribed round and round the thing while the other runs up and down. A low trick, I call it. But she said, after we'd been talking about this use of the fourth dimension and she'd given me the demonstrations I described to you—she said there was other knowledge in the inscriptions."

"I've got that down," she said. "The report is—comprehensive."

"Say I was verbose, and be done with it," he snapped with momentary irritation. "All right, you've got it down. Knowledge she dare not use, and dared not even define to me."

"Which would be——?" she asked, ignoring his brief outburst.

He shook his head. "There was so much," he said. "The actual secret of life, the inter-relationships between electricity and light and etheric vibration, transference of personality from one human being to another—how much wasn't there! And if she's got——"

"Told you she dared not use it," she reminded him.

"Not now," he said, "but what of her to-morrows? She may begin to experiment with that other knowledge as she's doing now with this of the fourth dimension. That woman may wreck the world, yet."

"Isn't that a slight exaggeration?" she asked quietly.

"I dunno, Miss Brandon. No—I do not know. How much she has there, and how much she dare do with it. She'd dare a lot."

"In other words, you will go back," she asserted—not for the first time—and smiling a little as she said the words.

"Have I got to tell you again that I will *not* go back?" he retorted with angry emphasis. "All right, Miss Brandon—there's no hurry about that transcription, and you can put it straight on file in case I ever feel like refreshing my memory about it. I won't bother to read it through before you file it. And those fresh inquiries?"

"Two divorce, one unspecified, two business problems, and what appears to be a squabble between two women, one titled," she told him.

"I'll look over the unspecified—you can turn down the others without my seeing them. Turn down *anything* to do with divorce—I'll never touch that dirty business of burrowing for evidence, as you know, and you need never mention them, but hurl 'em back.

He took the letter she handed him, and went off to his own room, to seat himself at his desk and, in a very brief while, decide that what she had termed "unspecified" would prove an attempt at getting legal opinion without paying for it. He marked the letter—"REJECT" in large pencilling, and put it down.

"We are not a charitable institution," he told himself. "We are Gees, out to do, not to get done. Rats to you, feller!"

Miss Brandon also talked to herself as she interposed a carbon between two sheets of typing paper, which would be headed—"Report on Visit to Troyarbour Hall, Dorset," when it got into the machine.

She said—"You *will* go back! I know you, better than you know yourself. You *will* go back to Troyarbour."

.   .   .   .   .

That same night, Sam Thatcher and Ephraim Knapper came out from The Three Thorns together at closing time, to walk the hundred yards or so that would take them to Sam's front door, hard by the church. The weather had changed since Gees had driven out from the village and revelled in the still clarity of October at its best. Now, with the moon three days short of full, light masses of wrack went hurrying north-eastward across the sky, and even down in this sheltered hollow of the downs little eddies of the wind that beat across the heights brought a faint tang of the sea with them. Sam Thatcher cocked his eye skyward.

"We'll hev rine, sune," he announced gravely.

"Aye," Ephraim concurred. "We c'n du wi' some wet."

"Aye, said Sam, "but it'll be tu laate. I lifted all my taters, an' they'm not nigh oop to sizeishness. An' my marrers—well!"

"Aye," said Ephraim, sympathetically.

Abruptly and involuntarily they staggered apart, as if a wedge of enormous dimensions had been suddenly thrust down between them. Sam emitted an—"Ow!" that was nearly a screech, and Ephraim grunted as if whatever had struck him had got him in the wind. Then the two of them faced each other, warily, angrily, each with balance recovered.

"Whoy'd yu du thaat, Ephraim?" Sam demanded.

"It wur yu," Ephraim responded harshly. "It wuren't me."

"Yu hit me in the belly!" Sam said wrathfully. "F'r tu pins I'd pound yu, Ephraim Knapper, till yu howled."

"It wur yu, I tell yu," Ephraim insisted. "*Yu* hit *me* i' the belly so my beer nigh riz on me. Whoy'd yu du thaat, Sam?"

"Dooant be a fule!" Sam urged. "Else, I'll pound yu, I saay!"

Then, both recovering breath, they became conscious of a faint scent that an eddy of the night wind drove at them. Such a scent as sometimes drifts to one's nostrils from a woman's hair—but the moonlight showed clear space all round them. There was a gap in the cloud wrack through which the pale light shone down, and from the back of the inn to Sam's doorway, and for the thirty yards or more of open ground to either side, was no human being but themselves.

Sam whispered—"Reckon I'll carry a Bible when I goo about o' nights. Wish I had a little'un—mine's a big owd thing."

Ephraim parted his lips to utter, perhaps, some similar vow, but whatever he would have said was lost. For from somewhere between the two of them

sounded the ghost of a laugh, deep-toned and musical
—the tiny semblance, as if were, of a woman's
laughter.

With bristling hair the pair of them stared at each
other, and Ephraim's teeth chattered as he stared.
Then with one impulse they faced toward their homes
and ran—aye, scampered, those elderly men, like agile
boys. One door slammed, another door slammed,
and Ephraim faced his wife, an elder sister of Martha
Kilmain, and fully as large and formidable as that
more prosperous postmistress.

"What on yearth is wrong wi' you, Ephraim
Knapper?" she demanded.

"She—she laughed agin," Ephraim half-sobbed.
"Outside."

"Stuff!" said Mrs. Knapper, angrily and con-
temptuously. "An' yu neenter reckon to smesh our
door, neether. What's wrong wi' you is beer, Ephraim
Knapper—beer! I've no patience!"

Ephraim removed his boots in silence, and crept
humbly to bed.

.   .   .   .   .

Two days later, Miss Brandon opened the morning's
letters, ignoring the fact that three of them were
marked "Personal." She had her orders from Gees
on that point: he had told her that, if he indulged in
any low intrigues of which the particulars were not
fit for perusal by her virgin eye, he would let her know
in advance, and had added that "Personal" on an
envelope almost certainly meant that the inquiry itself
was a dud. So she opened them all.

One she put aside from the rest, and, after perusing
and sorting them, some for answer by herself, and

some for Gees' attention, she returned to considera-
tion of this separate missive, to which a pinkish, blue-
stamped slip—a cheque—was pinned. She read the
letter again:

Messrs. Gees,
   37, Little Oakfield Street, S.W. 1.
Dear Sirs,
   We have been instructed by Mr. J. St. Pol Naylor
that the enclosed cheque is not to be paid on presen-
tation. We therefore return the cheque herewith.
                              Yours truly,
                    p.p. Barkminster Bank, Ltd.
                    —— —— —— —— ——
                                   Manager.

Try as she would, Miss Brandon could make
nothing of the signature: it was as illegible as, if not
more illegible than, a doctor's prescription, and she
gave it up to think over the letter.
   She wanted to hold it back—she even went so far
as to question whether she herself could pay the
eighteen guineas into Gees' account, and so prevent
him from knowing that Naylor had—to put it col-
loquially—bilked him. But it could not be done:
she had just bought her new fur coat for the winter.
No, he would have to see it, and then—she knew
what would happen. Oh, yes! She knew, very well!
   When, as was his habit, Gees came to lean in her
doorway, give her "Good-morning," and suggest a
matutinal cigarette—which she sometimes accepted—
she held the letter with its enclosure out to him mutely,
and he advanced to take it from her and read it. Then,
dropping it from before his eyes, he gazed steadily at

her till she felt herself blushing. She wanted to hide from that gaze—anything but meet it.

"Now say—'I told you so!'" he growled savagely.

"Well, I did," she admitted, and reached for the telephone.

"Quite right. And quite right that you did, too. Eleven o'clock—no, tell 'em twelve-fifteen. I'd nearly forgotten that I promised to look in on my father this morning. Twelve-fifteen, Miss Brandon."

"Very good, Mr. Green."

With the letter in his hand, and with no question about the rest of his mail, he stamped off to his own room. Miss Brandon spoke into the telephone receiver—

"Tunnicliffe's? Yes, Mr. Green's secretary speaking. Mr. Green wants his Rolls-Bentley sent to Little Oakfield Street by twelve-fifteen, please. Yes. You'd better put the hood and side-curtains up, as it's such a wet morning. Thank you very much—good-bye."

As she replaced the receiver she reflected that she ought, really, to have told them to fill the petrol tank. But they would probably do it without being told—they serviced Gees well, knowing that his account was always paid promptly and that there would be a good chance of losing his profitable patronage if they failed him.

"It will be really wet on the downs," Miss Brandon told herself, observing how little rivulets ran down the panes of her window. "I don't want it to bother him, but I hope it drowns her!"

IX

MUDDY rivulets made shining, yellowish ribbons of
the ruts in the lane: rain fell with heavy, inexorable
steadiness. The wind had died away, even out on the
open road, and here, after turning off for Troyarbour
in late afternoon, Gees drove in a stillness troubled
only by the steady surr-rr-r of the downpour and the
noises that his car made along the way. Though, in
different weather, the light would have held some
while longer, it was already dusking as he faced a
steady curving of the ascent, for the heavy cloud,
unbroken from horizon to horizon and so low as to
curtain the tops of the downs ridges, masked away
altogether the last of the sun's slanting rays. There
would be a moon: full moon to-night—no, though,
to-morrow night.

The uninstructed, and sometimes even the instructed, of old time used to attribute magic to the
full moon. Had he and Ira Warenn been right in
agreeing that there is no such thing as magic? Listening to the surr-rr of the rain as he drove carefully
along the narrow way, he decided they had not. Some
things in life never lose their magic: a scent may
drown reason as a leaping wave may drown a life:
the cadences of a melody may give infinite happiness
—or infinite pain: a flower, impressing itself on one's
consciousness, may carry one into another world, an
Eden of stored memories. Magic? Everywhere in life!

No magic, though, in the heavy tumbril, drawn by a single horse, that a turn of the ascent revealed ahead of him. Inside the tumbril stood a boy holding the reins, and in some part protected from the rain by a sack drawn hoodwise over his head and shoulders. Gees heard him say—"Whoa—whup!" in a Boanerges roar, and the horse leaned back into its breeching so that the vehicle stopped—with no room for passing. The last widening that Gees had passed was a good hundred yards behind him, now: the arc of clarity that his wiper made on the misted windscreen showed that the next was not more than ten yards beyond the tumbril—if that boy had had quicker wits, he might have swerved in and left room for the car to pass. But Gees saw too that it would be impossible for the horse to back the tumbril up the slope to that next widening. He himself would have to back down to the last one he had passed— or else sit here all night.

He opened his door to yell—"All right, come on! I'll back," and, slamming the door again, put in reverse and began a gingerly retreat, trying to see through the fogged square of talc at the back of the hood, and so prevent himself from over-running the curve he had rounded to sight the tumbril. The boy drove on again with whups and whoas and sundry other instructions to his heavy shire gelding—as it turned out to be when Gees saw it more closely. He kept a twenty yard interval—fortunately, for Gees found himself in the end over-running the widening that would permit the tumbril to pass him. He backed another ten yards or so, then stopped, put in first speed, and went ahead, swinging well over to his left to make room for that clumsy vehicle.

Very well over to his left! It was the second day
of rain, and trickling rivulets from the ruts had over-
flowed on to the soft patch of ground that made the
widening, and softened some part of it almost to bog
consistency. Gees felt the car canting over as the near-
side driving wheel sank in, and unwisely thrust in the
accelerator pedal. Down went the wheel to axle depth,
and the differential, spinning the sunken wheel while
the off-side one, on firm ground, remained stationary,
told him that the car was bogged. And the tumbril
passed him, the hooded boy standing like a scarecrow
inside it, with never a glance at the leaning car. Gees
yelled—"Hi, you!" in vain as he opened his door
to get out—and instantly got in again to put on the
waterproof he had slung over the back of the seat
next his own. When, proofed against the downpour,
he eventually emerged to inspect the damage and make
up his mind about things, the tumbril was on the
point of disappearing round the curve that he had
ascended to meet it.

Not worth while, running after it. Even if he could
get the boy to turn about at the next widening and
come back here, that one farm horse could not tow
the car out. A first glance showed that both front
and back near-side wheels were down to their axles:
the car was undamaged, but needed a breakdown
crane to get it on to firm ground again.

Not much more than half of the rainy daylight
remained, now. The car would be safe here till morning—would it, though? Would some other hooded
boy drive a tumbril into it as it stood? How far had
he still to go to reach the shelter of Todd's Three
Thorns? Blast that fool of a boy! No, though, he
could hardly blame the boy for a soggy patch in the

lane widening. Well, blast the idiots who made a widening in a bog patch! And he had to walk, splash through the mud of the evil-surfaced lane, to Troyarbour. It was his nearest refuge—unless he spent the night in the car with one rug. Unthinkable, that.

He reached in and switched on the off-side side light and the tail light: there was plenty of juice in the battery, and the small amount of current those two lamps would use would not affect the starter in the morning. He got his small suitcase out of the locker at the back of the car, put in all movables and relocked the compartment, remembered to take the ignition key out, and locked all four doors. Then he began to plod his way along the lane to Troyarbour, and the rain and the night came down on him as he squelched wet-footed on his journey, inventing fresh curses each time he sank a foot in a mud-hole.

Until, on his left, showed the lone farmhouse he knew, a blackish oblong against the grey indistinctness of rising ground that sheltered it. Light showed through a blind that had been drawn down or across the window of the room he knew, and, less clearly, came out from the narrow central hallway, indicating that the front door was standing open. He paused for a moment, and knew himself wet and chilled—and, on foot, it was a long way yet to Troyarbour inn. Not a long way in a car, nor, really, on foot in normal weather, but on such a night as this. . . . And that cowslip wine, as she had called it, was a cordial to make one forget the small irritations of life. Cowslip wine! If she had waved a cowslip over it, that was as near as the flower had got to the fluid. It drew him a couple of steps toward the open door—

Resolutely he turned and went on his way. It would not do—he had come here to settle accounts, in the full sense of the word, with J. St. Pol Naylor, not to measure wits against this witch, or join in with her to wage the feud she maintained against Naylor. No! Not for a barrel of the stuff! Rest and food and drink at Todd's, then to get the car pulled out of the mud back there along the lane, and to beard Naylor and make him realise that he could not play the fool.

Moonrise, evidently—the greyness of young night was lightening, now. And the rain was lessening, too. Abruptly Gees walked into a white wall, a blanket of fog, warm and close-clinging. He took four more steps, five—and stumbled against a bank. The side of the lane, obviously, yet he had, as far as he knew, been keeping a straight line toward Troyarbour. He set off again, and found himself up against—was it the bank on the opposite side of the lane, or on the same side?

Conscious that he had lost his sense of direction, he stood a moment to reflect, and decided that, if he went very slowly, and kept quite close to the bank, he would eventually get either back to Wren's farm, as they called it, or to Troyarbour, according to the direction in which he was now facing—and whether he were facing toward or away from the village was more than he knew, after those two stumbles against the bank—or banks—bounding the narrow lane: if his eyes had been completely bandaged he could not have been more surely deprived of sight than by this suddenly-enveloping fog.

Step by slow step, taking care to keep to the slope of the bank, and not leave it for the comparative level of the middle lane, he went on—or back? He could not tell, until he stepped out from the blinding reek as suddenly as he had entered it, and saw again the dark oblong of the farmhouse, now ahead of him and to his right. Here was no fog, only the grey gloom of heavily-clouded night with a full moon: he looked back, and saw only the same grey dimness: no sign of fog.

What was wrong with him? There *was* fog, surely, between him and the village! The front door of the farmhouse was closed, now: he had a momentary mind-picture of Eve Madeleine—Miss Brandon— regarding him with ironic amusement: he had been so sure he would not go back, and here he was, almost on the witch-woman's doorstep. Verily, Eve Madeleine would be amused, if she knew. But it was not his fault: it was—what was it? For along the lane, to- ward the village, he could see nothing that looked like fog. Yet. . . .

Out there in the rain, gazing at the one lighted window as he stood in the now softly-falling rain, he remembered the tale of Gunnar the Bald, who went a-viking in his long ship after he had incurred the wrath of Skal, an Iceland witch. Gunnar had laughed at Skal's threats of vengeance, and had sailed out on what looked like a prosperous voyage, until, on a night of full moon, blinding, clinging fog had dropped over the ship as he held to the steering oar, and in it he had piled the vessel on the rocks of Orkney and found his doom—the doom the witch Skal had promised him. Men of Orkney had waited on the beach to repel the ravager, and, so the legend went, they *had seen no fog!*

Yet, Ira Warenn had agreed, there is no magic!

In some way she had learned that he was returning to Troyarbour, and wanted to assure herself, perhaps, that he did not intend to side with Naylor
against her. Perhaps that was it: if not, what did she
want of him? By the look of things, if she who was
garnering secrets of old time had mastered that of
blinding one by a semblance of fog, she wanted to
stop him from passing her house, wanted him to come
to her, not go on to the inn. He said aloud—"Very
well—we'll see!" and devoutly prayed that he would
see, all the way to the inn. He was not going any
nearer that house of hers. No, not if he had to wander
in the wet darkness until dawn, or go back to the
car and sleep in it. Magic or no magic, he was not
to be beaten by her.

By now, though, he was dog-weary: a mile of
plugging through the clinging, slippery mud of the
lane in the falling rain was equivalent to four or five
miles of decent walking: where he was not wet with
the insidious trickling of the rain, he was conscious
of an equal discomfort of perspiration, for no water-
proof-maker ever yet learned to ventilate that garment efficiently, and Gees felt not merely moist, but
soggy. He set off again for the village in sullen
wrath.

And there was *no* fog. On and on he tramped, till
he knew himself far past the point at which he had
stepped into the blinding white wall and lost himself,
and the night lightened, for the moon was now climbing up the sky and raying on to the layers of cloud.
No fog: not even the lightest of mists. He said aloud
—"Beaten you!" and laughed.

Was it an echo? Was his laugh deep-toned and
musical, a sound to bring one to a pause, with a little

thrill that was half pleasure in the lure of the sound, half apprehension lest one's most secret thought was being interpreted? He barked out a single derisive— "Ha!" and plodded on, and from some fold of ground the "Ha!" came back to him—yes, that was echo, and nothing else. Which proved that the other had been something else—someone else.

Now he saw the lights of the inn, and breathed easily. Now he had the door open, had entered the bar-room, and Todd gaped at him. Disregarding the five worthies—Fred Carphin had evidently been forgiven, for he was back there with the others—Gees dropped his suitcase on the brick floor with a thud, and faced Todd.

"Whisky," he said. "A half-tumbler of whisky —and gimme a syphon if you have one. I'll make the mixture myself. Gimme the bottle—I want something more than a mere double. And the same room?"

"Cert'nly, sir," Todd answered, and put down bottle and glass. "You—you mean to make a treble, sir, I take it."

"*I'm* taking it," Gees told him. "Very nearly neat, too." He poured a good half-tumbler, and filled up from the syphon. "Put it on my bill—don't rob yourself over it, either. Ah!"

Feeling in his pocket, he brought out, not the currency note that Todd had expected to see, but a folded slip which he opened up and read

"Lucky I forgot to throw it away," he remarked. "I suppose your post office isn't open at this time of night, though?"

"No, sir. It wouldn't do to knock Martha up, either."

"One might get knocked down, eh?" Gees remembered the Amazonian proportions of the postmistress. "Well, in the morning will do."

He pocketed the slip again. It was a receipt from the Blandford garage at which he had filled his petrol tank that afternoon. A wire to them in the morning would bring out a breakdown lorry which could lift the Rolls-Bentley back to use. Then he would not feel so lost.

He produced a ten-shilling note. "Draw those chaps a pint apiece, Todd," he said, "and have what you like yourself—take it all and the whisky out of this. You haven't got a bath-room, I know, but could you build me a good fire to sit over awhile?"

"Well, sir——" Todd looked dubious over it—"Mrs. Hodden's gone long ago—she comes in by the day. But—if it'd do, there's my sittin' room—I got a fire in there. It's—well, not over tidy."

"I don't care a hoot in a coal yard about that," Gees told him. "Let me take this bottle along, and tell me how much you want for it—later. I've got a fit of the shivers, and want to hug a blaze and set my insides on fire at the same time. You get me?"

"Come through this way, sir," Todd invited, and lifted the bar flap. "I'll see to them pints an' all the rest after I got you fixed up. But if you got them wet things off, sir, it'd be——"

"I know exactly what I want!" Gees interrupted snappishly, and tucked the whisky bottle under his arm. "Just lead me to it, and leave me to it. Otherwise I shall swear at you—I'm feeling like that."

A sewing machine and a pile of fluffy fabric beside

it, evidently hastily abandoned on the centre table
of the "sitting room," were the first things Gees noted
on following the landlord in. Then he saw a door at
the far side of the room, and understood why Todd
had rattled the handle of this door, and coughed,
before opening. It gave the lady of the stockings time
to get away.

There was a good coal fire, and an armchair which
had only two broken springs when Gees tried it. He
seated himself and huddled over the fire, shivering
visibly. Todd eyed him with some anxiety.

"Wouldn't you be better in bed, sir, with lotsa
blankets?"

"You go back and draw those pints," Gees retorted,
"and I'll go when I feel like it. Unless I'm in the
way here."

"Not a bit, sir—not a bit! I was thinkin' what'd
be good for you. It look like you got a reg'lar chill
comin' on, to me."

"Buzz off, Todd—pints all round. Don't fuss."

Alone, he finished the whisky, and poured himself
a second stiff dose, which he sipped crouching over the
fire after stirring up a good blaze. Then he was aware
of the blonde he had seen before, standing beside his
armchair with a mass of clothes of some sort over her
arm.

She said—"I 'ope you'll' excuse me, sir, but Mr.
Todd told me 'ow you're feelin'. If you was to lock
both doors, now, an' then strip an' put these on—
there's a blanket you could wrap round yourself,
too. You'll get your death, sittin' in them wet
things."

"You should worry!" Gees retorted, with angry
rudeness.

"I—I do apologise, sir," she said timidly. "I didn't mean to—to—I only thought you'd feel better like that——"

He stood up, then. "Little lady," he said, "it's I who have to apologise. I'm very grateful to you for your thought and kindness to me, and I'll do exactly as you say—to prove I'm sorry for what I said. Except—with people like you, I don't think I need lock doors."

"Just as you like, sir—thank you, sir. For not bein' angry, I mean. An'—don't be angry, sir, please —do hurry up an' get outer them wet things, an' I'll see to your room for when you wanter go up."

She dropped the bundle from her arm to the floor and fled. Gees looked at the closing door, and shook his head.

"If Todd isn't good to you, child, he ought to be shot," he said.

.   .   .   .   .

"Well, sir——" Todd answered the question hesitantly the next morning, as Gees looked up at him from behind a mighty plateful of bacon, eggs, and mushrooms, "she was one o' them what answered my advert f'r a cook-housekeeper, an' the only one what'd come to a lonely place like this. Father dead, an' there's a stepfather. Useter knock her about, an' she stood that. But then worse, if you understand."

"Easily," Gees agreed. "I had a hot water bottle last night."

"That was hers, sir. She reckoned you oughter have it."

"That's why I mentioned it—I thought as much. Y'know, Todd, there are some things you can't buy in the best and biggest hotels—things that count for a lot more than those you do buy."

"I'd never call this a hotel, sir," Todd protested.

"It's a pub, which is a far, far better thing. I want you to thank the little lady for her very great kindness to me, after I'd been very rude to her. She's made me ashamed of myself."

"No need for that, sir. I'm sure she—Phyllis, I mean—she said she thought you a very nice gentleman, an' you oughter have the hot water bottle. So she filled it an' put it in for you."

"Things you can't buy," Gees said musingly. "Tell me"—he wakened to normality—"what staff is kept up at the Hall?"

"Staff?" Momentarily Todd looked puzzled at the abrupt question. "Well, sir, there's five maids, countin' in the cook, an' Phil Hodden an' a boy f'r the gardens, an' Hanson—he's groom an' looks arter the car. Which Mr. Naylor don't use the car much —don't go out a lot, except ridin' wi' that big hound o' his tailin' along behind."

"And what sort of hound is that?" Gees inquired.

"I dunno what sort exactly, sir. If you crossed a bloodhound wi' one o' them big wolf-dogs—them Russian animals, I mean, you'd get somethin' like it, I reckon. Nervous, shy sorter brute it is."

"Greyhound and borzoi, you mean," Gees suggested.

"That's it, sir—bor—bortzoy. Like you said. But heavier—it got a very broad chest an' big quarters —a big hound. Savidge, accordin' to Phil Hodden, but it stick close to Mr. Naylor when he's out ridin', an' don't take no notice o' anyone else."

"Oomph! Is there a telephone at the post office?"

"No, sir—not for people to use. I believe Martha send the telegrams by telephone, but customers can't talk on it."

"Okay, Todd. I shall probably be staying again to-night."

"Thank-ye, sir." And Todd, realising the statement as dismissal, went out, after which Gees finished his breakfast and in turn went out, over to the general store and post office, where Martha Kilmain produced a telegraph form at his request. He filled in the address of the Blandford garage from the receipt in his pocket, and wrote—

"Rolls-Bentley car bogged beside lane leading to Troyarbour. Please send breakdown lorry with crane to rescue same—better include two stout planks. Wire time when lorry may be expected to Green, The Three Thorns, Troyarbour. Reply paid."

Martha counted the words three times, and figured out the cost on a piece of brown paper. When Gees had paid her, he went back to the inn and waited in his room for the best part of two hours. Then a small boy brought the buff envelope, and he opened it and read—

"Expect lorry 12.30," and a signature.

He slung his waterproof over his arm and set out. The day was grey and still, with slight haze over the distances. When he passed Wren's farm, he saw no sign of life about the place, but, on looking back before he had passed from sight of it, observed Ephraim Knapper plodding heavily down the slope behind the house, probably returning from some sort of work for his dinner hour. Cultivated land showed behind the outbuildings, and above it, fenced away by wire, sheep grazed: probably Ira Warenn made a reasonable living out of her tenancy, than which no farmer could hope to do more, in these days.

"But she's no concern of mine," Gees told himself resolutely, as he went on to retrieve his car.

X

"I DIDN'T CALL"

THE two men in charge of the breakdown lorry were happy: Gees had seen to that, after ascertaining that the Rolls-Bentley was undamaged, except for a slight distortion of the near-side rear wing, the back edge of which had rested on the ground when the wheel sank in, thus lessening its curve over the wheel. A trifle, that.

Now, with the breakdown lorry setting off toward home, Gees pressed his starter button and headed the other way, toward Troyarbour. He passed Wren's farm with a glance that showed him no evidence of either human or animal presence about the place, drove down to and through the village and, at about two-thirty in the afternoon, passed through the gateway of the Hall—the beautiful Italian gates stood open, this time—to pull up, as before, opposite the entrance. And, as before, Nettie Carphin answered his ring at the bell.

"To see Mr. Naylor, please," he asked. "The name is Green."

"I'll see, sir," she said. And, without inviting him to enter, turned and left him. She also left the door open, but he did not enter. From the step he eyed the trophies on the walls, and presently Nettie returned and faced him, primly, even woodenly.

"Mr. Naylor is not at home, sir," she said mincingly.

"Uh-huh!" Gees sounded not at all perturbed.

"You gave him my name?" He made the question one of slight anxiety.

"Yes, sir—I mean"—he had spoilt her composure, and she went scarlet under the steady gaze of his eyes—"he is not at home."

"Well, will you take a message for him?" he asked, friendlily.

"Ye-yes, sir. I could do that," she assented.

"Well, just go and tell him I didn't call. Just that —nothing more. Mr. Green didn't call. Will you tell him that?"

"Yes, sir." She appeared to find nothing strange about the message.

"Thank you. That's all."

He turned and went, to find no Peter in his car, this time. He got in and drove away, and, as he went, realised that no Peter was necessary, to-day. He would go to Ira Warenn, make common cause with her against the bilking squire, as he now called Naylor in his own thoughts, and not leave Troyarbour until he had made the man sorry for himself. Not the amount, but the way in which he had been robbed of it, took Gees to the limit of anger: he had made over twelve thousand pounds out of one of his cases— illicitly, but safely and with no compunction—and a mere eighteen guineas would not have spoilt his sleep. But, he told himself, no man should play a trick like that on him and get away with it—and the very fact of his allying himself with Ira Warenn, as soon as Naylor knew of it, would put the wind up the man: he was afraid of her, Gees knew: he would be still more afraid when he knew that the man he had thought worth summoning to aid him was allied with her—obviously against him.

So deciding, Gees pulled to the right when he got to the village, and ran the car into the open shed, placing it next Todd's wagon, as on the night of his arrival. Inquiry in the bar produced cold ham, not a factory product, but really home-cured—as rare a thing in these days as a Niel rose or a Verge watch—with pickled onions, home-baked bread, Dorset butter and Cheshire cheese so ripe that only a connoisseur would risk it. A truly Olympian lunch, in fact, and with that as lining Gees brooded over a cigarette and a final half-pint of bitter, and then set out for Wren's farm.

He had no plan of campaign in mind, but was prepared to be guided by circumstances—and, possibly, by Ira Warenn. When knocking at the front door of the house produced no result—three knocks, crescendoed from *forte* to *fortissimo*—he went round to the back, and found the girl he wanted to see in a badly-soiled blue overall, feeding maize to a gawky brood of last spring's chickens, with Adolphus squatting on his hunkers beside her and watching the proceedings with faint interest. The boar stood up and wouffed as Gees rounded the corner of the house.

"Sit down, Dolph!" his mistress bade severely, and he obeyed. She said—"I'm sorry I couldn't come to the door, Mr. Green. Adolphus would have snatched one or two of these fowls, if I'd left him with them, and having begun to feed them I must finish."

"Of course," he assented. "The genus *sus* is omnivorous, I know. I've seen three small chickens go down a pig's throat before he could be driven off the brood. They got into his stye."

"And Adolphus is no exception," she observed calmly, shaking the last of the maize out from the

wooden bowl among the fowls. "I was going to get
out of this dirty rag and take him for his afternoon
exercise, now. Was it anything important you wanted
to see me about?"

"Supposing I join you on the walk, and talk it
over?" he suggested.

"If you wish. Just one moment, please."

Unfastening the belt and three buttons of the overall, she stripped it off, and took it and the bowl to
place them on a bench beside the back door of the
house. Then she faced him again, dressed exactly
as he had first seen her, except for flat, low-heeled
shoes that, to his thought, marred the effect—they
were not dainty enough. She said—"That's all. I
am quite ready. So is Adolphus. Where would you
like to go? I generally make a two-mile tramp of
it."

"I'll leave direction and distance entirely to you,"
he answered. "All this country is new ground to me—
the very existence of so remote a place as Troyarbour
is still incredible to me. Its isolation."

"It was not always so," she told him. "Main roads,
as you know them, are comparatively new things, and
in old time this lane was a respectable road by com-
parison. It has not kept abreast of the times, not been
'taken over' as the phrase goes, and widened and
made up, but is still the private property of Troyarbour Hall for nearly all its length. And the squires
of Troyarbour do not want the place to grow."

"It won't, while that lane remains what it is," he
declared rather grimly. "But aren't you going to
get a hat?"

"Why should I? It isn't raining—and if it were
I wouldn't care. I'll take you up to the crest that

gives the place its name, and you shall see all of Troyarbour. Have you time, though?"

"As much as you care to spare," he answered.

"This way, then. Come along, Dolph! And don't eye those chickens like that!" She spoke the last sentence with severity, and the boar, understanding perfectly, fell in behind the pair of them as she turned toward the slope which went up from behind the farm buildings.

"You can estimate what the place was by the size of the church," she remarked as they walked slowly, bent-kneed, up the steep slope. "I believe the same thing applies to Norfolk and other agricultural districts where the population shrank after the Black Death. This church seats five hundred—used to seat them—and now the whole population of Troyarbour is not more than a hundred and fifty souls. That is, if they all have souls. One has doubts, in some cases."

It was difficult to reconcile this easily-speaking, self-possessed woman with the bizarre girl who had poured what she called cowslip wine for the two of them, equally difficult to realise that one so plainly of the world beyond this village was a tenant farmer's daughter, and now a tenant farmer herself. So, silent for the while, Gees reflected, and she turned her head to smile at him, with evident amusement.

"It is the same person," she said. "Sometimes, you know, I wish it were not. Wish I were not—fated and fey, as I am."

"We make our own fates, Miss Warenn," he said gravely.

"A brave saying, but not quite true," she retorted, rather wistfully. "'We are ever and always slaves of these, the suns 'that scorch and the winds that freeze.' Not literally, but—let's talk of other things, if talk we must. Why did you want to see me?"

"I came back here to see Naylor," he answered, "to collect a debt that he refused to pay—refused insultingly. Now he has refused to see me, sent a message that he was not at home. I sent back a message that I didn't call. In other words, declared war."

"And what have I to do with that?" she asked thoughtfully.

"When I was here before, he wanted me to steal or in some way get possession of your axe-handle for him," he said. "Had an idea, because I once succeeded in doing a service of sorts to a man he knows, that I would undertake anything—even theft."

"Well, mumps to murder—you are the 'Gees' who put that advertisement in the papers, aren't you? And that *might* include theft."

"It said I was prepared to tackle anything from mumps to murder, not commit either of them," he pointed out. "Let me give you a hand."

They had reached the summit of the ridge under which both Troyarbour village and the farm sheltered. Before them rose a steep-sided mound running parallel with the crest, an obviously man-made earthwork of some sort, thirty yards and more in length. Gees took the girl's arm, and set his feet sideways for grip on the grassy steepness. They came to the narrow top of the mound, and Adolphus went to the end farthest from the village. Ira Warenn, still held, looked up at Gees.

"I know why you don't let go," she said.

"Because—in case you're wrong—there's the Hall in full view, and if Naylor sees us together like this, he'll begin to squirm," Gees told her. "This apparent intimacy will emphasise it."

She leaned toward him and laughed. "I know," she said. "And this ridge"—she pointed along the top of the mound—"is where the three trees used to stand. Thorn trees, three in line. When we Warenns had in our hands the high and middle and low justice, they had their use."

"Such as——?" he asked.

"That end"—she pointed ahead of her—"was for men, and where Adolphus sits was for women. The condemned. The tree at the end was drawn in toward the one in the middle by ropes. The convicted criminal was stripped, and stretched between the two trees by wrists and ankles. Then the ropes that had drawn the trees together were taken away, and the living body hung there like a cord. There was a man who took three days to his dying, stretched between the trees."

"What had he done?" Gees asked. "Stolen a rabbit?"

"I will not tell you what he had done," she answered. "It is on one of the parchment rolls in the chest, with a quaint old drawing of his punishment. If he had lived six days, the punishment would not have been too great. Think, now! In these days the great majority of people obey the laws, and live normal lives. In those days there *had* to be terror for those who broke the laws as that man broke them. It was in Stephen's time. My people held to Queen Maud."

"How do you know so much?" he asked abruptly.

"I know very little," she answered, after a brief pause. "My father taught me most of it—he was a very wise man. And he sent me to Tours for a year —the year my mother died. And there are books, English and French. When my work is finished I shall go out from this place, live differently. Practise all I have learned in theory."

"Your work?" he asked.

She leaned still closer to him, and pointed toward the Hall. "It is there," she said. "You know. Like you, I want him to see us in apparent intimacy, to fear me still more. Part of my work."

"Of your hate, say," he suggested, and smiled— with her head almost under his as she stood, she could not see the smile. "And there's Troyarbour down under us, quite probably seeing us and drawing its own conclusions. If you go ghosting to-night as you did when I was here before, you may hear mighty judgments on yourself—on us."

She laughed softly—just such a laugh as he had heard in the bar-room of The Three Thorns. Then, standing away from him, she pushed the night-dark hair back from her temple, and he saw a patch of discolouration—a bruise, evidently, on the whiteness of the skin.

"You see?" she asked. "It is not painful now, but it was at first. A proof of how little control I have. I stepped out, along that fourth line, just as I did the night you were here. And thought to step back into my own room—the one you have seen—but in actual fact came back between Ephraim and another man. Pushed them apart from each other as they were walking home, and so got this bruise. And"—

again she laughed, softly and long—"each of them thought the other had done it. They were going to fight—it was so funny that I couldn't help laughing aloud, and that frightened them so much they simply fled to their homes. It was night, you see. And in that fourth direction there is no night, no darkness, because one does not see with the physical eye."

"One does not see——" He repeated it incredulously.

"I told you why you still wanted to hold my arm, up here," she explained. "I knew, last night, you were determined not to come near me, and blinded you as if you were in a fog, and turned you back—and then let you go. It is all quite simple—one sees in a different way. I could only explain it fully if you were able to comprehend that fourth direction of movement—but then I should not have to explain. You would know as I know. I might show you, teach you——"

"Control of this fourth dimension?" he asked.

She shook her head. "I have not yet got control of it," she answered. "Give you comprehension of it, say, such as I have myself. I think, with your greater knowledge, you could get control, and perhaps in turn teach me. Because—I have no right to what I know of it."

"No," he said, very soberly. "You are rather like a child sitting on a ton or so of high explosives, playing with the switch that might blow you to fragments at any moment. Something like that."

"I'm cold!" The way in which she shivered proved it. "Ephraim will be going home soon, too, and I want to see him before he goes. And Adolphus has had his exercise, and I've shown you all Troy-arbour."

He looked down, and saw the village in its two separate yet connected hollows under the downs, with the Hall in yet a third hollow, and the lane that wound toward the Italian gates—closed again now, those gates. And the lone farmhouse with its out-buildings, quite apart from the life of the village, as she was apart from it all. A witch, perhaps, but in this climb no more than a girl like other girls—except for her hair and eyes, which were unlike any other that he knew or had seen. The mentality of her, for this hour, was so normal as to make him doubt the qualities he knew existed in her, or the power over which, as yet, she had only partial control. He took her arm again.

" 'The suns that scorch us, the winds that freeze'," he quoted after her. "Yes, you're very little more than human, in reality. You've found something that might change the world, and you not only can't use it, but would put it to a small and personal use if you could."

"To what use would you put it?" she asked, rather sharply.

"I wouldn't use it to destroy one man," he answered bluntly. "I wouldn't use it to scare simple minds like those I find in the bar-room of the village pub. I might try to put it to real use."

"What is real use?" she demanded, with a bitter tinge to the question. "Could you make men other than what they are—could you change the cruelty and selfishness that rules the world? I seek to destroy one man—I admit it, because it is my purpose in life, something greater and stronger than myself. If you gained full control of this I know—this power of movement that sets one free in a way you cannot comprehend—and taught it to others, what do you think would be the result? Some country—this country, perhaps—would use it to master other countries, make itself the most powerful in the world and in the making inflict ten times the suffering caused by all the wars of the last five hundred years. I know a little, and with that I *think!* Mankind is not yet fit to hold this knowledge, but must suffer more, learn more of self-control. I think I told you—along that line, beyond the three in which we two have moved to reach this point over Troyarbour, there are greater intelligences, greater powers. I have communed with them like one talking to gods through a veil."

"And——?" he asked, impressed by her intensity.

"They see man as a pitiful thing," she answered. "As I see Adolphus, there, waiting to swallow my chickens if for a minute I release my control over him. A being that insists on putting appetite before ultimate good. Oh, there are exceptions, I know, but can you point me to one nation that will not try to beat down its neighbour for its own advantage, or one corporate body that will not crush and destroy any smaller competitor to swell its own profits?"

"No," he said, after a pause for reflection. "I'm afraid I can't. But you, with your small aim, are hardly the one to accuse others."

"I do not accuse—I state," she retorted. "As for my own aim, it is not in my control. I *have* to follow it, accomplish it. That, I know, you cannot understand. And I'm cold—let us go down."

"At least," he said, as he took her arm again and with her began the descent from the mound, "you're human."

"That—which also you won't understand—is the worst of it," she said. "The Norns—or Erda herself, perhaps—bound us all with that chain, or else Dark Lagny herself might have accomplished all that is left for me to do. There are times when I wish——"

Near the comparative level of the ridge, she slipped, almost fell, and reached up—for a second or less he felt her arms round his neck. Then, as he would have held her, she was not there, but he was alone. Adolphus the boar, following them down, vented a savage grunt and came charging at Gees as he gained level ground. Fury blazed in the little, sunken eyes of the boar's head, and his protruding tusks seemed to stand out as Gees stiffened to meet the raging attack, knowing that, weaponless, he had little chance against the beast. It was within a couple of yards of him when he heard Ira Warenn's voice, saw her materialise between him and the boar. Yet it was not mere materialisation. As suddenly as she had ceased to be in his hold, she was *there*, solid and real, no ghost that became visible, but a woman who stepped from somewhere and stood between him and the charging brute, which recoiled so suddenly as to fall in trying to turn, and slid ignominiously along the grass, with a squeal that told how it had not yet overcome hereditary porkishness, nor got back in full the courage of its wild, far-back ancestors. The girl pointed an accusing finger at it.

"Bacon!" she said, with vibrant anger, and Gees wanted to laugh. Adolphus lay on his side, and put his forepaws over his face.

"He knows what I mean." She turned to Gees. "It's my lowest term for him, the one I use when he has done wrong. As great a punishment as using a whip on him. I—I had to take that step to save myself from falling, or else—I didn't think he would blame my disappearance on you. He couldn't understand it, of course, and his piggy brain had the impression that you had destroyed me, so he tried to destroy you."

"I see." Gees got back the composure he had almost lost in the fearful moments of the boar's impending attack. "You didn't think I had strength and balance enough to hold you up."

"I knew, when I tried to save myself by holding to you, that you must not hold me up," she answered coolly. "Shall we go on down?"

"By all means," he almost snapped, and began the descent toward the farmhouse, leaving her to follow as she chose.

She said—"Follow on, Dolph—to heel!" and came level with him. So they went down and down, and came to the comparative level on which the house and buildings were set. There at the back of the house stood Ephraim Knapper, and as they came toward him he scratched his head and replaced the old hat that his fingers moved in scratching. It was a gesture of bewilderment, almost—or so Gees saw it. Ira Warenn half-turned and, without speaking, gestured the boar with a pointing finger toward a pen, clean-strawed, of which half was roofed over—and under the roof the straw was thick enough for the animal to burrow and hide in it. He entered, as meekly as a newly-whipped dog, and as she closed the door of the pen and shot the bar she uttered the one word—

"Bacon!" at which the beast ran under the roof and
hid in the straw.

She turned to Knapper. "Feed him, Ephraim,"
she bade.

"Aye, Miss Wren," he answered. "The sow's
bedded, wi' her litter."

"Thank you. When you have fed Adolphus, you
may go."

"Thank, ye, miss. I'll 'tend to him."

She went, then, round to the front of the house, and
Gees went with her. By the front door she paused,
thoughtful.

"Do you notice that these men never drop their
aspirates?" she asked. "Their dialect does not include that perversion of speech."

"I don't think theirs is a perversion," he said.
"But I was questioning in my mind—it's nothing,
though."

"Just nothing! A trace of mockery marred the
music of her voice. "But I'll tell you. We Warenns
have held this farm since our castle was destroyed
—you were thinking of how my father owed rent
when he died, and so Jerome Naylor came to threaten
me. It was not that we could not pay, but that
my father would not pay, till the roof had been
put back on the barn. You see there is a roof on
it now—my father demanded what was due from
his landlord before he would pay what was due from
him. And—what I need, I have. You understand?"

"That it isn't safe even to think, with you," he
answered.

She smiled, the smile that was more in her eyes
than on her lips, and again he recalled Naylor's

definition of her as "allure unutterable." She said—
"Most of your thoughts are deep red or even violet-
purple, and still quite transparent. Only the black
and grey are beyond reading. But all this is new to
me—I am still learning."

"Learning what?" he asked, with the harshness of
incredulity.

"If I told you, you wouldn't understand—yet," she
answered.

"Yet?" Echoing the word, he looked full into
her eyes, and knew he would never be able to
determine their colour. In that, though not in the
shade of colour, they were like a phosphorescent
wave he had once seen in the Mediterranean—once
and never again. A hue that does not belong on
earth, an indescribable beauty of light: so, but of
darkness rather than of light, was the depth of her
eyes, a dark radiance to which he could put no
name.

"I believe you will," she said. "If—listen!"

He heard it—the musical, yet terrible, clanging
resonance that she had said came from the sword in
the chest, the singing sword. He asked, when it died
down—"What does it mean?"

She shook her head. "I have not asked," she
answered. "I have not been told. I—the wine—will
you come in with me? I need warmth—the wine.
Will you—drink it with me?"

"Why?" he asked prosaically.

"Because I am afraid—the sword's song. Will
you?"

He nodded assent, and she led the way toward the
door. Following her, he entered the house. The song
of the sword had ceased. Daylight was just beginning

to fail, and the comfortless furnishings of the room he knew were losing some of their dinginess as dusk softened their outlines. The girl said—"Wait," and left him standing by the carven-lidded chest, seeing its age-gleaned sheen as almost luminous in the first beginning of night's gloom.

XI

ENCHANTMENT

SHE returned, and, facing her, Gees saw that she had brought the squat bottle, and the two glasses that—according to her—a Varangian had taken home with him from Byzantium. He asked—"What do you want with me?" and even to himself the words sounded querulous.

She asked in turn—"What do you want with me?" and he heard laughter in the question. It angered him, unreasonably.

"Nothing!" He almost shouted it. "You and your pigs!"

"And Peter—don't forget Peter." She sounded not in the least perturbed by his wrath. "Peter?" She made a call of it. "Oh, Peter!"

A flurry of movement, a black shape that leaped to her shoulders, and sat regarding Gees with baleful, greenish eyes, more fully alight than the gloom of the room warranted. He said—"I knew it all the time—you are a witch. And that isn't a cat at all—it'll turn into a bandersnatch any minute. Or a tove—a slithy one."

"It's the wrong season—they're summer creatures," she said calmly, and tickled Peter's ear as he sat back of her shoulders and purred, like a sawmill cutting hardwood. She took up the bottle and withdrew its cork, to poise it over one of the two flimsy glasses.

"That's for yourself, because you're cold," he said. "I know—that stuff is a fire that trickles down to your toes. But I'm not cold—don't fill the other glass. Is it cowslip wine again?"

"No," she answered, deliberately. "This is the liquor Freya poured for Odin, the potion that made him give up the Ring which hid her from the giants, so that they took the gold instead of her as their price for building Valhalla. It is the charm with which Dark Lagny bought her lovers. Do you want to know more about it?"

"I do," he said with dry irony. "Are you trying to buy a lover?"

She filled the second glass, and held it out to him. "Drink, and tell me," she retorted with equal irony. "Am I so cheap?"

On that, he took the glass. "I'm sorry," he said contritely. "I had an idea—never mind. To—to the best of you."

"What you think is the worst may not be," she told him. "I am what I am, and—but to you, Mr. Green—Gees, I believe you call yourself, though why that should be I don't know."

"It's all my names," he explained. "Gregory George Gordon Green—God help us all! Inevitable, when you come to think of it. Gees to you from henceforth —and here's to you—Ira."

He drank, and noted that she too drank. The liquid was a fire, a comforting luminance within him: he felt almost somnolent under its instant influence, and nodded his pleasure at her, smiling the while.

"That's good," he said. "You're a real pal. Sounds rather incongruous with what you really are, and know—but I mean it. Just that. I'm warmed from crest to toenails—feel quite cheerful, all at once. You *are* a witch! You know exactly what suits your victims."

"Quite so." As he put the empty glass down on the table, she took up the squat bottle and refilled it. "If I were a normal person, I should have offered you tea," she said. "Would you like tea?"

"In face of this far, far better thing that I drink— no," he answered, and took up the glass. "I prefer— enchantment."

"Is it?" She refilled her own glass. "Simple warmth, I thought—and I was cold, up there on the ridge of the three trees. How can there be enchantment in a mere drink?"

He heard derision in the question, and looked through the glass at the window. The fluid was not still, but a current circled in it from its surface to the bottom of the glass, a turning wave as if water sought to mix with oil. He asked—"Can you quiet that move- ment? I believe you did quiet it, in the stuff you called cowslip wine."

"This is that stuff, as you call it," she said. "Yes— look again!"

He had lowered the glass to speak to her. He held it up again, and the wine in it was still. He said— "You are a witch, obviously, and though this is out of the same bottle, it is a witch's potion, as dangerous as any of them. As you are—I've known it all along."

She laughed. It was the laugh he knew, the laugh he had heard when the worthies in Todd's inn had doubted whether it had actually sounded to them. For a moment he saw her as mistress of old wisdom— whether she had gained it fairly or by stealth was nothing to him, for he wanted it for himself. And he would be a very Ulysses, using her attraction to him to win her knowledge. So he told himself.

She said, very quietly—"Yes, I am a witch."

"Then I'm a wizard." He took up the glass she had filled for the second time. "And this—Byzantium, you told me. Their secrets went to Venice, and we get Venetian glass. But this is finer, more delicate. You know—forgive me for saying it—I don't like this room of yours. When we were coming back from looking at Troyarbour—the Hall included—you said 'What I want, I have.' That means—this?"

With a gesture he condemned the shabbiness and discomfort of the room. And, as she looked almost angrily at him, added—"It's not good enough for you. Jewels should be set—don't you understand? If, as you said, you can have what you want, why are you in such a setting as this? It doesn't fit you. Do you see?"

She said—"Will you bring that glass with you?" and, talking up the glass she had filled a second time for herself, moved toward and through the doorway. Peter the cat sat still, as if knowing that he had no part in this adventure. Gees, taking up his glass, and noting that the ugly little bottle remained on the table, followed her across the narrow hallway, into the other main room of the ground floor.

"What I want, I have," she said, turning to him as he entered, and reaching past him to push at the door. It swung closed, and he heard the latch click. Enough light came from the window to show him the room.

Sea-green walls, and rugs of deep crimson on the floor, fleecy rugs into which one's feet seemed to sink: a wide divan at the far side of the room from the

door: two little ebony tables—or stools—·before the
divan, on one of which was placed a bowl of dull
red lacquer. The cover over the divan was of deep
crimson silk, and cushions thrown on it were the colour
of the walls. There was an armchair that appeared
to rival the one Gees kept in his office for clients, as
far as depth and comfort went, but this was upholstered
in deep crimson velvet cord, and held more green
cushions. The only picture in the room hung over the
divan: it was a water-colour of some southern European
or perhaps Eastern fishing harbour, and against the
harbour wall were moored two small boats, each with
its sail set as if about to put to sea. One sail was
green, and the other deep crimson. And in the picture,
as in the room, the two colours did not clash, but
harmonised: the effect was one of luxury, yet not of
sensuousness. It was a room in which to think rather
than feel—so Gees saw it then.

"Yes," he said. "I see. And—that other room?"

"To give an impression," she answered coolly.

"I see that, too. But you don't want to give me
that impression."

Her eyes smiled. "You are the first man to enter
this room since my father died," she said. "Will you
put your glass down—here?"

Moving toward the divan, she put her own glass
on the ebony stool beside the lacquer bowl, and Gees
placed his there too. Then she turned and stood facing
him. She seemed suddenly hesitant, even nervous.

"I want to—to try an experiment with you," she
said. "It was for that I tried to make you come to
me last night——"

"What was it—that fog?" he interrupted. "Not
real fog."

"No. It was in your eyes only. Some time, I'll tell
you how it is done. Now, as I said, I want to try
an experiment with you."

"And if I say I won't let you?" Momentarily his
distrust—even fear—of her came back. She was a
witch: she had blinded him in an attempt at compelling
him to come to her—for what?

"I want to find out if it is possible to take you with
me—to take anyone with me—into the other world
I am beginning to learn," she explained. "You see,
when I enter it, all I am wearing goes with me.
Do you remember Wells' story of the invisible
man?"

"And how he caught cold because he couldn't make
his clothes invisible." He nodded understanding.
"But you can—you do, I know. Disappear clothes
and all, I mean. It's one of those matter-of-fact details
that wouldn't occur to one's mind, but an important
one all the same. But how do you propose to include
me in this?"

"This way." She moved so near as to stand touching
against him. "Now put your arms round me as if—
as if I were buying a lover. So!" She reached up,
and he felt her arms go round his neck—and the
scent of her night-black hair, lying against his lips,
was like a breath out of Eden. She said—"So hold
me——" and he felt her strain and press closely to
him in a tense embrace that he knew was quite passion-
less: even as he held her thus he knew he was only
subject of an experiment.

For a moment—or an age—she took him with her.
The room disappeared: without moving he had been
moved, and while he was still conscious of her clasp
he knew fear, great and terrible. For she had drawn

him into a world of such light as does not exist on earth, of sounds beyond the range of the normal human ear, of colours infra and ultra, such as the human eye cannot perceive: a world in which were vast Presences, comparable with nothing that he knew, and beyond all description. There was in that state neither time nor distance, but he was beyond and outside them, not in space, but in an infinity in which he could take hold on space and roll it up, hold it in his hands and look at any part of it—if only he could get past the tremendous fear that bound him to helplessness.

The Presences of which he was aware passed through and interwove with each other, yet were separate. He was one with Ira, clasped to her in inextricable embrace, yet a world away from her. And they two, one yet separate, were ants in a cathedral so vast that its confines did not exist for them—and why he had the sense of a cathedral he could not tell. He was before and behind and under and above Intelligences beside which the human mind is no more than a thousandth part of an atom, and They were passionless, Their consciousness of him was that of a vast reason considering the minutest bud on a twig. For Them, he existed, as for a man a grain of sand exists—and no more than that. And They were Many, yet One—in this state was neither separateness nor unity, for there was no space, and no time, but infinity in which all things are one, all consciousnesses one, yet all are separate, for where space does not exist there are both unity and separateness, yet there is neither of those two. And he knew that, although space did not exist, yet it was *there,* as time was there, and both were no more than thoughts in the minds of these Presences, incomprehensible as these were to three-dimensional mentality, just as Athanasius found his Trinity incomprehensible. In that timeless, spaceless state, Gees knew that until he entered it he had always considered the Athanasian creed an example of unconscious humour, but knew now that the saint had had a glimpse of this fourth perpendicular along which he, Gees, had been moved, and in the light of that glimpse had tried to define his belief, knowing it beyond definition as he tried.

In the light of that glimpse! Light unbelievable, colour incredible, a feast of glory in which desire failed, and adoration for the Maker of these things became too great for bearing. Sound that went past mere music, since it far exceeded the gamut of the human ear, and rolled in on his consciousness as the triple chord of the universe, comprehending all music and all discord, for music and discord were one, but discord was harmony in this infinity, since it was comprehensible as part of the vast plan of things. And this, he knew, was but a fourth dimension: what of the fifth, and sixth—and all that range which lies too far beyond space and time for even a fourth-dimensional Presence to comprehend it? Gees knew, in the infinitesimal part of a second that was yet an age, since it was out of time, that there are gods and gods, and yet greater gods, all subservient to and subjects of the Ultimate, the Power beyond sight and comprehension even of the Presences that interwove yet were seperate in this state that he saw with other than his human eyes. Beyond time and space, beyond even infinity itself, is God, Who rules and creates all gods that are within fourth-dimensional comprehension, and beyond man's understanding.

He stood alone in the green and crimson room, straining nothing against his breast, holding nothing, but still conscious of the scent of Ira's hair against his lips. She was not there: his tensed arms relaxed, fell to his sides, and he said—"Damn!"

She laughed, such a laugh as he had heard in the bar-room of The Three Thorns, and he saw her—he would not have said that he saw her appear or materialise, but that he simply saw her—standing by the foot end of the divan. She shook her head, and said—"No."

"And what does, that mean?" he asked, raspily.

"That I can take my clothes, but I cannot take you or anyone else with me," she answered. "I tried. Oh, I tried! I wanted you to see. and understand. Because I know you could understand, if you saw."

"I did see," he told her. "So much—it would be impossible to tell you all. If I hadn't been so terribly afraid, I might have seen more. Talked to Them, perhaps. Yet They were too big to talk."

"Afraid—yes." She stared at him. "Then you *did*—I did take you! Oh, I'm so glad! So very glad of it! Just—it wasn't a moment before I lost you, couldn't feel myself holding you, but——"

"No," he said soberly in the pause. "It was not a moment. Where there is no time, there can be no moments."

"And you saw—you heard——?" She went on staring, tensely.

"Yes. This was what I meant when, as you said, I wanted you. I did—wanted this you have given. I was one with you, and, yet you were not there with me. Do you know? And I was terribly afraid."

"You have me, now," she said. "Completely. If I took you so far, up to the fear. That is the first of it—I can go past it, now, and take hold on the ends of a distance, fold it up and move across it without moving as I must, say, to come to you here——" she took a step toward him as she spoke. "When I am more advanced, more sure, I shall be able to take hold on the ends of any distance, fold up the world itself for my use. Do you see? Put Kinchinjunga in a valley of the Andes and step from east to west. See the whole world as an illusion, and know that space in the sense in which we live in it does not exist. Dark Lagny knew it, found the infinity outside space."

"And died on a cross outside the wall of Eboracum," he said.

"Because she let human love and human passion deflect her from that greater purpose," she told him. "If one fails, one pays."

"You will pay, in any case," he said grimly. "What you showed me is the summit to which Adepts attain, and they reach it after passing through the last gateway in the Path. You think to step on to the Path somewhere near its farther end, to steal in by a side door and miss out all the work of initiation. You will pay, heavily."

"I will, as you say, pay," she retorted. "Not heavily, but as the gods ask—I have got past fear. If you went with me, you knew fear, just as I knew it when I first took that step out of space and time. Fear held me in paralysis, unable to commune with the beings I saw, unable to use the knowledge I had. Then I stepped past fear, and now learn—learn more and more. To be able, as I say, to roll the world up like a paper strip, and move from east to west in a step. Out of time and space—to be a god with the gods of that dimension, ever greater, ever more beyond this world you know, and in the end——"

"Go on!" he bade harshly. "How far will you go, in the end? You small three-dimensional thing like myself—how far will you go, when you claim equality with the Presences I saw?"

"To control of life itself," she said. "To use of another thing scribed on the Rod for me to read. To the use of time, not compulsory movement in it, from youth toward age, but to control of time, life——"

"They thought that in Atlantis," he interrupted, "and the greater gods of the fifth or sixth dimension moved one step, and rolled Atlantis up and put it under the sea. So they will roll you up and put you—somewhere outside space, where you cannot do this harm to the world that you plan. Because mankind is not yet fit—you know it!"

"I have passed fear," she said evenly. "Mankind? No! Here and there one—one like you! One who *can* pass fear, and in the end—the end I mean to reach—stand up beside the gods outside space and be one with them. Interweave with them, be eternal——"

"Die!" He made a vicious exclamation of the interruping word.

She laughed, and for the first time he heard no music in the sound. "You have not passed fear," she said. "I have. And so I know."

"You are a thief and an interloper," he said harshly. "You own that you use this power—this knowledge, rather—to destroy another human being. Little as I like that being, I tell you you are wrong—you will not be permitted, with that use of the knowledge as a base, to go on to the point you want to reach. You will—die!"

"And then? She laughed again, and all the music of it was there in the sound. "What is that, when one has seen and moved outside space, as I have? I tell you, I have passed fear. I am Dark Lagny, say, the essence of me indestructible—what is death? A passing out from space—all that is me goes on, lives, where there is no time, where the beauty that is behind my physical self will be my joy—and the joy of the Presences into which I am interwoven, though they are separate from me. You—you who have not yet passed fear—you put your arms round me when I asked, and I put mine round you. We were one, but separate—I felt you close to me, and you were apart—when for the thousandth of a moment I took you with me, up to the gate of fear, you were ten worlds away, and yet you held me. This is the mystery—when you have passed fear it will be no mystery to you, but you too will be one with the gods of that world."

"Are you yet one with them?" he asked sombrely.

"I am a child, tottering and clutching at the ends of small distances as that child totters and clutches at chairs and railings, while it learns to walk in the world in which it will presently run alone," she answered. "This is a great new knowledge, and I learn it step by step. Stumble, and so learn a little more. Bruise myself——" she lifted her hand to push back her hair, and so exposed the bruise on her head—"and learn a little more. Grow toward use of that movement as we all grew in childhood to the use of our legs and arms, slowly and with pain and trouble.

But surely, toward finality. To grow up in that world beyond the world—that world which cuts across this world and is an unseen part of it—or rather, this seen world is a line drawn through the infinite, a little picture painted on the greatness which lies outside space. Beyond breath and the beating of the heart, beyond warmth and cold—all that is a thought in the mind of the infinite, not real at all. Life itself is not real."

"It is all we have," he objected. "I live—you live."

"We are thoughts of those Minds," she told him. "You have not yet passed fear, as I have, and so you cannot see clearly. You have not talked in the speech that is beyond words——" Abruptly she ceased speaking, as if she knew she had said too much.

"I have this life to live," he said soberly. "I shall live it according to the best—and the worst—that is in me. If you put your arms round me again to drag me into that state I saw, I'd fling you off—I say it is not permitted for you or me or anyone to enter that state, or try to pass out from space into a state where space is not. Go on trying it, and you're doomed —damned! You are worse than the spiritualists groping to establish communion with the dead who have passed—you try to rank yourself with the life a stage beyond the astral. Yet not life—it is more than life, a higher rung on the ladder of eternity. A piece of the vastness that lies between the stars—you try to hold it as if it were a bar of chocolate or a peppermint drop! This world of sense and sight, woman, is not for you to play with, a mere jack in a game of bowls."

"I have never played bowls," she said coldly.

He roared laughter at her. "Oh, get back a sense of humour!" he adjured her. "See yourself, very lovely and very human, and stop being a witch! *Be* human! Give yourself to living interests—you might be so very wonderful, and you're just a thing of fear."

"I tell you—I have passed fear," she insisted.

"Oh, to the devil with that! You yourself may have passed fear, but you play tricks—make others fear. Those poor devils down at the inn—what business have you to upset the current of their lives with what they hear as a ghost laughing at them? What business have you to blind me with what looked like fog? You've got no *right* to interfere with other people's lives—that's where you're all wrong."

"I own that I had no right to blind you," she said slowly. "I wanted you here—wanted to try the experiment I have just tried with you, because there was no other within reach—I couldn't ask Ephraim Knapper to put his arms round me and hold me as you held me. Could I? You know I couldn't. Which was why I tried to get you back, make you come here to me. As for the rest of it—I got hold of the ends of that small distance—it was an experiment. When I laughed, it was because I couldn't help laughing——"

"The human trying to be superhuman, and being no more than human after all," he interrupted. "So you'll fail all along—you *are* no more than human! If only you had sense enough to see——"

"What?" she asked, as he did not end it.

"Yourself. Were you Har-Ees, back there?"

"Har-Ees?" She echoed the name uncomprehendingly.

"She made Byon-Ge forget that he was Adept—and because of the sin those two sinned—their attempt

at putting unfit man on a level with the Adepts—
Atlantis was drowned," he told her.

"That is not on the Rod—it is all new to me," she
said. "I am not that—what did you call her?"

"Har-Ees. It sounds ugly at first, but if you think
it a few times, it's a name that clings and stings."

"You are a man." She smiled up at him as she
stood, very near him. "And your judgments are
harsh—perhaps on this Har-Ees as they are on me.
Yes, I think I like that name. An echo, in a way
of . . . Gees."

He looked down into her eyes, and realised as he
saw into their luminous depths that complete darkness
was very near. How much time had he spent here
with her?

He said—"Good-night, Miss Warenn," quite con-
ventionally, and went out, leaving her standing there.
He had left his hat somewhere, but did not know
where to look for it. Nor would he look for it. He
went out from the house, and down toward the village
and the inn, hurrying before she could blind him with
fog, or in some other way force him to go back to
her.

He was afraid of her, terribly afraid of her!

XII

ROLLO

Two lines of Browning's *Abt Vogler*, other than those he had quoted to Miss Brandon, went with Gees as he tramped determinedly toward the inn: two lines, at first, and then the precedent two, so that the four ran in his mind—

"Novel splendours burst forth, grew familiar and
       dwelt with mine,
   Not a point nor peak but found and fixed its
       wandering star:
Meteor moons, balls of blaze, and they did not
       pale nor pine,
   For earth had attained to heaven, there was
       no more near nor far."

He repeated it—" 'No more near nor far!' " And added—"He knew. Oh, yes, he knew! I don't know, but I have seen."

He went on: back there at the farm, she was calling to him to come back: she was a witch, and he could feel the call, but he would not go back. No, there was no magic, only applied science—but the woman had power. He would *not* go back.

A voice came out from the gloom—"Good evenin', zur."

"Good evening," he answered friendlily, even ingratiatingly. "Who is it? You sound as if you knew me."

"Thadger, zur—Zam Thadger, they moztly calls me."

"Ah, yes! I've got you, Sam. A bit stiff in the joints, by what you said the other night, but still able to sink the odd pint."

Sam Thatcher chuckled. "Zo be it come my waay," he agreed.

"And what are you doing outside The Three Thorns this time of night, if I might ask?" Gees pursued, keeping step with slow-moving Sam.

"Mus' Timms got a cow calved—I works for Mus' Timms," Sam explained. "Cow's calved—mozly they calves arter midnight, but zhe wur moor conzidable (Gees divined that he meant to say considerate) an' dropped en. Rackon I arned a pint, stoppin' laate."

"And now you're going to get it," Gees suggested.

"Arter I put missis quiet," Sam said. "I goes hoam, an' then—my pint. Wunnerful good f'r the innards, is beer."

"Is that so?" Gees put a vast amount of curiosity into the query.

"Yu be gooin' to see Mus' Todd, zur," Sam said, with cold dignity. "I'm gooin' hoam. Gi' you goo'-night, zur."

He branched away, though he might have continued another score yards with Gees toward the inn doorway. The ironic question had got under his skin, evidently, and Gees regretted it. One had to be careful with these men: they were on their own ground, and he was a mere furriner among them: furriners must not take even verbal liberties.

Within a yard of the inn door he stopped abruptly. Those two glasses: they still stood, filled for the second time, on the little ebony table. Rather, they had so stood when he left the green and crimson room. She would have moved them by now, emptied them.

It was nothing: rather it was an absurdity that such a trifle should recur to his mind as if it had some importance. In the tremendous moment through which she had impelled him to live, he had forgotten all about the refilled glass, and now he had a feeling that he ought to have drunk its contents. A curious fluid, like nothing he had ever tasted or smelt. Dark Lagny's brew, Ira had said.

Resolutely he put it from his mind, and opened the inn door to enter. Three of the worthies, Carphin, Hodden and Cowder, had already begun their evening session, and they gave him grave "Evenin', zur," as he moved toward the bar, a greeting that he returned cheerfully, while he took in the man who stood, one elbow on the bar and a glass beside it, a new figure in the place, as far as Gees was concerned.

A middle-aged man in shabby but evidently well-cut brown tweeds and heavy brogue shoes, muddied and—by the look of them—seldom cleaned. From under an ancient and slightly greasy-banded soft felt hat his grizzled, bristly hair showed, and under it his smallish grey eyes had a humorous cast, while between them his nose was beaky and slightly purplish. His hands were small and well-shaped, not the hands of a manual worker. He said, as Gees approached— "Good evening. My name is Firth, from that mansion across the green. Since we don't get a stranger here every year, I thought I'd drop across."

He was likable on sight, and Gees said, pointing to his half-emptied glass—"Good evening, Mr. Firth. Will you have another? My name is Green, from

London.   And I feel like a pint of bitter, Mr. Todd!"

"A distinctive name and a comprehensive address," Firth remarked drily. "And a welcome invitation——" he took up his glass and emptied it. "Yes, I will have a half-pint with you, Mr. Green. Thank you."

"Ah!" Gees watched Todd busy at the barrel on trestles behind the bar, and put down a half-crown. "Good spot for a rest cure, this."

"One needs some interest," Firth remarked. "Mine's bugs."

"You—er—farm them?" Gees asked blandly. "Or trade them for—what?   It's a specialised line, of course."

"Collect," Firth told him. "I had a big practice in South London—I'm a doctor by profession—and my health gave out just as a legacy came to me from a grateful patient. So I bought the house on the other side of the green, intending to put in week-ends here. That was six years ago. The fourth week-end didn't end—I'm here yet."

"Collecting bugs," Gees ended for him, thoughtfully. "Well——" he took up his pint—"here's to bugs. Dorset bugs. And you."

"Your very good health," Firth responded. "I was always more inclined to entomology than to the physical mechanism of my fellow man, and there are some fascinating things to study in this district. An entirely distinct variant of the small red ant—I did a monograph on it that got published and fetched Sir Hercules Madison down here to see my slides of the brain and thorax—you know his name, I expect?"

"He is a new one on me," Gees confessed solemnly. "Another enthusiast, I take it. In your particular line. Bugs, that is."

"Sir Hercules is the leading authority—the final court of appeal if any question arises," Firth told him. "Ah—good evening, Thatcher."

Sam, entering, said—"Evenin', zur," and advanced to the remote end of the bar from the two against it, to call for his ha'f pint. He added, severely, to Gees—"I zeed yu avore, zur," took his glass, and retreated to seat himself with his cronies.

"Staying long, Mr. Green?" Firth inquired friendlily.

Gees shook his head. "Just a flying visit," he answered.

"Fine car you run. Not much use for it here, though."

"No-o." Gees breathed the negative softly, uninterestedly.

"I see you've already found the best view about here," Firth remarked, with a shade of nervousness at introducing the subject.

"This afternoon, you mean," Gees observed calmly. "I'd hardly say I found it. I made what you might call a personally conducted visit."

"I don't know if it interests you," Firth said, still more nervously, "but every soul in this place has talked that walk of yours over."

"Including yourself?" Gees asked with ironic amusement.

"Having nobody to talk it with me, I am the exception. Do have a refill with me, Mr. Green. I feel like one more."

"Very hospitable of you. Yes, I will—another

pint, Todd. I was very well aware that I made myself conspicuous. Not for nothing."

"No?" Firth looked his curiosity at the statement.

"No." The retort was final, indicated that the subject
was closed.

"Ah! Umm-m! I was remembering, just before
you came in, that it will be five years to-morrow since
her father—since Cornell Warenn died. And each
anniversary the daughter goes to the churchyard—
the only day in the year that she goes near the church
—and puts a hawthorn branch on the grave. Shrivelled
leaves and berries and all on it, and nothing else. An
odd idea, I always think."

"The lady might think bug-collecting an odd idea,"
Gees said drily.

"Oh, quite probably she does! I see very little of
her—hardly ever run across her, in fact. There is
no doctor in the place, as you may guess, and I volun-
teered to attend her father in his last illness. She—
accepted my services. There was nothing to be done,
really. A man's heart gives out on him, and that's the
finish."

"So," Gees remarked. "There was, I believe, a
case here in another direction. Pneumonia at mid-
summer, or something like it."

"At the Hall—yes." Firth looked as if he would
question the reason for Gees's interest, but did not
question. "That was sheer foolishness. I had nothing
to do with it—a Blandford practitioner was fetched
over, and then a London specialist. From what I
could understand of it, there was predisposition in the
first place—pulmonary weakness—and the lady went
out in a thunderstorm, didn't change her wet clothing
in time, caught a chill, and—well!"

"And the child?" Gees asked, after a pause.

"Ah! I think all the health inspectors in the county tried to find out why that happened. Naylor had taken the child to London to see what could be done about developing astigmatism, and I think the bacilli got at her there. She was a very delicate little thing, puny and undersized. He brought her back and—it was diphtheria killed her. She might have got over the fever—probably would. May have caught it in London, and then again it may have been flies. Infecting milk, or food—something. A terrible thing for him."

"A terrible thing for any man," Gees observed.

"Yes, but—if you'd seen him before he lost those two—contrast that with what he is now! An utterly different man."

Gees remembered the album of photographs Naylor had bidden him look over. But, he reflected, though Ira Warenn had claimed (in some measure) responsibility for Naylor's losses, it appeared by what Firth said that they were due to natural causes. There remained the death of his favourite dog, but a veterinary surgeon had attributed that, too, to a natural cause. Here was ground for some relief.

Why? He pulled himself up sharply. Why should he feel relief over acquitting her of having caused Naylor's losses? And could he acquit her, in spite of what Firth had said? She had powers, as she had proved to him this afternoon, and they might extend in other directions. Not only this afternoon, but last night: she had been able to produce the illusion of a fog and with it had almost driven him back to herself: what other illusions could she produce—had she worked against the dead woman and child, produced illusions that had caused their deaths? Willed them to die—willed the child within reach of infection, and the woman to a folly of carelessness that had killed her?

Past telling, he knew. He was still silent, reflecting over it, when Todd moved along behind the bar to stop opposite him.

"'Fraid we couldn't git much for ye to-night, sir," he said in a confidential aside not intended for Firth's ears. "There's plenty sausages, an' the eggs, an' the ham—I tried to git some fish, but he'd sold out all but a couple o' little haddicks which was mostly skin."

"Then you can make it sausages and eggs and ham," Gees told him. "I'll have whale on the half-shell some other time."

"Come across and share a bone with me to-morrow night, Mr. Green," Firth invited. "It would be pleasure to eat with my fellow-man."

"Now that's very kind of you," Gees answered, "but I don't know if I'll be here to-morrow night. Still, thank you all the same."

"If you are here, say. Just walk across to my place—you can leave it open, and join me at my meal if you turn up by seven-thirty. If you don't, I shall understand that you can't. Leave it so."

"That sounds brotherly enough," Gees answered, "and if I am on the spot and able to accept, I shall be very glad to join you."

Declining another refill of his glass, Firth bade good-night and went out, and Gees remained by the bar until Todd should announce that a meal was ready for him. The worthies along the side of the room talked among themselves, with the deliberateness of their kind, and in tones evidently not intended to reach his ears: that they talked at all while he was present showed that they meant to accept him among them, though strictly on furriner status.

Jacob Cowder spoke: "Dangersome. No doubt about it."

"Reglar zavidge," Phil Hodden agreed after a lengthy pause. "Git wuss, it du. As sune fly at ye as look at ye."

Gees listened intently: were they discussing Adolphus the boar? But no: the next remark proved that they were not.

"It mind him." Sam Thatcher delivered a judicial opinion. "While it mind him, it don't hu't nobody. An' if Zquire ain't got a right tu taake a hound when he goo ridin'——"

He left it at that, and the end of the sentence needed no vocalisation. A silence, and then Jacob Cowder, the original complainant as nearly as Gees could tell, voiced another protest—

"It *look* dangersome," he said. "I 'ouldn't keer f'r en to coom sniffin' round me. Them teeth look a hem tu sharp, f'r my likin'."

Todd leaned toward Gees. " 'T's all riddy, sir," he announced. "Phyllis done ye four sausages—they run six to the pound—an' four eggs, an' ham along of it. That'll be enough, sir?"

"If it isn't," Gees answered, "I'll shout. Four sausages and four eggs——" he passed behind the bar as Todd lifted the flap—"God help us all! To say nothing about the ham!"

"I reckoned, sir, seein' yu had that long walk this

arternoon, yu might be sharp-set f'r yure vittles. I *hope* it'll be enough f'r yu."

"You can have faith as well as hope," Gees told him. "I've already found out that charity is no stranger in this pub, so you're safe on all three. I think I'll say good-night, because by the time I stagger up to my room after that meal I shan't be. able to speak."

"Like some tea wi' it, sir, or another pint?"

"I never mix my drinks, Todd. Tea on beer! Unthinkable!"

"I'll bring it along, sir. Right at once."

.   .   .   .   .

A clouded morning, with moisture in the air—there was no rain, as yet—and thin scud driving over the heights which shut in Troyarbour, telling that the outer world was troubled by a wind, though here in the valley was stillness. Gees slept late, found yet more eggs and ham awaiting him on descending to the "coffee room," and, having eaten, went out to the shed at the back and gazed at his car. The amount of mud it had collected on the run along the lane indicated that a hose with plenty of pressure behind it was the only means by which cleanliness could be regained without scratching the gloss of the surface, and he shook his head at the car and gave it up. Went out and along the winding branch of lane that would take him as far as the church. He wanted to see the church. By-and-by, when he got rid of his present almost somnolent indifference, he would plan what to do next to make Naylor regret stopping payment of that cheque. When he had got the eighteen guineas, he would entrust it to Todd with instructions to dole out pints to the worthies for as long as it lasted. They need not know who was responsible for the munificence or why it was bestowed on them: a sort of fund, with Todd as trustee. . . .

The church proved uninteresting. There had been brasses, but no more than the studs in the stone remained. Of memorial tablets he could find none. As nearly as he could tell, the fabric dated no farther back than the sixteenth century: in all probability, when the castle of the Warenns had existed where the Hall now stood, there had been a place of pre-Reformation worship as part of the establishment. This church had replaced that earlier gathering-place.

Well, that was that. Some Naylor had put in a stained glass window to the memory of Eleanor his wife, and, knowing a little about the colour-values of medieval stained glass, Gees felt that this squire of Troyarbour had done his early-Victorian worst—or the craftsman who had done the work had done *his* worst. There was a collecting box for foreign missions in the porch, and Gees grinned at it. Sam Thatcher and his friends treated furriners warily. So would he, Gees.

He saw a curly tail, termination of a line of bristles, whisk past the nearest buttress of the church as he emerged to the mugginess of outer air, and remembered Firth's remark to the effect that Ira Warenn came near the church once a year, to place a branch of hawthorn on ·her father's grave. An odd sort of tribute, but no concern of his—she did as she liked. And bringing a boar pig into the churchyard—well, it was her boar pig. Nothing whatever to do with him.

He went slowly, thoughtfully, back toward the inn.
Should he leave Naylor to his own devices—apparently there was no means of getting at the man—and
run the car out and go back to London forthwith?
He could be discussing fourth-dimensional experiences
with Miss Brandon soon after lunch time—he could
discuss anything on earth or out of it with that girl,
he knew, and she never let him down. And Naylor
and his eighteen guineas meant nothing, in reality:
only the humiliation—if it were that—of being "done"
had fetched him, Gees, back here. It was a petty
reason for coming all this way, when one thought it
over. Yes, he would go back, rule out Troyarbour
and all in it from his scheme of things, and find something more worth-while in some one of the inquiries that
reached his office by each day's post.

With that resolve he quickened his pace. Merely
to throw his pyjamas and other belongings back into
the suitcase, back the car out of the shed after settling
up with Todd, and——

In the after days, he never cared to think much
of what followed on that resolve: it was too ugly, too
nightmarish. . . .

Jerome St. Pol Naylor came riding on a big chestnut hunter, riding down from the Hall toward the
main village and the frontage of the inn. It was a
powerful beast that he rode, up to far more than his
weight, and, following him, came the hound to which
the worthies of the inn had alluded in their talk the
preceding evening. A hound with a muzzle that, Gees
estimated, would touch him at the waist-line—and he
was just over six feet in height. A vast-chested brute,
with tapering, almost borzoi fineness of jaw-line—but
behind the muzzle were eyes deeply sunken, bloodshot

and furtive. And on its great paws the beast slouched
heavily, as might an overfed Great Dane—it was no
lightly-stepping hound, but of mastiff build, powerful
and formidable.

The girl Phyllis came out from the post-office, just
as Naylor rode past the doorway. Looking up at
him as he passed, she had almost missed sight of
the great hound, until it nosed up to her, sniffing at
her as she went across the grass toward the inn. At
that—Gees was just emerging from the lane toward
the church, then—she screamed and struck at the
brute, and her open hand landed on its muzzle. On
the instant it leaped and had her down, screaming
horribly: its long teeth fastened in her shoulder, and
it shook her slight form as a terrier shakes a rabbit—
and Naylor swung his horse about, his crop raised
while he shouted—"Rollo! ROLLO!" He might
as well have shouted to the wind or the racing clouds
over him: the hound had something to worry, and
took no heed of him.

Running toward the prostrate girl and the great beast
that worried her, Gees heard behind him a voice—it
was not loud, but had a carrying power that threw
the words down into his consciousness—"Dolph! Kill
that dog! Kill, I say! The dog! Kill!"

A ridiculous pattering of tiny hooves, the split
hooves of swine, and the boar went past Gees—he
himself was running, but that lightning charge left
him as if he might have been standing still. He saw
the line of bristles on the boar's back stand up as it
passed him, saw its charge, and saw that the great
hound released its hold on the now unconscious girl
to face this assailant—and Naylor tried to strike at
hound and boar, but could not get the horse to face

them. It swerved and wheeled about, and Gees had time to think the rider a poor horseman while he saw the fight between hound and boar.

A brief fight. Adolphus charged in, a flying fury, and from the snapping of his jaws a tusk took the hound low and behind the thorax, disembowelling him so that his entrails fell and tangled under him. Yet he lived, and, living, got a jaw hold on the boar's hide, just behind the shoulder, where he hung on and worried, dying as he was—till Adolphus, with an incredible turn of his thick neck, got the hound's muzzle between his mighty jaws, and crushed it with a sound of splintering bones. Blood poured from the wound the hound had made in his shoulder, and, pig-like, he squealed at the pain and sight of his own blood, but took a fresh grip after squealing, farther back toward the hound's neck, and crushed its head to pulp. By that time, both Gees and Ira Warenn were abreast the combatants, and she said—"Well done, Dolph! Oh, well done! Brave Dolph! Well done!"

Bent over the unconscious girl, by that time, Gees was aware that Firth, the ex-doctor, was bending over her too. Firth said—"Get your hands under her, Mr. Green. Lift her and hand her to me—both lift, and get her up into my hold. I'll carry her home and dress this bite." And, on that, Gees lifted, and got the limp body into Firth's arms, to see him walk off with it toward his double-fronted house as if he had been carrying a small child.

A sound of trampling, thunderous hooves—Gees started up and back, and saw that Naylor was trying to ride down Ira Warenn. Stark murder looked out from the man's mad eyes, and his riding crop was

lifted to strike the girl down—but within ten paces
of her the big chestnut came down to stillness with
a thudding of its forefeet, and stood, shuddering
like a human being. So Gees saw the power she
had over animals, and remembered Farmer Timms'
bull.

She said—"Not so, Jerome Naylor! Look there!"
She pointed at the headless, mangled remnants of the
dead hound. "Will you kill more of your servants?
Shall I set my pig to kill your horse?"

"Ah, witch! Devil woman—you curse! You
spawn of hell!"

He slid down from the chestnut, and, terrified by
the smell of blood, it turned and galloped away toward
the Hall. Naylor ran at the girl, his eyes blazing—
it came to Gees as a curious reflection that he had
never seen eyes literally blaze until that moment—
and the riding crop upraised to strike her down. A
baresark fit was on him: he saw nothing but his enemy,
the personification of Dark Lagny, and he, Oger's
son, was bent on her destruction—until, like the horse,
he was within striking distance of her.

Then he stopped, and Gees knew that in this baresark fit the man was all animal, not human at all.
And Ira Warenn had power over animals, such power
as is given to few. Jerome Naylor stopped dead: the
crop thudded to the ground, and he pitched forward
on his face, senseless. It was the culmination of the
fit, end of his madness.

The boar licked at his bleeding shoulder. Ira Warenn
said, caressingly—"Dolph—come here! Good Dolph!
Come here!" And the beast got up and went to her,
blood trickling from where the hound's jaws had
closed in its hide. She scratched along its back. "Oh,

good Dolph," she said again, and there was honey in
her voice. "If you were human I'd love you, Dolph
—and you're just a beast! No, don't touch it! Come
here! Don't touch it!"

For with a little "Wouff" that was half a question
the intelligent brute had turned to sniff toward where
Naylor lay still. It turned back at Ira's command,
and Martha Kilmain, the postmistress, stalked primly
out from her doorway, gathered up Naylor in her
mighty arms as if he had been a baby, and with him
stalked back and disappeared among the cheese and
lingerie and bacon and boots and stationery and
cigarettes and all else that her multifarious store contained. She vanished: a curious circle of villagers
looked on the mangled heap that, so little while ago,
had been a living beast: looked on Gees, and Ira
Warenn, and the boar Adolphus that licked and licked
at the lessening flow of blood from its wound—and
occasionally looked toward Martha Kilmain's doorway,
or toward Firth's front door—closed again, now—as
if to learn what had happened with regard to the
savaged girl, or the baresark man whose fit had ended
in unconsciousness.

Ira said—"You didn't do anything, but you couldn't
have done more than you did—or didn't. There
wasn't time. I want to doctor Dolph. Do you mind
much if I take him back, now?"

"Who am I to mind?" he asked acridly.

She shook her head. "The one man who let me
take him to dare the unknown," she answered. "I
know you are going back—will you come to say good-
bye to me before you go?"

He looked hard at her and answered—"I am not
sure."

She laughed—and the music of the laugh stayed with him until he saw her again. She quoted, very softly—

> "Time stoops to no man's lure:
> And love, grown faint and fretful,
> With lips but half regretful
> Sighs, and with eyes forgetful
> Weeps that no loves endure."

He said, with ironic amusement—"Don't they? How do you know?"

"Empirically," she answered, and let the one word stand alone.

"Maybe. Has it struck you that we are the hub of a wheel made of staring Troyarboreans—I made that word all by myself, and it's up to you to applaud me. But I don't like quite so much audience. What do we do next? I mean, to get out of this publicity?"

"What do you want to do?" she asked.

"The intelligent and hospitable Todd told me there would be chops for lunch. That, if I know him, means half a sheep, or thereabouts. The village is listening, on that outer circle. Be careful."

She reflected over it. "Four o'clock?" she asked at last, with a gleam of human mischief in the eyes he had known, so-far, as no other than boding and fateful.

"Four o'clock is the nearest hour I'm to," he said. "Work it out, and subtract yourself plus me from the answer. Plus, remember!"

She said—"You are a fool."

"Columbus discovered a continent," he retorted. "I think you've gone one better. You said four o'clock. I say four o'clock. Two minds with but a single time."

"You idiot!"

"Why the pronoun? Don't be redundant."

She left him. Adolphus stopped licking himself, and followed her, and Gees went slowly, indifferent to curious gazing, toward the inn.

XIII

IRA, HERSELF

"Y'SEE, sir, poor little Phyllis—I reckon them chops ain't fit f'r yu tu eat. I done 'em meself, but she's all hu't an' shook up be that blasted brute—an' I ain't done no taters. Yu'll ha' to overlook, sir—I'm all shook up too. Y'see, Phyllis——"

"That'll do, Todd. I'd sooner eat raw chops or none at all than see you worried like this. You go and look after the girl—stop bothering about me. I can look after myself—it wouldn't be the first time I've done it. Stop bothering, and hustle back to her."

"Mr. Firth's lookin' arter her, sir. An' all you're payin' me, an' me not lookin' arter you like I ought——"

"Todd, if you say one more word I'll heave a chop at you—I can spare one without bothering, and two if you don't shut up. Buzz off!"

With a stare that became almost a grin before it ended, Todd went to the door. There he said—"If you want anything, sir——"

"Yeah, peace and chops," Gees interrupted. "Leave me to it, and go and keep an eye on that girl, as——" he ended the sentence to the closed door—"I know you're yearning to. Naturally."

An inquiry, later, told him that the girl would recover from the shock of the hound's attack in a day or two: she had some sort of heart trouble, Firth said, but it was not serious—some valvular affliction over which he would have gone into physiological details, but Gees restrained him with—"Spare the lay mind, feller. I'm a helpless orphan in a foreign land, when it comes to anatomic idiosyncrasies. Be kind to an infant and leave me in peace."

Firth smiled. "And you're coming along to eat this evening?"

"If the gods are good. Do we talk bugs?"

"We talk whatever you like, from metaphysics to football coupons and how to fill them in," Firth said, and smiled.

"Brother, you're human," Gees told him. "I've always wanted to know how you fill in a football coupon. And you're going to tell me? I'll be along before seven-thirty, or bust. Count on me."

Four o'clock, Ira Warenn had said. It was half-past three when Gees told Firth to count on him, and set off on foot for Wren's farm.

As he went along the lane, he questioned dubiously whether he could make Ira Warenn realise the cause of his light and apparently unfitting foolery, when they had faced each other with nothing but the mangled carcase of the hound left as evidence of the swift sequence of events—nothing, that is, but the gaping circle of spectators. In her—"You are a fool!" he had heard angered protest against his levity, yet had persisted in it—because he had had to drive out from his mind the picture of Naylor, mad and awesome as he charged at the girl with the riding crop upraised, and fell senseless. All the rest of the swiftly-moving sequence, the hound's attack on the girl Phyllis, the death of the hound itself, lifting the unconscious girl into Firth's hold—all of it was no more to him than a scene from a play. But Naylor—he had had to drive the picture of the man from his mind, somehow, force his thoughts into another channel, and had taken that apparently unfitting way of doing it. She would not see that, he felt: she had not seen it at the time. Well, it was done: he had himself fully under control again, now: facing her for the last time before setting out for London (for he had finished with Naylor, and the eighteen-guinea cheque might go hang!) he would not attempt to excuse himself. She could think what she liked——

Abruptly came the realisation that she had dominated all that sequence of events: he had to admire her for the way in which she had kept her head, impelled the boar to save Phyllis and destroy the hound, and then controlled first the horse and after it Naylor himself, rendering both impotent against her: they had had no chance, but had receded from her as waves from a rock. Yes, a rock: she had lost no iota of her composure. He, Gees, had been shaken by the sight of a man gone baresark, shaken so that he resorted to a small foolishness to cover away his loss of self-control: she had stood apart from and over all that had happened, unmoved and dominant.

Pale sunlight emphasised the shabbiness of the farm-house frontage. Emphasised, too, the ridiculous appearance of Adolphus the boar, not lying down, but sitting up as he leaned against the wall not far from the doorway, with a big patch of plaster over the wound the hound had made behind his shoulder. He turned his head to give Gees a look in which was permission to pass in, and there was in it, too, an admission that Adolphus was exceedingly sorry for

himself. Loss of blood, probably, accounted for his
state.   Lying beside him was Peter the cat, in his
fashion keeping watch over the pig to see that he came
to no harm—so Gees saw it. Or had Ira Warenn posed
the pair of them there for him to see? Never before
had he seen a pig look sorry for itself, but Adolphus'
expression was unmistakable. She could render
animals almost human, so much power she had over
them.

The door was open, and he saw her advance along
the narrow hallway, clad now in a fleecy frock that
had the colour of the walls in the green and crimson
room, and he saw that she was wearing the pendant
of the turquoise-blue stone, and high-heeled shoes that
toned in with the colour of the frock.   She said—"I
thought you would have had the car," with no pre-
liminary greeting.

"I haven't," he answered baldly, standing on the
doorstep and facing her.   "If you mean you thought
I should drop in on my way to London, I've got an
appointment to dine with Firth this evening. The
man who took that girl off to dress her hurt this
morning."

"I know." She drew back a step. "Do come in,
won't you? So you will be here till to-morrow." She
spoke the last sentence over her shoulder as he followed
her along the hallway, and turned in at the doorway
of the green and crimson room. Following her, he
said—"Yes, I shall be here some part of to-morrow,
at least," and detested himself for the banality of the
reply.

The door of the room closed slowly, with no aid
from either of them, and he heard its latch click.
She asked—"What is on your mind, Mr. Green?

Something—I can see it. Something . . . disturbing you."

"It is disturbing," he answered. "The fool I made of myself and you called me this morning, and you—splendid. You were splendid."

She shook her head and smiled, the smile that was of her eyes and left her lips uncurved. "I was terrified," she owned. "It was all so swift—all passed so suddenly. I was terrified—whatever I did was automatic, outside myself. You—you helped by being silly, talking as you did. The relief of it—something to divert my thoughts."

"That makes you still more splendid," he told her.

She laughed. "What is this—a mutual admiration party?" she asked ironically. "Or a farewell?"

"Neither, I hope," he answered, and put emphasis into it.

"No?" Still more of irony sounded in the question. "Will you stay here in Troyarbour to see the end of Jerome Naylor, or shall I come to you in London? Our two ways have touched on each other, but they must diverge again. You know it as I know it."

"I do," he agreed soberly. "I'd never travel your path. It ends—I told you where it ends, when you showed it me."

"And I told you that is nothing to me," she answered defiantly, half-angrily. "Told you, too, that I have passed fear. You have not."

"What made you quote Swinburne at me to-day?" he asked abruptly.

She shook her head. "It came into my mind," she answered. " 'Time stoops to no man's lure.' Just that. The rest that I quoted—his music, nothing else. It has—had no meaning. For me in relation to you, I mean. Where there is no beginning, there can be no end."

"Quite so." He made it an acrid comment. "And now, all being said, do we say good-bye? Or am I being boorish to my hostess?"

"Till we have said good-bye, all is not said," she retorted.

"Not worthy of you, that, Ira," he said gravely. "It's the sort of thing an *ingenuée* might heave at a casual partner at her first dance."

"Perhaps—but I meant it. All is *not* said!"

Her eyes were but a little distance from his own: she gazed full at him as he spoke, and he too gazed, intently, yet still he could not determine the colour of the eyes. They smiled—only the eyes. The scent of her hair reached him, and with it came back Naylor's description of her—"allure unutterable." It was true.

He said—"You are a witch. A witch—dangerous."

"There is no magic. You agreed—there is no magic. Would you like some tea, Mr. Green? Ephraim Knapper's boy will have to go and milk the cows, soon, but I can get him to make us some tea first, if you'd like it. He's my housemaid, which is why the other room looks so terrible. Would you like some tea?"

"No. Tea in here would be like a starched collar round Adolphus' neck. Like treacle on that frock you're wearing."

"Do you like my frock?" She was no witch, but all woman, as she asked the question. "I put it on specially."

"It's—well, the mere man always says the wrong thing if he tries to say anything about what a woman wears. And now I think of it—what became of the stuff in those glasses?"

She looked puzzled. "What stuff? What glasses?" she asked.

"When I went away from here, we left two full glasses there——" he pointed at the ebony table on which still stood the red lacquer bowl—and, pointing, saw in the bowl a powdery greenness that he knew might be incense of a sort. "I remembered them, after I'd gone, and—it was just an inconsequent thought——" He broke off, rather lamely.

She said—"Yes. I put the contents of those glasses in a flat bowl, and Adolphus was very happy. Quite muzzy, in fact."

"The swine actually appreciated the pearls."

She frowned. "I don't like that. It speaks despite, and you know as I know that the pig is nearest to man in brain content, not to be despised. I couldn't say to any other class of animal—'Kill that dog!' and know he would not harm the girl the dog was trying to kill. Adolphus is my brave and loyal friend, more than any dog."

He said, acidly—"I apologise. To Adolphus."

"Sit there." She pointed at the divan, at a point opposite the ebony table on which stood the bowl. "Wait."

As he moved to obey the order, she turned and left the room. He saw the door swing closed behind her, and heard the latch click. He knew there was a magic in this room, in spite of her denial of the existence of magic: it was in some way separate from the normal world outside—time itself was different, here. Turn-

ing as he sat, he looked up at the green and crimson sails in the picture: was the green sail part of
the painting, or did it move, an actuality rather
than a flare of colour against the background of
white wall and blue sky?   Blue like the stone she
wore on her breast, white like the whiteness of
her neck, green like the frock she had "put on
specially."   She was a witch: this room was a witch's
parlour——

She returned, bringing the squat, ugly bottle and
the two glasses of paper thinness, with stalks like
threads. They had known, when those glasses were
fashioned, how to render glass tensile and malleable—
the secret had gone with that of Roman cement, of
interweaving living trees, of taming African elephants
to servitude.   When she put the glasses down on
the ebony table he took up one to look at it, and
the bowl of it quivered on the impossibly slender
stem.

"Supposing I broke it?" he asked.

She took up the other glass, and tied a knot in the
stem, to put it down again with the bowl awry. "Well?"
she asked.

He took up the glass, and found that he could untie
the knot as if it had been made in a length of cord.
He said—"I don't think I like you, Ira. Is the moon
made of green cheese?"

"There isn't any moon. It's just as much an
illusion as time and space—as you and I are here.
We are thoughts in a greater mind—all is a thought
in a mind past our knowing—we are not, nor have
ever been. And yet we are——" She poured the
crimson fluid into the glasses—"and that is. Instead
of tea—you wanted this."

He asked—"How did you know I wanted it?" and laughed a little.

"Because you remembered, and asked about it. Drink—with me."

Lifting the glass, he felt it quiver on its stem, and drank hastily. As before, he felt the warmth of the drink, a tingling sweetness that yet was acid, a sensation rather than a taste. When he put the empty glass down, she put hers down empty beside it, and refilled them both from the bottle. Then she seated herself beside him on the divan, and the two filled glasses stood before them.

"Let me tell you," she said. "Once on a time you were in a green and silver room—not green and crimson, like this. You had an illusion with you, and with her you drank—as you drink this wine of mine. But that was a magic drink, and you lost yourself— the illusion willed you to lose yourself. Is that not so?"

"How do you know? Yes, it was so, but how do you know?"

"When you and I held each other, I took you beyond space, for a moment. I saw all your mind, all your thoughts and memories, like a picture. Things you yourself have forgotten—do you know that nothing you have ever done or said or thought is lost? That it is all *there*, painted on the fabric of your brain?"

He nodded assent. "Yes, I know that. Memory may be faulty, but it is all there, as you say. And you could see it?"

"Your secretary—I don't know her name. The girl who died, the man you brought to justice—they hanged him for murder—an old man I think is your father— a woman who saved your life one night, and a falling aeroplane that was lost in the sea. And money you took——"

"You are most decidedly a witch," he interrupted. "Stop it!"

"It was there for me to read. I have passed fear. On the farther side of fear is power, sight, hearing— you felt them all as possible. I know them as realities. And you—you with your greater knowledge of all that lies this side of fear—I want to persuade you to share that other side with me. To be one with me in it."

He shook his head. "That is forbidden," he said. "I'm going to end my human life in three dimensions, not risk destruction trying to fathom the fourth, as you do. I tell you—it is forbidden."

"I say it is not!"

"So Har-Ees said, and wrecked a continent."

"What became of her?"

"How should I know?" He sounded almost querulous. "I'd say the fishes scraped the meat off her bones, if any fishes were left alive after the convulsion that destroyed Atlantis. She died with the rest of them. Very few escaped—your ancestors must have been among them."

"I think you know all there is to be known on this side of fear. And if you with your knowledge passed it—if I could make you come past it and find your way as I am finding mine—Oh, don't you see? We two might fold up the world, rule it—be gods in it!"

"The eternal thirst," he said slowly. "Power— whether fit to use it or no. Damnation! I have known women, and it is always the same. Power over a man—the sense that they can control and hold him down—or else power such as you want. You're so great, and yet so small. You are *all* the same, you women! To give as pleases you, and to take when it pleases you to take—and apart from your pleasure a man may wait and question and hunger— you want *power!* You'd have me share in this dominion—Ira, you're wonderful, were wonderful to-day, but you're a woman, and you want me to follow along your path!"

"Well?" She put a mocking note into the question.

"To please you. Not that I and you may rule the world, but that *you* and *I* may rule. I've trouble enough to rule myself."

She took up one of the two glasses and handed it to him. "You are irrational," she said. "Drink again, or I'll offer you tea."

He laughed. "It's getting late," he said. "Ephraim's boy must have gone milking by this time, and you'd have to make the tea yourself. Still—here's to Har-Ees, and Dark Lagny—and you!"

He drank, as she drank with him, the second glass. For a moment he resisted the spell, knew why the glasses had been left filled when he had last gone out from this room: there had been no need of them, then, for he had not refused Ira's "experiment." Now, while the moment lasted, he knew that she had taken this drugging means of making him repeat it, and then questioned inwardly—why should he resist? For the effect of that second drink was such as to nullify cold reason, and leave in its place contentment, almost indifference. So much so that, when as before she put her arms round him for that strange, passion-less embrace and willed him to hold her, he felt little more than that she was good to hold, even in such a fashion as this.

"Still!" She whispered the word. "Let me take you past Fear."

.   .   .   .   .

So for the second time she tried to take him with her beyond time and space, but this experience was not as that other had been. He knew himself one with her, yet separated from her by all infinity. He knew light beyond light, sound beyond all sound, and the scent of all the flowers of Eden blended in with reek from the fires of hell—yet hell itself was a part of the great scheme of things, and so part of the great heaven that was, and yet was not. All incredibilities were real, and all realities incredible. He saw a point of radiance far off and, gazing at it, knew it was near —knew that he looked into the light of her unknowable eyes. He shaped the thought—"I lose and find you," and she was not near, but removed from him an infinity—she receded so far that he could not see her, yet she was warm in his hold. If only he could get past Fear, he would comprehend this mystery.

Fear! A shape that had no shape, a Thing that stood inexorably between him and knowledge. He knew that in this second experiment she had failed even more than in the first of them: in that, she had so far taken him with her that he was very near on moving as she moved, near on comprehending the relation between that fourth direction of movement with the three that he knew. Now, there was a world that he saw and felt and smelt and heard, a greatness that comprehended so many dimensions as to have none—and it was not for him. Fear stood before it, as the angel stood in the gateway of Eden. There

was a long and difficult pathway leading to another
gate by which one might enter, a path untrodden by
this witch's feet: she was a trespasser who had no
right there, one who at some point would be judged
for her trespass, and for the lawless use of the knowledge she had gained from the Rod.

In some part of this experience he was able to see
her and comprehend her misuse of her knowledge. It
was and yet was not wilful misuse: that she perverted
it to so small an aim was a defect bred in her race
from the days of Oger and Wulfruna, a cancer of the
mind that she could no more root out than an oak
can root out the mistletoe which lives on its sap. She
had to pursue that feud to its end, he saw, to adjust a
balance that ought never to have been disturbed. He
could see her and see this of her, then: after, back
in normality, he could not comprehend it: only in this
abnormality could he see why it had to be: between
them, she and Jerome Naylor must redress the balance
that Oger and Sigurd the Volsung had thrown out of
truth.   In this again was a mystery, for in human
experience two wrongs can never add up to a right:
but beyond Fear is neither wrong nor right, he knew
while this state lasted: all is, all has ever been, and
all will be—a completeness in which apparent right
and apparent wrong are both, equally, fulfilments of
infinite law, opposed facets in infinite order, and of
equal value in it.   Only beyond Fear, at a point
which he could not reach, was this apparent
contradiction reconciled: for him, it must remain
uncomprehended.

And now he sank down and down, out from light
and sound and scent into a darkness that was infinite
as the light had been.   He lost all consciousness of

Ira's holding him, tried desperately to retain hold on himself and stay this plunge into measureless depths. Down and down and down, past all worlds and suns, past the outermost nebulæ of space, past all of space itself, and far, far past time. Into nothingness—was this death?

XIV

THE MADNESS OF JEROME NAYLOR

SOMETHING cold and wet across his forehead, and a tang of brandy in his mouth. Lifting his hand, he found the thing on his head was a wet cloth, and he pulled it off, turning his eyes to see Ira Warenn kneeling beside the divan on which he now lay flat—and the room was lighted by an incandescent paraffin lamp which stood on one of the little ebony tables. So gazing at her, he saw that in her eyes which he had not seen at any other time: there was no witch left in her, only human woman, and in this guise she had a power that he felt.

"You—I was so frightened," she said tremulously. "For you."

Slowly he sat up, and swung his feet over the edge of the divan to sit beside her. He felt no ill effect after what he knew, by the lighted lamp, must have been a period of hours. He asked—"Frightened? Why should you be? I've been asleep, I suppose?"

"I—couldn't waken you," she told him. "You were like one dead. And so—the brandy and the cold water—I was terrified."

"You, who have passed Fear," he said slowly. "You—afraid!"

"For you—whether I had taken the spirit of you so far that it could not return. Because—you don't know the way as I do. And you lay so still, breathed so very little. I tried all ways——"

211

He made no reply, but sat looking before him until she bent to look up into his eyes. She asked—"What are you thinking?"

"James Watt," he answered, and left it at that.

"I—the man who discovered the use of steam, wasn't he? Why—what were you thinking about him?"

"You're something like what he must have been," he explained. "I think, when he had made his discovery, he had a vision of all the world changed by it—of a great stir among people when they knew this new power was released for their use. A means of swift travel, power to replace human effort in a thousand ways—Oh, I don't doubt he saw it all, almost as we know it to-day. Just in the moment of discovery, and then found that it would not come to its full use in his lifetime—that man had to grow up to it, slowly and even painfully. He was the pioneer who opened the gate, but it was not for him to pass through the gateway, fully. He sowed, that the later centuries might reap."

"I think I understand," she admitted, rather wistfully.

"You, like him, have found a new power," he went on. "You think you can take it to your use and roll the world up in your hands—after you have in some measure used it to destroy an enemy. You see yourself greater than any other, and I think, in trying to get me to share the greatness, you have discovered how small you are—how far from complete use of this power. As you yourself said, a little child trying to walk, staggering and clutching at things to hold you up. Not in your lifetime, Ira, will this use of a fourth direction be achieved. I think myself that mankind will never achieve it—will not be permitted to play with the world in that way. I *think* that. It may be that a generation or two hence a man or woman here and there will have grown up to the use of this knowledge—this tremendous knowledge. But until then, until one or more come fit and ready——"

"I want to tell you you are wrong—and I can't," she said. "I don't know. I feel, after this experience with you, that I have not fully passed fear. Else, I should not fear the singing of the sword—I do fear it, because I cannot understand it. And when you lay there, dead all but the breathing and the beating of your heart—Oh, my dear! My dear! That I had left you there—lost you!"

"Why the emotion?" he asked drily. "There was none when you held me to take me with you, and asked me to hold you. It was all—practical, part of an experiment outside emotion."

"I wouldn't——" she leaned forward and spoke whisperingly, her face averted from his sight. "I wouldn't let you know——"

"No?" He kept to a matter-of-fact tone. "Why let me know now?"

"Because—so near on losing you, I myself learned. That I'd made you hold me as a lover might hold me, and held you, knew what might be, if . . . don't you understand? The first man's arms, the first man's strength, wakening me—why do you make me tell you? Cheapen myself to you by telling you—why do I tell you? That I seem now not to belong to myself—if you could know what it was to me to look down on the shell of you, and knew the man himself far off from me——"

"Very far off from you," he said soberly. "Worlds and worlds and worlds away from you—away from all human things. So far that I asked if the darkness were death. Beyond any point you have ever reached in stepping out from the dimensions I know. Beyond all that is."

"So near death! And I—my folly made it."

"You will give it up?" He put eagerness into the question. "Give up this forbidden knowledge—forget it? Be just a woman?"

She shook her head. "No. How could I? Dark Lagny's daughter—how could I? I would be two, not one, and one of the two should be—I would have said all for you, but you have no need of that one, I know. And I must go along the path I have entered, but——"

"Yes?" He spoke the question after waiting a long time.

"But if—if at some future time——" she turned as she sat and looked full into his eyes—"you will never lose me, now. Not that you have any need of me, but I—you will never lose me. When I can walk freely in that other state, I shall come to you at times, to find whether you have any need of me. *Any* need of me! The me that you held and in holding wakened —I am fully woman, now. The me that could take hold on the ends of a distance for you and give you sight you could not get apart from me. I see a hundred ways in which I might be of use to you—or, perhaps, mean to you something other than use. Not now— when I have come to my full power. Because then I shall be able to see into your mind, not need to wait for your words."

"Power," he said sombrely. "And again and always —power!"

"No! Something else. Something greater than power."

She leaned toward him, and he knew the scent of her night-black hair, reached out to draw her nearer —and then she sat erect as a knocking sounded on the outer door of the house. Gees stood up.

"Who else is here in the house?" he asked.

She shook her head. "Nobody. After Ephraim and his boy have gone, I am alone here. Why? Why do you ask?"

"All right," he answered, and relaxed from tension. "You said that nobody else comes into this room. I was thinking of you—for you. I—shall I stay here while you see who it is?"

She nodded, and, rising, looked up at him. Abruptly he drew her close and kissed her, all of a lover's kiss. Felt her shuddering response, and the insistent, almost fierce clasp of her arms—she was all woman for that moment. The knocking sounded again, a more imperative rapping on the panel of the door.

"I shall come back to you," she whispered, and left him. And, looking at his wrist watch, he saw that it was ten minutes past eight. Firth would have had dinner alone—it was too late to go to him, now.

Ira Warenn went along the hallway and opened the door. Little light came out from the doorway of the room in which she had left Gees, and she could see only the indistinct shape of a man facing her from the step. And, since she had left the door of the green and crimson room open, all the colloquy was audible to Gees as he waited.

"Excuse me, miss—it's Hanson, from the Hall. To ask if Mr. Naylor has been here—if you've seen anything of him."

"I have not," she answered evenly. "I should think this is the last place he would visit, after to-day, surely."

"P'raps it is, miss—I don't know about that. It was Mr. Firth asked me to come and ask you, half an hour or so ago."

"And why—what is all this about?" she demanded coldly.

"Well, you see, miss——" the chauffeur-groom sounded apologetic over it—"after—after Mr. Naylor had that sorter seizure to-day, an' Miss Kilmain took him into the post-office—Mr. Firth was looking after that girl from Todd's place at the time. When he'd got her fixed up and taken her across—this is what he told me, miss—he went to the post-office to see if he could do anything for Mr. Naylor. An' he found Mr. Naylor laid out senseless—he said Mr. Naylor was sick like a man is after concussion, an' then just laid out dead to the world, so Mr. Firth left him like that. Then I come lookin', down from the Hall, because Mr. Naylor's horse come back without him. An' Mr. Firth told me Mr. Naylor'd most likely be all right soon, and then he'd either walk back up to the Hall, or else if he wasn't fit Mr. Firth'd let me know, and I'd come down with the car to take the master back. You see how it was, miss, me waiting for him to come back?"

"Yes," she answered. "Go on—what happened?"

"I come down with the car just before it began to get dark, miss, and when I went to the post-office Miss Kilmain said Mr. Naylor'd come round about a half-hour before, and went out seeming sorter strange in himself—like as if he was still a bit dazed. So I thought he'd gone home to the Hall, and drove back up there. But he wasn't there, hadn't been there, and I thought how Miss Kilmain said he looked when he went out from her place, and what Mr. Firth said about concussion, and drove back down to Mr. Firth's place. And he told me he'd seen Mr. Naylor walkin' up this way, just before I'd got to the post-office with the car, and reckoned it wasn't his business. An' then Mr. Naylor didn't come back an' didn't come back, so I turned the car out again and come along here to ask you, because there was nowhere else this way he *could* go, unless he went all the way out to the main road."

"I have not seen him, and know nothing about him," she said.

"Well, I hope you'll pardon me for troublin' of you, miss. I don't really think he could be here, but thought it as well to ask you."

"Quite right, Hanson. But I'm afraid I can't help you. I've seen nothing whatever of Mr. Naylor since Martha Kilmain picked him up and carried him off this morning, before I came back here."

"Well, thank you very much, miss—and that about Miss Kilmain taking him up like that is what helps to worry me about him. Because, you see, miss, not long ago two of her couldn't have picked him up and carried him like they say she did. He's fair fallen away to skin an' bone these last few months, an' if he's off his rocker an' wanderin' about the downs in the night like this, it'll be real bad for him."

"I'm afraid I can't help you in any way, Hanson."

"Well, thank you very much, miss, an' I won't worry you any more, but hope he turns up all right. Good-night, miss."

He turned away, and she closed the door on him. Presently sounded the whirr of a starting car, the hum of its low gear, and then all sound ceased. Ira faced Gees, back beside the divan.

"Are you quite, quite sure you are yourself again?"
she asked. "Quite sure I haven't harmed you with
my—my experiment?"

"Quite sure—Ira," he answered, and smiled at her.
"But this—I heard all that man had to say—this
business of Naylor."

"His business, not mine," she answered. "I have
played on him to some purpose, it seems. He is very
near the end, now."

"You claim—well, authorship, for this?" he asked.

She nodded assent. "I foretold the deaths of the
dog, and the woman, and the child," she said. "Fore-
saw, and made him think I caused them all. Planted
fear in him—fear of me. It has been enough. He
knows the baresark tendency will develop in him—it
is enough. He himself has developed it by fear—I
have not. Do you see?"

"Mere auto-suggestion," he remarked. "Yes. But
how did you fore-know those three deaths? That was
not auto-suggestion."

"No. It is part of the knowledge that is on the
Rod. A commonplace fortune-teller—if genuine—has
some small fragment of that knowledge. Is able to
see—it is not foretelling at all, but realising that there
is no such thing as time. Perhaps you can understand that a little better than you could before you
came here to me."

"Thanks to you, I can," he said soberly. "Even
the fortune-teller gets a little way outside—has a vague
consciousness of the ways you know. Yet not a consciousness at all. Is actuated unconsciously."

"You are a very wise man." She smiled as she
said it.

"I am not, but——"

He ceased speaking, and listened. She too stood tensed. From somewhere outside the house came a sound that was between a shriek and a roar. She said "Adolphus!" and started toward the door. Gees followed her, out from the room and to the back door of the house.

She opened the door, and a flaring light rayed toward them, a reddish glow from the blazing straw with which Adolphus' pen, placed well away from any other building, was littered. The piles of it in which the boar burrowed for warmth, normally, were masses of red blaze, and the maddened animal, squealing and roaring in terror, raced round and round the pen, by his movement fanning and accentuating the flame. Ira called to him—"Dolph! Dolph!" in agony of entreaty and fear, and ran toward the sty, Gees following, but knowing that neither he nor she could do anything in time. And, as she neared the pen, Adolphus charged with the fury of maddened despair, and smashed down the stout wooden railings on the side farthest from the house. Gees saw him by the light of the burning straw, his hide hairless and half-roasted, and then he had plunged away into the darkness.

Ira called—"Dolph! Dolph—Oh, come back! Dolph?"

But it was useless. Man is the only animal that can comprehend and use fire—to all others, even the bravest and strongest of them, it is a thing of terror, a cause for madness. The boar plunged away downhill, toward the only thing he knew that would hide him from this hell—the pond at which the farm animals drank—water. They heard the splash as he went in, and a choking, gurgling noise that stilled. Again there was nothing about them but silence, for the straw

had burned down to a still glow. And Ira called—
"Dolph? Dolph?"

Gees went down toward the pond, and now she
followed him. He struck a match, and saw the boar
floating, senseless or dead, out of his reach. He would
have waded in, but she held him back.

"No," she said. "He's dead—I could see when
you struck the third match. Shock—it isn't the burns
that kill, ever, but the shock. Dolph is dead—I know
it. Come away. Leave him."

He stayed to strike another match, and hold it high
over his head. The night was still, deathly still with
a light haze clouding the air, and the match and its
reflection on the water showed the boar floating, still
and hairless and pink from his burning—dead!

Ira said—"Let us go back. My father chose him
out and began his training. Does it sound silly to
say I counted a pig among my friends?"

"I once made a friend of a dog," Gees said.
"Adolphus was more than any dog, from what I saw
of him."

"Dead!" She took his arm and leaned against him.
"Where do they go? Shall I see him again? Dolph!
Loyal Dolph! Oh——" Abruptly she flung her arms
round Gees and broke into a passion of sobbing. "I
have so little—so very little—I who have all the world
to play with! Do you know? I—hold me for a little
while! Let me grieve for him! I—I——" she forced
herself back to self-control—"you see me silly. Tell
me—it was only a pig! My—my pig!"

"A living thing that looked up to you," he said
gravely. "Not silly, Ira—no real affection can ever
be silly, whether you spend it on a doll or a child or
a pig—it is all one thing. You love."

She drew back from his hold, and turned toward the house. "I am beginning to understand," she said. "Yes. Because I love."

They came to the opened back door, and she looked along the passage, which cut straight through the house to the front. She said—"But I closed that door!" and stood looking along the hallway. Gees too looked, and saw that the front door stood opened wide.

He said—"Naylor!" and almost leaped into the hallway, leaving her behind. In long strides he reached the doorway of the room into which she had shown him when he first entered this house, and, opening the door, went in. Utter darkness, but he struck another match and held it up: the oaken chest lay front downward, and its carven lid was smashed and splintered, and soiled by the trampling of muddied feet. He heard Ira in the doorway and extinguished the match.

"Don't come in," he said. "Nobody here—don't come in!"

As he turned toward the door he heard her footsteps recede, and then she returned, bearing the lighted lamp from the other room. She stood holding it while she looked down at the broken chest, and then put the lamp down on the table. Gees lifted the chest over on to its base, and heard the clank of metal. He saw the shimmer of the sword blade, and the rolled parchments, but of the axe with the scribed haft of narwhal horn there was no trace. Beside him Ira looked down.

"He thought I was alone here," she said, very calmly and quietly. "He lighted the fire over Adolphus to draw me out from the house, and then came in to get the Rod. While we were out there he took it——"

She broke off and stood with her head bent toward the chest, listening. Gees listened too, and heard the first faint beginnings of the sword's singing. A noise like trumpets far off, very far off, as it might have been a little echo of the noise of trumpets. Swelling, broadening and gaining in power, as if an army marched hither from the far confines of the world. Until it was a song, a terrible song of power and hate and strong purpose, a melody to drive men mad. A clangour that grew to its ultimate limit, as if the marching army went by, and faded down and down and down until again it was no more than the faintest of echoes, dying away to nothingness.

Gees looked at the girl, and she stood smiling at the rifled chest.

"I know it now," she said. "I don't fear it any more. It is not for me, the doom in that song, but for him. The end is to Dark Lagny, to me. To us Volsungs and children of the Hammer. The sword has spoken, and the last of Oger's race goes down the way of death."

"And the Rod?" Gees asked practically. "You set such value on it."

"All that is written on it I know. The value I set on it was that *he* should not have it, while he was still able to profit by the knowledge written on it. He has stolen it too late—nothing that is on it is of use to him, because doom marches on him, now."

Gees asked—"How do you know?"

"The sword has sung for the last time—it will not have a voice again, because I have read that song." She took up the lamp. "Let us go back to the other room. I know, I tell you. To you, perhaps, all this is foolishness, but I am Dark Lagny's daughter."

He followed her, and she put the lamp down on the ebony table near the head end of the divan—on the other, the bowl which contained the herbs of incense stood, and with it the two glasses. Gees stood irresolute, and she turned to smile at him.

"Two words of yours, when I grieved over Adolphus," she said. "Do you know, already that is a long while ago? Something of the past?"

"Yes, I think I do know," he answered.

"My little pig! I have Peter left—my cat. Nothing else."

"No? And what were those two words of mine?"

"You said 'You love.' I have no fear, no shame in telling you that is true of me. Because of it, I would even let Jerome Naylor go free of me and of any more harm, so much am I softened by it—but it is too late for that. I might even——"

"What?" he asked, after waiting for the end of the sentence.

"No—not that. I will follow this path of mine, find my way along the direction you will not know— do not wish to know. And be all I see I may be, far greater than any other living, greater even than the Adepts. Equal with the Powers outside and beyond space——"

"That's near on blasphemy," he interrupted harshly.

"Come to you as and when I will, perhaps unseen and unfelt by you, but *there!*" she went on, as if he had not spoken. "Because—I have no shame nor fear, I tell you—because, unloved by you, I love. If——"

"If?" he echoed, at the end of another long pause.

"Once more put your arms round me, and kiss me— one moment of all you have to live. That I may tell you—not in words."

He held her, and she was a flame in his hold, an

infinity of passion-swept tenderness. There needed no words to end that "If"—and then she thrust him away.

"Now go," she said. "You know. When I in my turn can look into your eyes and say as you said— 'You love,' I will not ask for power. Because the greater good will be mine. Now go—no more words. Go."

He went out to the night, and back toward Troy-arbour and the inn.

XV

THE LAST FANTASY

THE haze of earlier evening had thickened to a chill, clammy reek as Gees went down toward the inn. Not so opaque as to be worth terming fog, but a vapoury swirl that, with moonrise at hand, whitened the slopes on either side of the lane. In it he saw ahead of him a wavering, bobbing point of light which, as he neared it, revealed itself as a hurricane lamp. The one who carried it stopped and held it high, standing in the middle of the lane, and Gees also stopped, feeling that he was undergoing inspection. He made out Phil Hodden's fringe of whisker behind the light, and said —"Good evening."

Hodden asked—"Yu zeed un, zur?" with no preface of greeting.

"Seen nobody," Gees answered, rather shortly. "Who is it you want to see?" Though, as he asked the question, he knew.

"Zquire, zur. Gorn all fulish, they zay, an' we be lookin' f'r en!"

"Precious little chance you've got of finding him, till daylight comes again," Gees told the man. "He'll probably go back to the Hall of his own accord, if you leave him alone."

He realised, almost as he spoke, that he had said too much, betrayed knowledge of Naylor's aberration. Hodden lowered the lamp.

"Whut du yu know, zur?" he asked, rather ominously.

"That I've seen nothing of your squire," Gees snapped in reply. "You tell me he's gone foolish, and you're looking for him. That's what I know. What else could I know about him?"

"I—I dunno, zur." Hodden sounded apologetic, now. "But yu been along heer, so I reckoned p'raps —niver moind, though."

He would have passed on, but Gees stopped him by getting directly in front of him. "What did you reckon?" he demanded sharply.

"I—him an' her—Miss Wren—I heerd all what happened to-daay—hur owd bore killed his dawg, an' if so be he wur like what he wor then, when he swore at Miss 'Wren—mad, like——" Hodden floundered over his explanation, badly—"an' yu been to hur plaace—I reckoned happen he went theer too, an' yu zeed en."

"I have not seen him since he tried to ride Miss Warenn down this morning, and the woman Kilmain picked him up and took him away," Gees said, quite truthfully. "What's more, I'm not looking for him —don't want to see him. You do as you like—good-night."

He stood aside, and as Hodden passed him with a rather sullen—"Good-night, zur," went on his way toward the inn. So far as sight or hearing had told, Naylor was nowhere along the lane between Wren's farm and this point, and Hodden would be out of luck if he went on searching in that direction. Naylor had got the Rod, and had not stopped short of arson to get it: he wanted no more than that from Ira.

Words she had spoken came back to Gees as he went on his way. "No shame nor fear. . . . Unloved by you, I love." That she should have spoken them, words that a normal woman would never have spoken, was comprehensible. All her knowledge of life was empiric—she was not to be judged by normal standards. Apart from the time for which her father had sent her away, she had dreamed here in a solitude, rather than lived, and while she dreamed had come on a knowledge which rendered her conscious of herself as a power. His own analogy of James Watt came back to his mind: she had seen this thing she had found as an acquisition that set her above all others: here at the first beginnings of the path she meant to tread, she saw herself so far advanced along the path as to be able to command, to ask and have. Inadvertently, in that "experiment" with him, she had wakened herself to full womanhood, and in consciousness of her power in other directions saw no difference between confession of that awakening and statement of her intent to make herself equal with powers beyond three-dimensional comprehension. Seeing herself as greater than all others, should she not command all others? Not yet did she realise that what she knew as a greater good than power is not to be commanded, but is wayward as the winds, given and taken away as the gods will.

He said—"You can't have both, Ira," and opened the bar-room door to enter. Past nine o'clock, and the table at which the worthies usually sat was bare and unused, to-night. Up by the bar stood a stocky being in dark box-cloth semi-uniform and gaiters, whom Gees guessed was Hanson the groom-chauffeur, and Firth. They ceased talking and turned to look at Gees as he advanced, and Firth shook his head.

"I waited for you till a quarter to eight," he said.

"Sorry," Gees answered contritely. "I—well, I simply couldn't make it. You said you'd leave it open, in case I couldn't."

"Quite so—that's all right," Firth told him. "And —you've heard that Mr. Naylor has vanished into thin air, I expect."

"Has he?" Remembering his encounter with Hodden, Gees achieved an air of surprise. "Since when? You don't mean——?" He broke off, leaving an inference that Firth might have meant anything.

"Since this afternoon," Firth told him. "He was in a sort of coma when I last saw him—that was on Martha Kilmain's bed at the post office—and after looking him over I decided he would stay like that for some hours. I saw it as the result of his seizure— you remember?"

Gees nodded. "Epileptic, perhaps," he suggested.

"Not it!" The denial was emphatic. "He's never shown any tendency in that direction. No. The symptoms appeared much more like those of concussion, to me."

"Except that he did nothing this morning to get himself concussed, as far as I could see;" Gees remarked. "One pint, please, Todd."

"That is so," Firth agreed, as the landlord took out a glass tankard and went to the barrel to fill it. "Martha Kilmain says he seemed dazed when he got up and went out—along the lane toward Wren's farm, or past Wren's toward the main road. We simply don't know where he went. About a dozen men have turned out to look for him."

"I went to Wren's and saw Miss Warenn," Hanson put in, "but she told me he hadn't been there.

Said, too, that he wasn't likely to go there, and there's no harm in saying we all know that's quite true."

"I don't see your dozen men finding him, except by luck," Gees observed. "An army might hide on these downs, to say nothing of one man. Especially in such a haze as there is to-night."

"I diagnose amnesia," Firth said. "And you're right, of course—it will be luck and nothing else if he's found. Quite probably he will turn toward the Hall automatically, and be at home by the time you get back, Hanson. If you want me, you know where to find me—it's getting late, and I think I'll get away home, now. I can do nothing here."

"Thank ye very much for what ye've done, Mr. Firth," Todd remarked. "Heer, I mean, for Phyllis. I took a look at her a while back, an' she's sleepin' quite comfortable. I'm much obliged to ye."

"She'll be none the worse in a few days' time," Firth said. "Fortunately, the hound broke no bones —that boar of Miss Warenn's was on him and took him off her in time. Wonderful animal, that—wonderful the way Miss Warenn has with animals, too. How she stopped the horse by looking at it, and——" He broke off and glanced at Hanson, rather trepidantly. Gees knew he had been about to say that Ira had stopped Naylor, too, but had thought better of it.

"Have one on me before you go," Gees offered in the pause.

"No, thank you—I'll get along. Good-night, all."

He went out and, a minute or so later, Hanson took up his drink and finished it, bade good-night to Gees and Todd, and went his way. Todd came and leaned on the bar, rather apprehensively.

"I dunno about cookin' f'r you, sir," he said. "Y'see,

Phyllis mostly does the cookin', an' I made a rare owd mess o' them chops."

"There will be some cold ham, and some pickles, and cheese," Gees suggested. "And what more could the heart of man yearn to absorb? In a minute. You're a furriner—I'm a furriner. What are they all saying, Todd? What's the general verdict on the situation?"

"You mean the frackass when the hound got mashed —glory be, what a mess that boar made o' that hound's head!" Todd responded. "Ground it up like I'd chew a bit o' toast! A savage pig is a terrible thing."

"Is that what they're saying?" Gees asked, rather caustically.

"It ain't, sir. I don't quite like what they're sayin', neither. Miss Wren's a pleasant young lady, f'r all I know of her—she's been right civil to me, the few times I've spoke to her. An' the nicest-lookin' lady betwixt heer an' Portland Bill, as the sayin' goes. Y'see what I mean, sir. Take one look at them eyes o' hers, an' you know she's *straight,* let alone anyone bad couldn't do what she'll do wi' animals. They know, do animals, an' it take a straight one to handle 'em the way she can. As f'r tales—well, to hell wi' tales!"

"Such as——?" Gees asked interestedly.

"Such as—but that warn't what I started to tell you, sir, nor what you was askin' me. She's like that, but thàt there Ephraim Knapper an' his boy, an' Tom Skinner the shepherd, an' Jerry Flint—live over t'other side o' Timms, Jerry do, so he don't often come in here. Them four is all what makes a livin' outer Wren's farm. Y'see what I'm tryin' to tell you, sir? Them an' Miss Wren herself—no more."

"It's coming to me," Gees answered. "Carry on."

"Well, sir, heer's Troyarbour, by the grace o' God an' Squire Naylor. So far's we know, he ain't got no relations—an' if he do have any, we don't know 'em. If anything happened to him—this is *their* way o' lookin' at it, not mine, sir—if anything happened to him, what'd become o' Troyarbour? He spent money like water on keepin' up the Hall, an' all the village live on him—'ceptin' of them four I named. An' there ain't one of 'em don't know there's war betwixt him an' Miss Wren. They've kept quiet about it, an' not took sides, so long as everything was all right—they reckoned he'd find some way to drive her out. But then she cursed him, the day her father died, an' his lady an' the child up an' died—both of 'em! Troyarbour says to itself—them two don't matter, so long as nothin' don't happen to him, it says. Our livin's safe, an' we're on a soft time, so long as *he's* theer up at the Hall, an' we ain't frettin' about she. But to-day was different. She faced him an' brought him down, an' I don't know if you know, sir, how old feelin' is kep' alive in out o' the way places like this? Lonely places, away from cinemas an' buses?"

"I can guess—all you're getting at," Gees told him. "Go on."

"We're furriners, sir, both on us, so I can talk to you about it. They're sayin', because she beat him down to-day—there's no sayin' she didn't beat him down, because she *did!*—they're sayin' she's got powers past the ord'nary—sayin' she's a witch, like there useter be years ago. Sayin' if she's let run on like this, she'll make that curse o' hers come true on him, an' then the Hall'll be shet up an' all the land he been farmin' 'll go back to sheep feed—an' wheer'll they all be f'r their comforts an' their livin's? I

don't say they'll *do* anything, sir—duck her or any
o' them old things they useter do to witches, but I
don't like the look o' things. Not at all I don't."

"They're in a dangerous mood, you think?" Gees
suggested.

"Not all, but some," Todd answered. "That theer
Fred Carphin—his Nettie got a soft job up theer at
the Hall—theer's them which says 'tis more'n a soft
job, but I dunno about that. Sam Thatcher—an' what
Sam says is took up by most. Timms, wi' the farm
next hers—he got a grudge about some grazin' ground
which he say oughter go wi' his land, not hers, an'
if her lease could be broke it'd go to him. I could
name ye dozens, all countin' their livin' outer the
Hall an' dead against her, an' if they don't find Squire
Naylor to-night, an' git outer hand—ignorance can
be mighty cruel, sir, an' we're a long way from police
an' law, heer. I dunno. It might be all wind an'
bluster, as the sayin' goes. It might. I dunno."

"I will have ham, and pickled onions, and cheese, and
the newest loaf there is, and lots of butter," Gees said
softly. "After that, Todd—this is for your ear alone,
you being a furriner like myself—after that, I'm going
to take a walk as far as Wren's farm, and heaven
help anyone who wants to keep his living if he comes
along there to preserve it! Collect the feast, Todd,
and I'll go along to the coffee room. And—while I
think of it—give my love to your little lady when she
wakes up, and tell her she has all my good wishes
for a quick recovery. Now get along—food, and I'll
love thee to the death, as Tennyson said. Then I'm
off—strictly between ourselves."

"Lord love you for a good 'un, sir. I'd hate anything to happen to Miss Warenn. An', come Christ-

mas, sir, we're goin' to get married, Phyllis an' me. Because she's the best little girl betwixt here an' Portland Bill, as the sayin' goes, an'—an' I've found it out."

Gees said—"Half a dozen pairs of silk stockings at five and eleven—I'll have to work it out. Half a dozen, anyway, Todd. Leave it to me—and if you don't turn that ham out one time, there'll be nothing of you to leave anything to anybody! You have been warned."

But Todd dwelt too far from a main road to appreciate the slogan. He went out of the bar as if Naylor's hound were still alive and close behind him, and Gees, lifting the flap for himself, followed at a more leisurely rate of travel. He knew he would be in time to greet the ham.

.   .   .   .   .

The moon, westerning, lighted the haze of luminance, and Gees, looking up, noted the flattened side of the orb and reflected that, once it had passed the full, it took on an aged look, like a man who has passed his vigour and is no more beloved of women. A sort of illustration of the fact that Time is the untiring foe—was it because he himself was growing past vigour that Ira Warenn had failed to stir him to response? Yet he was young, as life goes, and . . . no, it was not that, but the purpose which she put before human desire and human tenderness. She wanted him for a purpose, not for himself: she wanted to make him one with her in that purpose—though she had wakened to consciousness of desire, she still relegated it to a secondary place, sought power over him and to make him one with her in the pursuit of power. If he let her, she would use him, learn through him——

Curious beings, women. Giving as it pleased them to give—and no more. Utterly unselfish when unselfishness was selfish—because it pleased them to be so— but never beyond that point. A woman could realise a man's hunger for her, find pleasure in it and hold him, hungering, while she pursued her own aims—and yet love as Ira Warenn was learning to love. Yes, curious beings——

A whispering noise on the night stayed his thoughts. The moonlight half-revealed a group in the shadows beside the bank that edged the lane, and he stiffened to rigidity, listening.

"Yu gotter hev light. Yu caan't du it i' the dark."

"The pond's theer. Yu'd see if she floated, sure-ly."

Fred Carphin, that second speaker—and the purpose of the speech was plain. A third voice said— "Whaat du we du, then?" and on that Gees moved forward, faced a dozen or so of men of whom each one carried a hurricane lamp—but the lights of all the lamps had been extinguished. There was light enough to reveal the faces of those who carried them, and among them all that of old Sam Thatcher stood out vindictive in expression, stubbornly sullen, resentful of this furriner's interference, and obviously defiant of him.

Gees said, quietly—"You men had better go home."

Thatcher said—"An' whu be yu to tell us?"

Gees walked up to him. "If you were ten or twenty years younger, you old fool, I'd tell you quite a lot," he said. "As it is, I'd hate to waken the lady you're planning to injure by making a row. Go home!"

"Me tu, mister?" Fred Carphin stepped forward and sneered at him.

He reached out and took the man by his two ears, and with one large foot swept the clumsy feet from their hold on the ground. Carphin went down with a thud and lay still, staring up as if he wondered what had struck him. Gees looked over the rest, and, without raising his voice, asked—"Anyone else? I'm all ready. Or will you go home, the lot of you, and stop this blasted foolery?"

"You'm sweering," Sam Thatcher reproved him coldly. "Yu got no call to sweer at we. We're duin' yu no harm, mister."

Fred Carphin got up, slowly. He said—"Yu just-about broak my baack, mister, sure-ly. Why'd yu du thaat?"

"Go home, the damned lot of you!" Gees said with soft fierceness. "Home or to the devil—get to hell out of this before I smash your silly faces! Blast the damned lot of you—go!"

They slunk past him in silence, and he counted them —eleven men to one. When they had gone, he took up Fred Carphin's lamp that had been left behind through forgetfulness, and felt it over, to ascertain that it was quite cold: they had wanted no lights for this errand.

He swung about at a faint sound, and faced Ira Warenn. The sound of receding footsteps along the lane had died out, but from the distance came the slight murmur of the men's voices.

She said—"Why didn't you let them? It would have been so funny. I wanted them to come in and try to take hold of me—and find there wasn't any me! Take just the one step I can take, and laugh at them."

"And make them still more bitter against you," he said sombrely. "I've been hearing—that's why I came to guard you——"

He broke off, gazing at her. Still in the green frock, which was grey in the moonlight—and the scribed stone on her breast was faintly luminous, a phosphorescent blue. He said—"You fool! You very lovely fool! You are lovely, Ira, and you're a child playing with the lightning. Thinking to use it to scare flies off a wall—why won't you get a sense of proportion into that head of yours—that very lovely head with the hair you stole out of Proserpine's garden? Do you know, the sight of you makes me go all poetic? If I had the brains, I'd sing odes to you, but that other side of you wants to roll up the world and play with it—and so you spoil yourself."

"For you?" She moved quite close to him and spoke softly, caressingly. "Do you mean I spoil myself for you?"

"It's night, Ira," he told her gravely. "I'd have you say no more than you would say in daylight. If—if ever this illusion turned to reality, I'd want you to be able to say in daylight all you think in the night. You're cold——" He saw her shiver—"go back home, and feel yourself quite safe. They will not come back."

"I—I am not afraid of them," she answered. "*You* are cold. Not as I am. I wish I were cold, not ignorant and silly. I want to be taught the language you speak, to know as you know."

He took her by the arm. "Home," he said practically. "Warmth and sleep—they're what you need. This fire of you will burn you out, child—you're too intense, wanting to crowd all life into an hour, all the time. Those secrets you learned are eating you up——"

"If you knew them—I want you to know them!" she interrupted.

"Yes, I know you do." He impelled her toward the house. "But I'm not perilling my life as I know it by asking all you ask of the gods. It isn't safe—you'll find that out if you keep on this way you've begun. Not safe, I tell you! And you've achieved your purpose, by the look of things. A night out with this cold clamminess will probably put an end to Naylor, and leave you gloating."

"That is not all." She moved along, his hand still holding her arm, to the doorway of the house. "You know it is not all, but only a prelude—I have to accomplish that, and then I am free to use all the knowledge I have gained. Secrets you cannot even guess——"

"Nor wish to guess," he interposed. "I refuse to play with lightning, refuse to go beyond normality. You have shown me enough."

She stopped and faced him. "It will soon be dawn," she said. "Will you come in with me for a little while? I think—all that the night must know is not yet done, and there is nobody but you I could ask to see the end of it with me. Will you come in?"

He stopped before the open door of the house, and saw the light ray out from the doorway of the green and crimson room. "Why?" he asked. "Why should I? It's very near on dawn, now."

"But—please!" Her eyes reinforced the request.

He followed her into the room he had begun to know, and moved toward the divan. She said—"No—don't sit there. I want you to see the picture. And to find out—with you to see."

"More of your magic?" he asked, gibingly.

"There is no such thing as magic—you know it," she said gravely. "Not—not in the material world. In the world of the spirit—yes. You wakened a magic

in me—but that is another thing, quite different, and
of no interest to you, I know."

"Do you know it?" He smiled as he asked it, but
she shook her head and pointed at the bowl on the little
ebony table.

"Will you light it—the stuff in the bowl?" she
asked. "Drop a lighted match? As—as Jerome
Naylor dropped a lighted match and robbed me of
a friend. I want to see—the picture will tell, if you
light what is in the bowl. Whether—please light it
for me."

"Why haven't you lighted it yourself," he asked
curiously as, taking out his cigarette lighter, he flicked
it and dipped the flame into the bowl, holding it down
to the powdered herbs.

"It would not be the same," she answered. "Some
day, I will tell you why. But now—yes, it is alight.
Stand back, here!"

He moved back beside her, reflecting that this was
the second thing she had promised to tell him some
day—she meant to hold close to him, then. So far
his reflections went, and then all thought of abstract
futures ceased as a cloud of greenish-blue smoke went
up and broke against the ceiling, hiding the wall on
which the picture hung, and billowing downward to
thin and cease to be, so that it did not quite impinge
on him or on the girl who stood quite beside him. So
they two stood, and the smoke thinned and thinned,
until presently he saw the picture again, two boats
moored against a quay—yet were *both* boats moored,
as he had thought when he first saw the picture?

He felt a crinkling of his spine as he watched, and
heard the girl breathing audibly, almost pantingly.
He saw the boat with the crimson sail move, and the

sail swayed as if in a wind. There was nobody visible in the boat, but of its own balance or yielding to wind and tide it swayed, or seemed to sway, and moved, swung about, and pointed first out from the picture— then, still swinging, out from the harbourage toward the greying blueness of the farthest horizon. As if it had been a reality the pictured boat moved, and moved, gathering speed and growing smaller, smaller, till the crimson sail was but a patch against the blue, a swaying, tossing patch that diminished and was now no more than a speck, with the boat beneath it invisible.

"Surely, this is the last fantasy!" Gees breathed.

"Nothing is real—nothing unreal. All things are, and yet are not. Look again!" For he had turned his head to look at her. "A painted picture—nothing more. Look again."

He looked, and saw the picture—one green-sailed boat against the line of quay. Still, a painted thing, flat against the flatness of blue sky that hazed to grey on the horizon. He said again—"This is the last fantasy. Oh, witch, how do you do these things?"

"I do not do them. They are. Now do you know why I asked you to come in with me?"

He shook his head, and gave her no other answer. The last faint curl of smoke rose up from the red bowl on the ebony table, and left only a fluff of white, dead ash. Ira went to the window and swung back the shutter. The greyness outside had lightened—it was now very near on dawn. She turned back and faced Gees.

"These are mysteries to you, because you will not go with me and understand them fully," she said deliberately. "That—the passing of the crimson sail —it was a prefiguring. I know what must happen, and it is very near. The last fantasy, you said, but what must happen—what I know will happen—is beyond fantasy. Will you come out with me? I think the time is very near—Jerome Naylor's end."

He followed her out from the room, along the passage, and into the chill of dawn's first beginning. The moon had set, but the white haze of night was growing whiter by reflection from the as yet unrisen sun. And there was in the haze a cold like the chill of death, as if spirits from the underworld had risen up to still the blood of men. A harsh, unnatural chill that was of itself a fantasy, as it might have been a breath from the ultimate coldness of sunless space.

XVI

THE HAMMER

The white reek thinned, but the cold remained, as
Gees followed the girl beyond the end of the house
to sight of Adolphus' burnt-out pen, the farm buildings
apart from the site of the fire, and, growing distinct
in the increasing light, the slope beyond, up which
he had walked with her to the long mound of the three
thorns. She waited for him to draw level with her,
and took his arm. He saw the fine white line of her
throat above the collar of the green frock, and her
hair a rippling darkness, uncovered.

"It's bitterly cold," he said. "Let me go back and
get you a coat or something." And halted, faced
toward the height they had climbed.

"No. This frock is warm—I'm not cold. Why do
you think for me like this? Why did you come through
the night to me as you did?"

"Because it seemed the obvious thing to do," he
answered. "I had an idea—and those men confirmed
it. You'd told me you were alone here—I couldn't let
you face anything of that sort alone."

"I have been alone a long while—until you came,"
she said. "I shall be alone again till I learn how to
come to you—to master the greater distances in place
of groping and stumbling over small steps."

"Leave it alone, Ira," he urged gently. "I have
seen enough to know—leave it alone, before you are
destroyed."

She shook her head. "Nothing is ever destroyed," she said. "There is change, but no death. You—you will go back to what you see as your sane world, and all this you have known in a little hollow of the hills will be to you no more than the shadow of a dream. You will' say you dreamed it, and none of it was real, because it is all outside your sane world. When you see me again——"

"Is it 'when' or 'if'?" he asked in the pause.

"Are you still afraid of me?" She asked the question abruptly instead of answering his.

"Of you the woman—no," he answered. "Of the witch—yes."

"And if there were no witch?" She turned her head to look at him as she asked it, and her eyes smiled.

He shook his head. "You won't give it up," he said, "won't be content with what you call my sane world. You'll always want to slip out along that fourth perpendicular, play with the stars and feel yourself something more than human—though you're not. It's like a drug to you, a temptation too strong for you. A wrong thing you won't give up until it has—destroyed you. Because it *is* wrong, and you know it."

"Yes, I know it. And I will not give it up," she owned.

"Child, you're cold! I'm cold too." He put his arm round her and held her close to him. "Why are we out here in this—this inhuman iciness? What do you expect of it? Come back to your room."

"No." She pointed up at the long mound on the hilltop. "There—it will all end there—all that began with Sigurd's dying. Soon, very soon. And this cold

—I cannot escape it, no matter where I go. It is a Presence, a very old Power. Soon—now!"

The last word was an exclamation, and again she pointed toward the height. Then Gees saw how a smallish figure climbed the slope, from some starting point between them and the village. A lonely little figure that went slowly, wearily upward to the mound.

"It is Jerome Naylor," she said. "Last of Oger's breed."

"We ought to stop him," he said. "The man is mad—quite mad. He must have been wandering about all night—he'll kill himself."

"He is too far off—we could not stop him," she dissented. "And he will not kill himself. He has the Rod in his hand, and while he holds it he will try to kill others, not himself."

Then Gees remembered how he, holding the axe-haft in his grasp, had felt the influence of the weapon, had consciousness that it had killed many men. He said—"You mean it makes him mad."

"Baresark," she answered, "and that is a madness, as you know."

He had a moment's mind-picture of Naylor on the horse, riding-crop lifted as he tried to drive the horse at her, and the murderous blaze in the man's eyes. It was in truth a madness.

"You brought it on him," he said accusingly.

"He brought it on himself," she contradicted. "Believed it would be, and so made it. That is his fate—watch, and see."

Holding her, he felt the cold about them lessen, and become no more than the rawness of dawn in a day of late autumn. The figure she had said was Naylor had reached the summit of the ridge, and now climbed the steepness of the mound. Gees said—"We ought to go up, make him come down and act like a normal man. This is——"

"In that state, and with the axe in his hand, he would kill us both," she interrupted. "A baresark man has the strength of five—you could do nothing, while he holds the axe. And—look!"

Naylor gained the top of the mound, coming out to distinctness against the lightened sky at the end on which, she had said, women had been stretched between the trees in old time. At the other, men's end of the crest, there grew a shape that was not a shape, a gigantic shadow like a djinn cohering from smoke to substance. It shrank to human semblance, became shaped, and was the figure of a helmed giant—Gees saw shadowy horns projecting from the helm, such as the Norse warriors of old time wore, and saw that the shape held a vast hammer in its left hand. And it was all shadow, a mere illusion against the sky that reddened for the imminent sunrise, something with no more substance than a cloud. Gees asked—"Am I mad, too?" and blinked to dispel this aberration of his sight. Uselessly: the shape was there.

Ira said—"We are children of the Hammer, Sigurd's children, and now the Hammer will destroy the Rod. Jerome Naylor has seen it—look!"

He looked again at her bidding, and shadowy Thor bulked against the skyline, so illusory that the redness of the dawn was scarcely darkened by his shape, so nearly real that he dominated the height like a crown on the brows of morning. He swung the vast Hammer lightly in his left hand, and his right hand beckoned the puny human with the Rod. The gesture was a taunt—Jerome Naylor saw it, and ran along the summit of the mound, with the axe uplifted in acceptance of the challenge. Then again, though to himself and not in words, Gees questioned if he were mad, for that other madman could see the shape. And Ira could see it, but she was mad in a different way, one in which she thought to step beyond limitations and be one with the gods who interweave and yet are separate beyond the three dimensions that man knows.

While Naylor ran, Gees knew past all doubting that hers was a madness which would bring her to doom. Knew it as, up to that moment, he had not known, and tightened his hold on her as if he would hold her back from the path she meant to follow. He said—"Turn back, Ira!" but she shook her head and pointed toward the height.

There Naylor faced the shape of Thor, and the great, shadowy Hammer that was now upraised, poised like a reed in the great Smith's left hand, and ever interposed between the shadow and the axe with which the baresark madman tried to strike. Again and again he tried to reach past the guard of the Hammer, of which the heavy head flicked with rapier swiftness, and Thor stood rock-like with head thrown back and face upraised to the sky, as if it were nothing to him to guard against so slight an attack as this. As he stood thus he sang, and again and for the last time Gees heard the song the sword had sung, but now it was a tiny echo that beat back and down from the day-veiled stars, a shadow of a song as the singer was no more than a shadow of a shape, yet it was strong and terrible, and while he listened Gees knew that the old gods do not die, for there is no death, only change. They pass to other place and other use, but they do not die.

For a moment Gees looked away from the summit
of the mound, his gaze diverted by movement lower
down, and saw men running up the slope of the down.
He counted five of them, men of the village who had
seen Naylor waving the axe in his madness, and went
to save him—so they thought—from himself. Gees
saw them, and then looked again at the warring
man and shadow silhouetted against the reddening
dawn.

The axe was wearying, moving more slowly, and
Thor's song was fiercer and more terrible. The vast
Hammer that he wielded as if it had been a feather
went up above his back-thrown head, came down like
a lightning-flash on the scribed handle of the axe—
and, as Naylor fell and lay still, the terrible song
ceased. The shadow that was Thor turned its back on
the fallen man, and went striding into the sunrise, a
deeper red on the redness of the sky that blended in
with the fierce colouring, and presently ceased to be.

The running men were near the top of the ridge,
now. Ira shivered and held herself close to Gees,
nestling for warmth. She said—"I am very cold.
You see—I have not harmed him. All this was fated,
foreknown and foredoomed before I was—before
Sigurd begot Dark Lagny. I am very cold—let us
go back. Else, if I went up there, they might say
I had struck him down—I in my strength against
him in his weakness. Come back with me for a little
while—a little while!"

He felt her shuddering with cold, and leaning more
heavily on him as they went back. Along the chill
corridor, and into the green and crimson room—he
saw again the picture in which only the one sail rose
over the quayside, and a fluff of white ash in the red

lacquer bowl. Had the smoke from the bowl bleached out that other sail, made the illusion of the boat's passing out from the picture? Yet he had *seen* the boat loosen from its mooring, swing about, and pass away.

Ira said—"Hold me—not for love, but for warmth. I am so cold, and you are warm, solid and warm. Close—hold me!"

So holding her, he saw faint colour come back into her face, and her lips that had been pale with the cold reddened again. He felt her arms tighten their hold on him, and her eyes looked into his before they closed as she yielded up her lips to his kiss. Yet in yielding challenged, asked, and gave—the very spirit of her, he knew.

"I am all woman, for you. Wakened, by you. No witch, to you. No longer my own, but part of you. Ask, and I give—to you."

He said—"Give it all up, then, Ira. Be content as you are. This is the greater good—you know it now. And you may tell me what I told you. There is no woman like you, if you will be just woman and turn back from all the rest. Ira?"

She whispered—"I may say—you love?"

"Know it——" again he found her lips and held them—"you!"

"I will come to you—no! If I give it all up, you must come to me! Can I? I hold it—can I let go?"

She drew back from him and stood, perplexed between the aim that had been hers so long and this new urge that the first man to hold her wakened. He knew that she saw beyond the hour, into the future in which the old knowledge would tempt her: he could sense the struggle in her mind, yet her next words came as a shock—

"For this, Dark Lagny hung on a cross outside Eboracum."

"So!" he said heavily. "Choose. This is all fantasy, but in it I love you, Ira. Choose you, the dark ways outside time and space that will bring you to an end, or . . . magic. They say Dark Lagny had many lovers. I would have you take one, and hold to . . . me."

A heavy knocking on the outer door of the house startled her to realisation of practical things. Leaving him with no word of explanation, she went out, and he heard her voice at the end of the passage.

"Good morning, Ephraim. The boar's stye caught fire last night, and he was so badly burned that he rushed into the pond and died there. I want you to get the body out and bury it—yes, at the far end of the apple orchard. Please. Before you do anything else. Then come back to me, and I'll give you your orders for the day."

"Aye, miss. But if he'm only burnt, the meat'll be good."

"Bury him, I tell you!" The order was fiercely harsh.

"Aye, miss. Yu says, an' I'll du it."

She came back into the room, changed, mistress of herself. For a minute or less she looked into Gees' eyes, and her own eyes softened.

"I must have time," she said. "You ask me to forgo so much. The patient search that has lasted years, the gain I have had of it, the sight of greater gain very near my hold, now that I have finished with Jerome Naylor. All this, and against it——?"

She made a question of the last sentence. Gees, chilled, shook his head: he knew, even then, which way her choice would fall.

"Against it, magic," he said. "The only magic there is, Ira. For me, to look at you and say—'I love.' Till you have made your choice, I will not say it again. Nor may you."

"Do you know how much we have lived through since last night?" she asked after a pause. "Adolphus dead, the Rod gone, Naylor beaten down as we saw, and this new wakening, greater than all the rest. I think even I am tired and need time to rest. And you?"

He knew he was tired, then—up to that moment he had not realised how great had been the strain of the night and its happenings—and of the last stupendous, fantastic, incredible happening in the light of dawn. He said, heavily—"I too. Yes. I shall see you again before I go, Ira. Be able to think clearly again—see you——"

With no further word he went out. As he went, he heard the clanking of pails—Ephraim's boy was going to his milking, Gees divined. A small, inconsequent thing—was anything in life other than small and inconsequent? One might live through what seemed great moments, but the small things of life went on all the time, inexorable, inconsequent, unescapable. Ham and eggs at The Three Thorns, a bed on which to sleep and sleep, to wake, perhaps, to sanity and normal things, other than this unreal fantasy in which old gods swung hammers. . . .

It was a long, long way to the inn. When he got inside, he said—"I want some ham and eggs, Todd—lots of ham and lots of eggs. Don't cook 'em yet—I

want a sleep, first. If you wake me before I've slept
it out, I'll murder you. When I've had it, ham and
eggs."

"Right you are, sir. Nuthin' went wrong, I
hope?"

"Exactly that—nothing. Because I know now that
nothing exists, but everything isn't. Do you know
your Shakespeare, Todd?"

"Not too well, sir. Wrote plays, didn't he? I
learned bits at school, an' that sorter stopped me
frettin' about him. When you get them things, an'
parse an' analyse 'em, they go sour on you."

"Quite so, but he wrote one great truth that I've
had rubbed in since I came to Troyarbour. 'We
are such stuff as dreams are made of.' You get that?
You're a dream—I'm a dream—all we do and say
and think is nothing but a dream, dreamed by—
what?"

"'Fraid that's away over me, sir. An' if that
brewer's man don't turn up with a load before noon,
you'll yet no bitter to-night, because you got to give
a cask time to settle arter the finin's is put in. I hope
he's somethin' more solid'n a dream."

"I will now stagger up to—dream," Gees said. "Ham
and eggs when I wake, but not till. Let me sleep
it out, if——"

Without ending the sentence, he went toward the
stairs' foot. As he went, he questioned whether sleep
were for him, in spite of his weariness. But, lying
down fully clothed as he was, he passed to dreamless-
ness almost instantly. Ira, warm and pulsing in his
hold, was a moment's recollection, and then she passed
—all things passed.

.   .   .   .   .

At some point in the day he wakened enough to take off his shoes and, rousing more fully with the movement, stripped off all he was wearing and got between the sheets naked as a bathed infant, the way he liked best to sleep. He did not look at the time, and so did not know if it were still morning or past noon, and, snuggling down between the warming sheets, went off again, to waken in darkness. Then he lighted the candle beside the bed and, seeing that it was past six o'clock, got out, yearned for the bath that the inn could not provide, and after a simple wash went down, to find Todd hovering.

"I was in two minds about comin' up to wake ye, sir," Todd informed him. "I reckoned you'd slep' it out long since, an' must be bad."

"I am bad. Which reminds me—how is the little lady?"

"She's pickin' up surprisin', sir. An'—I hope it's all right wi' you, sir, but I told her you called her that, an' she near on cried wi' pleasure. You know what women are, sir, I expect."

"I don't, you don't, and nobody ever will," Gees told him. "The eternal puzzle. Well, you tell the little lady she's all that and then some, and I'm glad she's getting better. And this little matter of ham and eggs—what about letting me do the cooking?"

"Oh, no, sir! I got Cowder's wife in to look arter Phyllis—I can't keep an eye on her an' the bar, openin' time. An' Mrs. Cowder's got the eggs all laid out riddy, an' the ham cut, f'r me to say the word. An' seein' you was up all night an' slep' all day——"

"How many eggs, Todd? The truth, and nothing but!"

"She got six laid out, sir. I reckoned——"

"Don't! You simply can't reckon. Tell her to divide by two."

"Two eggs, sir?" Todd looked his lack of comprehension.

"Yes, two eggs, and then throw one at the wall. Then the quotient will justify the divisor. All right— never mind! She needn't throw it. If I find more than three, I'll do the throwing, and then you'll have to get some new wall paper. In other words, three eggs is my limit, and the ham must correspond, not swamp 'em. I want to be able to see the eggs between the ham, if you get me. Can do?"

"I don't quite get you, sir." He looked still more puzzled.

"Can—you—do—that?" Gees breathed deeply between each pair of words. "Can you ensure that I get no more than three eggs, and that said eggs are visible under not more than a reasonable amount of ham—which reminds me. The difference between a ham and a hammer?"

Todd frowned. "I don't get that, sir," he said, puzzledly.

"If you saw a great big man playing hell with a great big hammer, and a tiny little man aiming at him with what looked like the bone of a used-up ham, wouldn't you know the difference between a ham and a hammer?" Gees inquired, looking intently at his man.

But that man looked no more than utterly puzzled. He said—"I don't get you, sir. It's some sort of joke, I reckon, an' maybe I'm a bit dim. A ham, an' a hammer. No, sir, I can't see it."

Some of the worthies, almost certainly, had been in

for the midday opening of the bar, Gees knew. He tried again.

"Your small man has got all there is left of a ham —this is a puzzle worth thinking over. He's got a sort of stick with a bump on the end—it looks just like an axe—and the big feller's got a mighty hammer —Lord help us, half a dozen of 'em saw it happen! And you can't see it? You don't know this one?"

Todd shook his head. "No, sir, I don't," he answered stolidly.

"Well, I'll tell you the answer." Obviously, the fantasy of fight up on the ridge had not come through as news to Todd, so Gees gave up trying to pump him. "You see, any professional can chew a ham, but for a hammer you need a hammer-chewer. Is that too dark for you?"

Todd said—"Any professional——" and blew up. In such a place as this, jokes were few, and the old ones had all the flavour of novelty. He gurgled, and choked, and then roared as he got his breath.

"Easy!" Gees warned him. "Else, my three eggs'll addle."

Todd took a long breath and steadied himself. "I'll tell her, sir," he promised. "I'll tell her that one, too—but she'll never see it, I know. An' I better get along—she's mindin' the bar till I go back, an' you know there's no cash register."

"God help us all!" Gees exclaimed fervently. "Hurry, man, and turn her loose on the frying pan. She can make me tea—weak tea, tell her. And when I've got rid of the taste of it I'll come in for a pint or so. Just to hear the news—you know!"

"There's a whole packet, sir. I'm glad I'm a fur-riner. A lot's happened since you went out last night."

"You buzz along, Todd. No cash register, you said. You also said eggs, and ham. Buzz along, and turn that woman loose."

"In one shake of a lamb's rudder, sir."

With which, assuring Gees that he was *persona grata* here, Todd went off, and Gees headed for the coffee room to wait for his meal.

XVII

THE SHATTERED ROD

"Such stuff as dreams are made of."

The miracle that Shakespeare was, the clothing he could put on common things, making eternal verities of his clowns, even! Sam Thatcher, and Jacob Cowder, seated at their nightly table with their cronies, had been in the knowledge of that world-genius, were figured as chorus in his work, for all time. They, too, were such stuff as dreams were made of—stuff for *his* dreams, fixed for ever in his prose of comic relief from the poetry of his greater genius. Here in the bar room of The Three Thorns sat Bardolph and Nym, the two Dromios, Lance and Speed, the same in essence to-day as when the world-genius portrayed them. So Gees reflected as, entering the bar-room, he saw the worthies—but only for a minute, to-night.

For, acting in concert with Sam Thatcher, one and all of them lifted their glass mugs, finished their half-pints and, rising from their seats, stumped solemnly to the door, and out. Firth, up by the bar, stared at the closed door as Gees advanced to join him.

"What's bitten them all?" he asked, more of Todd than of Gees.

"A slight disagreement I had with them this morning, I think," Gees answered him before Todd could speak. "With them and a few others. I dunno, Todd —if my coming in here is going to rob you of custom

like that, I'd better take my pint back to the coffee
room and stop there."

"Not you, sir!" Todd protested emphatically. "I
make more outer you bein' here than I do outer what
that lot'll spend in a week. They takin' one night off
ain't goin' to hurt me. You just stop where you like.
A pint you said, was it, sir?"

"One—as a beginning," Gees assented.

"Make it the end as well, and come across and
eat with me," Firth suggested. "Atone for your
previous dereliction."

"I'm sorry, but I've just stoked ham and eggs to
the limit," Gees answered. "My first meal to-day,
and I made it a big one."

"Too bad!" Firth shook his head. "To-morrow
night?"

"If I'm still here—it's very good of you to persist
like this. But I doubt whether I shall be here—probably leaving in the morning."

"You'll stay for the inquest, I suppose?"

Gees achieved an expression of surprise. "Inquest?"
he asked.

"Squire Naylor," Firth explained. "It'll be almost
formal, apart from my evidence—I was the only quali-
fied medical man anywhere near. Last night—first
thing this morning, rather. They didn't find him, and
he appears to have wandered about all night and
climbed to the top of the downs this morning—before
sunrise. Mad as a hatter—must have been, by what
the men who saw him say."

"How—what makes them think that?" Gees asked.

"He'd nothing more than a thin indoor suit on—
and out in the cold all night, never going near the
Hall, as far as can be told. In the very first of the

morning he climbed up to that height overlooking the village, and he'd taken some sort of old battleaxe —he's got trophies by the dozen up at the Hall, and I expect he took this one down some time or other, and picked it up again after he left the post-office yesterday. That's the only way to account for it—nobody else has any African or Eastern stuff of that sort round here, as nearly as I know. Anyhow, he got to the top of that long mound, and there, they say, he did a sort of war-dance or something, waving the thing about while half a dozen of them climbed up in the hope of catching him and getting him back home and to bed. But they didn't."

"No?" Gees asked, and knew that, even if those men of the village had seen the shade with the Hammer against which Naylor had fought, they would not have believed their own eyes.

"No," Firth said. "Before any one of them could get near him, he slipped and fell—they couldn't see exactly what happened, because of the slope, but I went up there to-day, and it looks to me as if he skidded on the grass—it's very slippery, as I found myself— and fell so that the old battleaxe, or whatever it is, struck him just over the solar plexus. Either the head or the shaft end—it doesn't matter which it was, and there's no telling, now. But the way I see it, he fell on to the thing with one end on the ground and the other striking against his breast, because the bone is driven in, and the bone handle of the axe is literally shattered to powder. By what I can see of the bit left in the axe-head, that shaft was very old and brittle, and it simply crumbled when his weight came on it."

"I see-e," Gees commented thoughtfully, and remembered how—if he could believe his own eyes—the

Hammer had shattered the Rod. Had that happened,
or had Naylor fallen as Firth deduced, splintering the
ancient bone or horn by the sudden impact of his
weight on the end?

"That, as I see it, finished him—he was stone dead
when the men got up there. Shock following on complete exhaustion. I'd like to dissect the brain, to see
if there's any possibility of getting at the cause of his
seizure—but of course I shall not be allowed to do it.
It seems to me that the mania, whatever it was, held
him to physical exertion up to the limit of his strength
till the very last moment. That happens in a good
many forms of mental derangement, you know. The
subject maintains a frenzy until he or she collapses.
Then coma—in his case, completely exhausted as he
was, death. He'd no stamina—there's nothing of him
but skin and bone."

"A tragedy for the village," Gees remarked, remembering what Todd had told him. "That is, unless someone takes over."

"As nearly as I can make out, he hadn't a single
living relative," Firth said. "That, I suppose, is a
unique case, or very near it. Unless he made a will,
it looks as if the Crown will benefit. But I must get
along. Don't forget to-morrow night, if you're still
here."

"I'll remember," Gees promised, and knew as he
spoke that the promise was an empty one, for he
would be back in London before to-morrow ended.
This fruitless "case" was at an end, as far as he was
concerned: Ira would go her way. . . .

He brooded over it, alone there with Todd, and
almost unconscious, for the time, of the man's presence.
She was wonderful, like no other woman he had known,

and he had been near on loving her in those last
minutes. Very near, until she chilled him with the
reference to Dark Lagny's end. And she would not
give up her quest for forbidden things, but would go
her way. Suddenly Naylor's words recurred to his
mind—

"Her ways are death."

He had been right. But—death to her too?

"You'll have another, sir—with me, this one?"

"Make it a half, then, Todd, just to drink your
health. And I shall be leaving in the morning."

"Hope you'll come this way again, sir, before
long."

"Ah!" Gees made the syllable non-committal, and
took up the refilled glass. "Here's happiness to you
and the little lady."

"Thankye, sir. An' all the best to you, wherever
you go."

.   .   .   .   .

Cars parked before the inn, uniformed police in
evidence, a sober, black-coated individual who, Gees
decided, was Naylor's man of law, and another who
was probably the coroner. Villagers turning out in
their Sunday best for the occasion—Gees backed his
car out of the shed in mid-morning, unchallenged by
any one of them, and turned it to drive along the
lane. Halfway between the village and Wren's farm
he swerved into a gateway and stopped: it appeared
the nearest point to the mound on which Naylor had
died, and Gees wanted to see that height again before
he left Troyarbour—not to return, he told himself.
He felt that he wanted never to see the place again.

He climbed, steadily, and reached the top of the
ridge. Climbed again, coming up to the women's end

of the crest where three thorns had once stood, and walking the length of the mound till he came to where Naylor had fallen. He knew it must have been at that spot, because of the whitish fragments of the axe-haft scattered among the dry, slippery grass. Tiny fragments, and even a whitish powder which proved that the haft had been as brittle as a stick of chalk. He had thought, as he climbed, that it might be possible to collect the splinters and reconstruct enough of the Rod to read its runes, but one glance at the rubbly whiteness scattered there told him that it was out of the question. Dark Lagny's knowledge was no longer to be read—unless those parchments in the chest held it. If so, Ira would guard them. . . .

He saw her as the thought came to him, saw her appear at the women's end of the crest and come toward him. Her hair was uncovered—he had not seen it otherwise—and she wore the green frock and pendant with the scribed stone. Her eyes were sombre as she faced him.

"I saw you," she said, "and thought you might go——"

As he would have gone, without attempting to see her again. The incomplete sentence told him she had known that as his intent.

"I am going," he answered. "But that is not to say I should have passed your place without stopping to say good-bye."

"No?" She gazed at him steadily. "But I knew."

He gave her no answer. At last she turned her head to look down toward the farm. "And so—I climbed the hill," she said.

"Was it necessary to climb?" He put a satiric tinge into the query.

"Yes," she answered simply. "I would not come to you here in that other way. I think now I shall never come to you, never see you again."

"Because you will persist——" he suggested, and left it incomplete.

She shook her head. "I do not know," she said slowly. "It seems now—now that Jerome Naylor is dead—all the purpose of my life is ended. All the purpose of my life is ended. Infinity is cold—*I* am cold! It is a mood, and perhaps it will pass. As you . . . pass."

Again he was near on love for her, and knew it. She was like no other—not in a whole lifetime would a man weary of the deep music of her voice, nor learn all that her eyes could teach. He said—"Ira, if you would but be all human, not—not——" and did not end it.

"I know. Do you know, I believe at one and the same time that I shall come to you, and that I shall not see you again? That to me is a mystery, but so it seems to me now. That I shall come to you——"

"Using that power you are learning?" he asked in the pause.

"Or, perhaps, as I have come to you here," she answered. "I do not know—it is all dark. And that I shall not see you. It is all dark, and I cannot see how these two things can be."

"Nor I," he said thoughtfully. "They are—incompatible, call it."

"When you have gone out from this place, and in thought look back, it will appear to you that none of these things happened—that you dreamed them," she said slowly. "Dreamed me—perhaps that is so, and you are dreaming now. Or perhaps I dream—you!

But to me some moments in the dream are real. The first kiss of a lover—so you kissed me. Standing with you to see how Jerome Naylor was struck down by the Hammer. Holding you, taking you out from Time to Sight, when you so nearly went past Fear, but drew back, not knowing how small is that step. For that moment, in the place beyond moments, you were one with me, and I hold it here——" she laid her hand for a second over her heart—"as real. I tell you this because I shall not see you again."

"Yet, you say, you will come to me," he reminded her.

"Yet I shall surely come to you. Because you came to me here and wakened another self in me, taught me—what have you not taught me? The world of the spirit in which the flesh must have part, consciousness that only when both are given full play is completeness possible, and that I may gain most only by giving most—if you have need of me. Now go—do not answer —go! Alone. Until I come to you."

He knew why she imposed silence on him, and went stumblingly down the side of the mound, to look up before he began the easier descent of the hillside, and see her standing, gazing down at him. Then he went on, down to the car, and drove past the farm, along the tortuous windings of the lane, out to the main road which meant normality. When he saw Blandford and the smooth rise of road beyond it, he began to question —how much of what he remembered, how much of what he had experienced there at Troyarbour, had been real? It had the quality of a dream already. Ira, wonder-woman in those last moments—

"I may gain most only by giving most—if you have need of me."

THE SHATTERED ROD   263

In that, he knew, she had voiced the completion of
her womanhood—she understood what few women
ever learn. *Was* she real, or a dream-figure in a
fantasy he had dreamed? Had there ever been a
Squire Naylor—did Troyarbour exist? Was *anything*
real?

". . . such stuff as dreams are made of. . . ."

A state that cut across this world, a state in which
were Presences beyond human comprehension—and
she, Ira, sought to comprehend them! A state in
which time and space were not, into which she could
move by taking one step. A step of the spirit? He
had not seen that she made any physical movement.

Incredible, all of it. Preposterous! But she was
very lovely, and if, some day, she should come to
him and bring with her the knowledge that only by
giving most might she gain most—

He heard the hum of his tyres on the three-dimensional, tarred metalling of the road. He was going
back to London, to his office, to more inquiries out
of which cases might arise, to Miss Brandon, sanity
and material realities. Out from a dream. . . .

·   ·   ·   ·   ·

"Ah, thank you, Miss Brandon." Gees took the
clipped sheets of typescript that the girl held out to
him, and nodded at the very comfortable chair which
stood at the end of his desk, a trap in which to im-
prison possible clients. "Do you mind sitting down
and talking this over with me? You digested that
report as well as typed it, I hope?"

"Naturally," she answered, with an ironic inflection.
"If you wish to bounce your ideas, the wall is
here."

She seated herself in the chair—or rather, sank down into it—as she spoke, and Gees resumed his swivel chair at the desk.

"I dictated it as fully and descriptively as I could," he said, "with a view to clarifying my own views—getting some sort of explanation. And find none. How does it strike you?"

"All capable of explanation," she answered. "Rational explanation if one—well, accepts certain postulates."

"As how?" he asked interestedly.

"What do you want explained?" she asked in reply.

"She—Ira Warenn, that is, because there is only one woman in this story—she vanished and reappeared in my sight, by means of her use of the fourth perpendicular. That is to say, she actually moved in the fourth dimension. That for a start."

Miss Brandon's brows drew together thoughtfully. She said—"Suppose we consider this Ira Warenn herself, as the start?"

"What do you want to consider about her?" he demanded.

"Your references to her in the report on the case."

"It isn't a case. I didn't do a thing from start to finish, and I made nothing out of it—got bilked of eighteen guineas that I'll never see, now. Practically speaking, we can't regard it as a case. Pass that, though. Let me hear you on Ira Warenn."

"Very lovely, according to you. Also a woman of exceptional abilities, an exceptional woman in every way. Very attractive. May I ask if you are in love with her, Mr. Green?"

"Ask anything you like—I want to bounce my ideas. I'd say in answer to that—I don't know. I couldn't tell you or even tell myself without seeing her again. Until I see her again."

"By the 'until,' you indicate that you are," she said coolly. "Now you have cited that vanishing and reappearance. She didn't."

"Oh, yes, she did!" he derided. "I *saw* it!"

"As I said just now, an exceptional woman in every way. That power over animals proves it—a woman of almost incredible personal magnetism, and therefore one possessed of tremendous hypnotic power. She used that power on you, made you see what did not happen, just as an Eastern conjurer will make you see a plant grow in a pile of dust in the course of a few minutes. It did not happen."

"Says you! All right, Miss Brandon, I want your explanations to compare with my own conclusions. The laughter that scared those yokels at the inn? How do you account for it?"

"Perfectly simple. She was outside, unseen in the darkness."

"She wasn't—it sounded *inside,* not outside at all."

"Ventriloquially. I think, Mr. Green, you rather let your practical self go to sleep over this. You know as well as I do what ventriloquists can do, the illusions they can create——"

"All right—all right, Miss Brandon. And when, as I told you in that report, she put her arms round me and got me to hold her—not for any emotional reason, as I said—when she took me into that other world where I saw and heard and smelt and felt independently of her—saw things past the farthest edge of human sight, and heard tones beyond the range of a three-dimensional ear——"

"In those first experiments on you," she said as

he paused, "she gained a certain hypnotic influence over you. In this, with physical contact to aid her, she completed the influence, and all you saw and heard and all the rest of it was impressed on your brain by hers. She is, as I said, a woman of exceptional abilities. Tremendous abilities, I might call them. But all within three-dimensional limits."

"Umm-humm! The practical mind—yes. The song of the sword?"

"You didn't hear it. She made you believe you did."

"The shape on the hill, with the Hammer?"

"Your doctor Firth gave you the rational explanation of what happened there. Apparently none of the men who tried to get to Naylor in time saw anything unusual—only you and Ira Warenn saw it. That is to say, by her hypnotic influence she created the picture in your mind, willed you to see it. And the axe-handle—naturally, if a strip of bone is preserved for ten or more centuries, it will crumble at the slightest blow. Just as the axe-handle crumbled."

"I've seen Belgae skeletons dug out at Mai-Dun, near on eighteen centuries old, and you could have used the leg-bones for walking sticks. They wouldn't crumble," he objected acidly.

"Dug-up bones—yes," she said. "They had been hermetically kept from the action of the air and changing temperatures, not subjected to them—as this axe-handle was subjected, apparently."

"Then you deny Ira Warenn's use of a fourth dimension?" he questioned, after a pause for thought.

"Time is the fourth dimension," she retorted coolly.

"Is it? Well, I grant you that. But this fourth—not fifth—into which she can move, simply abolishes time. In it, there is no such thing as time—as I saw it. In it, time and space do not exist. You don't move from one place to another in a fraction of a second, because there are no seconds. You *are* here —you *are* there—and neither 'here' nor 'there' exists. In, infinity, you don't move at all, because you are part of infinity, which is beyond space. Where there is no space, there can be no movement. Do you see?"

"I see that you're merely accepting the hypnotic trance she thrust upon you, Mr. Green. You'll be telling me next that she took you from this world into eternity, and you somehow managed to get back."

"My dear girl——"

"I am not your dear girl!" she interrupted promptly.

"All right—all *right!* Let me get on with it. I was going to say—you are in eternity here and now. The reason you don't see yourself so is that you are bound by time, dragged along by time, handcuffed to the illusion we know as time. There is the value of this fourth perpendicular, as soon as man is spiritually fit to comprehend and use it. In his present state of development, he'd merely tuck a big gun under each arm and sail out along the fourth perpendicular to slaughter his fellow man, or else go out invisibly and spread false reports to rig the stock markets and so make his pile by ruining the said fellow man. But to get back to what I was saying, the main value I can see in the use of this fourth perpendicular is that of absolute freedom from time, erasure of it from among the dimensions we know."

She shook her head. "That's too deep for me," she said. "You must grow old, surely? Humanity can't be eternal."

"But it *can*, once it's released from time," he insisted. "I took in half a lifetime of impressions, of new knowledge, in the timeless instant I spent in that state with her, and Fear alone barred me out from experiencing the other half. I was no older for it, or no more than a second older, when I saw her standing apart from me instead of holding me as at the beginning of the experiment."

"Still I say it was all hypnotic," she persisted. "That she has unique hypnotic powers, and used them on you."

"And on Naylor, you'd say," he suggested.

"Undoubtedly. She herself told you—according to this report—that auto-suggestion brought him down to—well, to death, in the end."

"I've a good mind to go back there," he said abruptly. "With your solutions for everything fixed in my mind, to see if you're right."

"To see Ira Warenn again," she amended, slowly and with almost a gibe in her voice. "To fall still more under her influence, and——" She broke off, and smiled, as if the rest needed no words.

"Do you consider me a man, or a child?" he demanded irritably.

"All men are children," she answered, smiling no longer. "Half the troubles of the world arise out of women who refuse to believe it. To hold a man, a woman must give and go on giving, as to a child. What is it I typed in this—her words as you dictated them? 'Gain most only by giving most.' Oh, she is very wise, this Ira Warenn! Yes, go back to her by all means. You will not regret it, while she realises that as her means of holding—as the only means there is."

"How do you know?" he asked curiously.

"Oh—what was your word? Empiric knowledge, say. Yes, empiric. Or perhaps, once, I gave and gave and gave to the uttermost. Gained nothing for myself, but found my reward in the giving. I don't mean—I counted for nothing, and knew it, but the giving was its reward."

"I shall not go back," he said with decision. "It is in your typing—or ought to be—she will go her way."

"Believing it will bring her to you," she commented reflectively. "Yes. I see. She is not as wise as I thought. Withholding, she could not hold: It must be complete—she must not withhold."

"Withhold what?" he asked.

"What have you asked of her? To give up that way she insists on following. And whatever you might ask——" She did not end it.

"You're seeing me as a sort of monument to selfishness," he said.

"You are a man—I meant that to apply to any man, not merely to you. The best of them, as well as the worst."

He thought it over. "We haven't got far with this discussion, have we?" he asked at last, rather caustically.

"Oh, quite a long way!" she dissented. "I've bounced some of my ideas and watched them flatten and expand—I'm intensely grateful to you, Mr. Green. But still I say all your experiences were hypnotically produced illusions, all originated in a three-dimensional mind—one of extraordinary capacities and powers, though."

"Is that so?" he drawled, with the trace of scepticism that, he knew, she always found exasperating. "And for me, all illusion—or delusion. But you haven't explained away everything yet."

"I've given you rational explanations on every point you've brought forward," she retorted with acid triumph. "What else?"

"How did the crimson-sailed boat unmoor itself and go sailing out of that picture? I saw that, clearly enough."

"There are two or three explanations." She spoke slowly, thoughtfully. "The most unlikely one is that there never was a crimson-sailed boat in the picture, but Ira Warenn foisted it on your imagination to impress you at the finish with its disappearance. A more likely one is that there are still two boats in the picture, but with her very great powers of hypnotic influence she has blotted one of them out as far as you are concerned. I mean, if I looked at the picture, I should see both boats, but she has rendered you incapable of seeing that one. Was that sail the only crimson in the picture?"

"As nearly as I remember—yes," he answered. "And it isn't a trick picture with clockwork mechanism or anything of that sort. Flat water-colour painting, and a very good piece of work at that. I noticed it particularly the first time I saw the room."

"With that one touch of crimson in it—yes. And she asked you to light some stuff that rose up as smoke and hid the picture from sight for a time. Which gives a third explanation. The smoke had a bleaching effect on the crimson pigment, and on no other colour. It bleached out the sail, and the effect started at the edges, so that you saw the sail grow smaller until it vanished altogether."

"Won't do." He shook his head. "I saw the boat swing about, and actually move toward the horizon. Like a real boat."

"You thought you saw that happen," she dissented. "You didn't."

"*I* see!" The causticism of those two words was almost vitriolic. "Now explain away how the cat got in my car, two miles and more from its home and at a place where they stoned it away if they found it—when I first went to see Naylor, I mean, and before I knew about Ira Warenn—except for what Naylor told me, of course."

She smiled, rather pityingly. "Can you or anyone control a cat, or forecast where it will go or what it will do? That particular cat happened to have wandered so far, and inspected your car. Found a warm leather cushion where you had been sitting, and settled down on it—quite naturally. Your being told that it was stoned away is evidence that it haunted the Hall at times, which accounts for its being there just then. A pure coincidence—and a most important one, as I see it, for when you told her about it you gave her the idea that started the whole thing. She managed to convey to you the first impression that enabled her to use hypnotic influence on you later."

"Excellent! All so very logical. Not illusion at all, but delusion. I've not only been led up the garden, but dumped in the ditch at the far end as well. We live and learn, don't we? Now tell me the why of it. She did all this—to what purpose?"

She shook her head. "Only one person can answer that question," she said. "Ask it of Ira Warenn when she comes to you, or—as I believe you will in spite of everything you may say—when you go to her."

He sighed, heavily. "I see. And my ideas won't bounce to-day—you're too beautifully, perfectly logical. Now——" he sat erect in his chair—"I think you've got some inquiries I haven't looked over fully. If you'll fetch them in—but do have a cigarette first, just to show there's no ill-feeling. Yes? Now a light. Good! And I'll come along to your room and go through the inquiries there. I've got an uneasy feeling in spite of all your explanations——"

He did not end the sentence, nor did she appear to expect him to define the feeling. In her room, he seated himself on the corner of her desk, as usual, and began a scrutiny of the letters she handed to him.

"All this—this Troyarbour business, I mean—was a mere waste of my time, from the practical point of view," he said. "Now let's see. Something with money in it—that's what we want, Miss Brandon. Lashin's of money—a real wad of mazuma. Let us be strictly practical."

XVIII

"I SHALL NEVER———"

FOR three days the subject of Troyarbour and all that had—or had not—happened there was completely ignored by Gees and his secretary. She knew quite well that he resented her explanations, and resented his resentment. Perhaps she resented still more the knowledge that Ira Warenn was in his thoughts, and it might be even nearer than mere thoughts: for, as she had told him, she had given and given and given, not only brain, but heart as well—to him, and he could not see it! She was too near him, she told herself: she must contrive some reason, other than that of holiday, of getting away for a fortnight or so. He might miss her, then, and realise all that she did for him. In that way, he might see her as essential to him, or might find that he could do without her. It would be a gamble, but——

Near on three years of almost daily companionship: it was inevitable, his taking her for granted. Also, it must be stopped.

Thus she reflected in mid-morning of that third day, after replacing her telephone receiver. Eventually, sighing, she got up from her seat at the desk and went along to Gees' room at the other end of the short corridor. He sat at his flat-topped desk with the morning's *Times* opened before him, and looked up at her inquiringly.

"Mr. Ferguson will be here to see you at three-thirty," she said.

"Ah! Umm-m! What did you make of him, Miss Brandon? Very Scotch, or just Scotch and soda?"

"The accent was there, but not noticeably," she answered frostily.

"Horace Ferguson," he mused aloud. "Well, since he's calling, we get the two guineas initial consultation fee, anyhow. Also we find out what it's all about. His letter told just as much as J. St. Pol Naylor's, and no more. Did you get a hint of the nature of his trouble on the telephone?"

She shook her head. "He wouldn't tell me, naturally."

"Wants to come straight to the fountain head, eh? Scotch—yes, and no. soda. Some fountain head me, too."

She frowned with obvious dislike for the levity. Not that, in a normal way, she would have resented it, for she liked his attitude to life. But for the past three days everything had seemed wrong—and she knew very well what was wrong, with herself as well as with him.

She asked—"Nothing else, is there, Mr. Green?" Coldly.

He said—"Let me see——" and gazed past her with a dreamily absent look in his eyes—an unseeing gaze—that she found intensely irritating. She wanted to box his ear.

But one does not box one's employer's ear if he merely sits and gazes into vacancy. She waited, standing before the desk.

A voice sounded to them, faintly, yet so clearly that Miss Brandon heard it as music, such a speaking voice as few women possess.

"I cannot see you. I come to you, but I cannot——"

It seemed to Miss Brandon that the voice did not cease utterance then, but was cut off, as if by the closing of a sound-proof door. She saw Gees start to his feet so suddenly as to send his chair crashing to the floor, and point past her toward the door of the room, and his eyes were wide with fearful expectancy. Then she turned her head, to look along the line that pointing finger of his indicated.

She saw, as he saw, a tress of rippling, lovely, night-black hair, suspended at the height of her own head, close by the wall of the room. A pace or more distant from the wall, still, as if hung by a thread —but there was no thread! Neither then nor at any later time could she tell how long both she and Gees stood in utter immobility, and the hair stood (so she would have expressed it) rather than was suspended there. She knew only that it seemed a very long time.

Then the voice again. In it infinite longing, and the pain of a desire forever denied fulfilment.

"You are there, I know. I come to you, but do not see you—do you remember? There is no return, for me! I shall never——"

Silence again. Miss Brandon started back with a little gasp of fear. For the night-black tress was falling, floating down, until it lay on the carpet. They two waited, still, expectant, but heard only faint noises from the streets outside—except that Miss Brandon heard the beating of her own pulse in her ears, a soundless sound.

Gees moved first. He came out from behind the desk, and went slowly toward the place where the hair lay, and, as he went, he held his hands apart and at full stretch before him—Miss Brandon knew what he expected.   What he hoped, she felt in her heart.   She saw him grope like one in utter darkness, heard him whisper—

"Ira?   O, Ira!"

Uselessly.   He won no reply, no sign of other presence than his own and Miss Brandon's in the room.   He stooped, took up the little scented tress—the scent that was Ira Warenn—and held it against his lips.   Then he crushed it in his hold, and looked at Miss Brandon.

"Well?" he asked.

She said, whisperingly.   "Not—not illusion.   I was wrong."

"She came to me—she did not see me——"

He went back to the desk and sat down, holding the night-black hair, so lately fallen from Ira's head as to seem still alive with her life, in his hand and gazing down at it.   He said—"No return.   She will never—I know.   It was forbidden knowledge that she had, and used.   And so They hold her, on the other side of Fear."

"She is—you mean—she is—dead?" she asked fearfully.

He looked up at her and smiled.   "There is no death," he answered.

"But—that—her hair—she was *here!*"

"No.   Only this—this I hold—won through.   The rest of her—she was never in this room, but was held back.   You would have to see as she made me see, and then you would understand.   Held back, and she knew—told me—'There is no return, for me.' There *is* no return!"

He sat looking at the tress he held: Miss Brandon too looked at it, and asked herself what must the

woman be whose hair was like that. All loveliness?
Like her voice, with its unforgettable cadences?

A sudden anger against Ira Warenn surged in Miss
Brandon as she looked at Gees sitting there. The
woman had gone her way, thrown away his love
because she could not realise that one must give all
and go on giving all, though she had known it. In
time, barred out past return, she would fade in his
consciousness, but she had hurt him, and for that
Miss Brandon hated her. Then Gees looked up.

"You must ring this Ferguson, Miss Brandon," he
said, "and put him off till—let me see! Yes, till the
day after to-morrow. At the same time, the day
after to-morrow. Yes. Then get on to the garage
—I want the car in an hour from now. Can you
sleep here to-night?"

"I—yes, I could," she answered wonderingly.

"Just in case, if—I'd want you to be here and
tell her I've gone to Troyarbour to look for her there.
To reassure her, ask her to wait. To tell her—maybe
she understands, now, and will give up that way of
hers because—well, one must give up everything to
gain what she came to me to find. So nearly came
to me, I mean. Do you understand?"

"Yes, I know. I'll stay here all the time till you
get back."

"Good for you! Don't be. . . . practical." He
smiled, and she knew gravity would have been better
to see than a smile like that. "Just be—be very
gentle with her, if——"

"I know, Mr. Green. And for your sake I
hope——"

He shook his head, smiling no more. "I have no
hope," he said. "She told me, there is no return. Still,

I shall go. That's all, Miss Brandon. You're a terribly good sport, and I do appreciate it."

When she got back to her own room, she had to wipe her eyes before she could see to dial the telephone number.

.   .   .   .   .

A thin drizzle of rain obscured the crests of the downs and spoiled that day as, in early afternoon, Gees drove along the lane to pull in before the frontage of Wren's farm. Except for the rain, it might have been his first coming to the place. Irene the sow was out in front with her litter, and fowls scratched and chirrawked over bits of grit and whatever else they found as justification for their patient industry. He got out from the car and knocked at the closed door: knocked again, and yet again, waited, and then, giving it up, went round to the back of the house. A sound took him toward the farm buildings, past the charred desolation that had been Adolphus' pen, and he found Ephraim Knapper, cleaning out the cowshed in readiness, probably, for the evening's milking. Ephraim straightened himself, pushed back his greasy old bowler hat from his forehead, and said—
"Arternoon, zur," in a questioning, friendly sort of way.

"Good afternoon," Gees responded. "Miss Warenn —could I see her? I've tried the front door, but couldn't get any answer."

"Happen she be zleepin', zur," Ephraim suggested. "I ain't zeen her go out, an' if she'd been goin', she'd towd me, I reckon."

"When did you last see her?" Gees asked.

"It'd be—lemme zee." Ephraim scratched his cheek for inspiration. "Aye, nigh on 'leven, it'd be. Zhe coom to back door theer—I wur fetchin' haay—she coom to back door an' stood a bit, an' went baack—dedn't zay northin', jes' went baack. An' shet the door. It wur nigh on 'leven when I zeed her."

It had been eleven o'clock, or a very few minutes after, Gees knew, when he and Miss Brandon had heard the voice—when he had seen the tress of hair that now was locked in the top drawer of his dressing chest at the flat. She had come to him.

"I'm going to see if either door is unlocked, Ephraim," he said, "and if I can get in, I'm going in. You don't know what may have happened to her between eleven o'clock and now, and she doesn't answer my knock. You can come along too, if you feel like it."

"Noa, zur, yu goo—I dooan't wanter goo. Yu knows her, an' yu looked arter her when they coom along that mornin'——" He did not specify the occasion, but Gees knew what he meant.

"All right. You carry on with what you have to do."

He went round to the front of the house again, and tried the door there with no more knocking. Unlocked, it yielded as the handle turned, and he entered the passageway. The doors of both the rooms that he knew stood open, and, standing between them in the hallway, he called softly—

"Ira? Where are you? Ira?"

But knew, as he called, that he would win no reply. After a pause, he entered the dingy room to which she had first taken him.

The chest, with the ruined bits of its lid down in front, stood by the wall. It was empty: the parchments and the sword had gone—charred bits of wood and blackish, leathery-looking fragments in the grate told what had become of the parchments, and he did not look to see what had become of the sword that would sing no more. There was nothing else that he wanted to see in the room, and he crossed the hallway to enter the room of green and crimson, and stand before the divan to look at the picture which, once, had showed two boats moored against a quay, one with crimson sail, and one with green.

Now, *no* boat remained. The line of the quay stretched before a white wall, and back of it were white houses, and the blue of the sky. To the right was the long perspective down which he had seen the crimson sail grow small and smaller, and vanish. Abruptly he turned and went out, remembering something Miss Brandon had said.

He found Ephraim again. "I want you to come into the house," he said. "Want you to look at something with me."

Ephraim stared at him, stolidly. "Me, zur?" he asked.

"You. Come along, man. Only for a minute or two."

Following him, Ephraim wiped his feet carefully on a tuft of grass outside the front door, and then entered the room where the picture hung. With a hand on the man's shoulder, Gees marched him before it.

"A good picture, isn't it?" he asked.

"Aye, zur. Right pritty," Ephraim conceded.

"And those two boats against the quay—at the edge of the water, there——" He reached out a finger to indicate the spot. "They're well done, don't you think?"

"Booats, zur? There bain't no booats!"

"Surely, man! A green sail and a red!"

Ephraim shook his head. "Mister," he said severely, "you'm seeing things! Theer bain't no booats, an' theer bain't no zails i' that picter, an'——" he turned, suddenly accusing—"yu knows it!"

"All right." Gees produced a half-crown, and handed it over. "I was only fooling. That's all—you can go."

Ephraim stumped his way out, muttering to himself, and for a little while longer Gees remained before the picture. Ira had told him that the passing of the crimson sail had been a prefiguring: had the green sail followed that same way, over the horizon, out from the picture? No return! "I shall never——" No—no return!

A flurry of movement, and Peter the cat did his great leap to land on Gees' back, settle there with dug-in claws, and begin to purr. Gees reached up to tickle his ear, and the cat pressed down to make a scratch of the tickle.

"Peter! Oh, Peter!" Gees said chokingly.

At a thought he went out to the car, the cat still on his shoulders like a necklet that reached only from ear to ear behind him. He turned and looked up at the house, and it was empty, dead. There was no return for her. He had known it when he set out on this journey.

He said to himself—"You can't steal a cat. A cat isn't property—you can't steal it."

He got into the car and seated himself at the wheel. Peter climbed down to the seat beside him, looked up at him. He said—"Yes, old chap, if you feel like it. Because she loved you."

. . . . . .

He left the car by the kerb and went up the stairs with Peter in his arms. It was then past eight o'clock in the evening, and Miss Brandon came out from his office room, not her own, to stand gazing at him and at the black cat in his arms.

"You won't have to stay the night after all, Miss Brandon," he told her. "I've brought a lodger, a permanency, unless he goes back on me. His name's Peter. Do you like cats? Cherry-coloured cats with rose-coloured weskits, like this one?"

She came forward and stroked Peter's head, very gently. "He's just lovely," she said. "Look—he likes me to stroke him."

Gees put the cat down on the floor. "I'll get him a basket," he remarked. "One of those round ones that'll just fit him when he folds himself up. And put a fat cushion in it—to-morrow. Oh, Peter!"

Peter looked up at him for a moment, and then went exploring. He went along to Gees' office room, and vanished inside it.

"You remember I told you about the picture?" Gees asked the girl.

She nodded. "And I said——"

"Yes, I know you did," he said, as she did not end it. "I got an ancient man to come in and see it with me—he'd not been hypnotised to see things that weren't there, or miss seeing things that were——"

"Don't, please!" she interrupted.

"All right—I won't. The green sail has gone too, now."

"I don't understand—any of it," she said perplexedly. "What—what will happen there now—at Troyarbour? At her place?"

He shook his head. "I don't know. It is nothing

to me. I know, past any question, that I shall not
see her again."

She said—"I'm so sorry, Mr. Green. For you."
Said it with absolute sincerity, but he made a little
impatient gesture.

"Get your hat and coat, girl, and get away home,
before I start weeping on your shoulder. These things
—the real things—one faces them best alone. And
I know now how real this was. Good-night, Miss
Brandon—don't hurry to get here in the morning,
after staying so late for me to-night. I do appreciate
it."

He passed her, then, going to his own room. Peter,
seated on the swivel chair at the desk, looked up at
him and emitted a very faint, small, questioning—
"Waow?" Then Gees went and tickled him under the
chin, and presently he began to purr.

Miss Brandon had lighted the fire in the grate. By
the look of things, she had intended staying the night
in this room, and not in Gees' bedroom on the other
side of the corridor. Perhaps she thought it would
be too indelicate, sleeping in his bed. He half-smiled
at that thought, and then, as Peter dropped to the
floor, the smile went out like a light that had been
extinguished.

Peter went to the door, and Gees, following him,
heard the latch of the outer door click behind Miss
Brandon. Some time, perhaps, he would again think
of her as Eve Madeleine, but not now—not to-night.
He saw Peter scratch at the door of his room, and
opened it. Peter went straight in, and, as Gees switched
on the light, he saw the cat standing up on his hind
legs, clawing at the top drawer of the dressing chest.
Clawing, scratching, pulling at it.

Then Gees went to the drawer and, opening it, took out the tress of night-black, wonderful hair. Not quite so wonderful now—*her* life that had been in it no longer made it vibrant in his hold, and when he lifted it to his lips the scent of her as he had known it was faded, almost to nothingness. He said aloud—"Ira? Oh, Ira!"

No voice answered. No voice would ever answer, he knew.

Peter, at his feet, looked up and mewed piteously, persistently. Then Gees turned about, half-blinded for the minute, and stumbled into the other room with the cat running round him, looking up and mewing, calling. Before the fire Gees shook his eyes clear, and for the last time laid the wonderful hair against his lips.

"For you, Peter, this. Lest you should go on remembering and grieving—calling to her. Because she loved you."

Bending forward, he laid the tress among the red coals. It shrivelled to nothingness with a little sound that was like a sigh. It had vanished, gone beyond return.

After a time Gees turned about, and saw that Peter had got on the seat of the swivel chair again, where he lay as if quite at home, quite content. When Gees scratched his head for him, he looked up and purred.

And purred—and purred. . . .

THE END

www.ingramcontent.com/pod-product-compliance
Lightning Source LLC
Chambersburg PA
CBHW020606260626
47157CB00003B/894